LET'S TALK ABOUT SEX

ROXANNE BLACKHALL

BLACK LABEL PRESS

No AI was used in the production of this book.

ISBN

Digital: 978-1-966882-07-7

This book is about sexual and creative freedom
and the radical belief that love is sacred
pleasure is powerful
and desire is not something to fear

For those who love boldly
fuck joyfully
and refuse to make themselves smaller

In uncertain times and always

CONTENT NOTES

Let's Talk About Sex includes explicit sexual content between consenting adults. It explores trauma recovery, emotional surrender, and the complexities of consent and control.

Additional themes include emotional abuse (past), public shaming, and professional/personal ethics. Readers sensitive to depictions of intense sexual dynamics or emotional trauma should proceed with care.

Please check the website for a full list of content advisories.

www.RoxanneBlackhall.com/content

SUNDAY, MARCH 22

LET'S TALK ABOUT SEX—EMERY

"The average adult penis is five-point-five inches long when erect."

My voice fills the room, but I'm not speaking. I'm standing in the most generic office I've ever seen, clenching my fingers onto the back of a chair so the man standing on the other side of the desk doesn't see my hands shaking.

No, my voice is coming from Connor Rives' iPad, propped on the desk, the screen glaring like an accusing eye. I can't look away. The sight of me in my usual black pencil skirt and red heels, one hip cocked, fingers showing what five and a half inches looks like, is too surreal. It doesn't help that I'm still in the same outfit.

"Hi, I'm Emery Nicole and this is..."

The audio isn't perfect, but it's clear enough to hear the ripple of laughter that follows my introduction. It's the sound of people easing into uncomfortable topics, and it's why I open how I do. Disarm with humor and use it to build trust.

It's worked for years. I know the faces in that darkened room, every one of them. Phones locked in secure pouches. Identities protected. Or at least, they should have been.

"How did you get this?" My voice comes out tight, breath snagging. The video shouldn't exist. But it does. Of course it does. Because what my career really needs is an unauthorized sequel to The Let's Talk About Sex Lady, now streaming on your favorite social media.

Connor Rives doesn't sit. Neither do I. Sitting feels like surrender.

He braces both hands on the desk and leans closer, filling my vision. He looks like every bad decision I've ever talked a client out of. Broad shoulders, sharp jaw, whiskey-hued eyes that promise nothing good. Temptation on two legs with a swagger that says he knows exactly what he's doing. My brain says no, but my body hums maybe. *Traitor.*

There's something about the way he holds himself that grates. He's all calculated control in a tailored suit. Everything about him, from his posture and expression to the take-charge tone of his voice, says he's already decided how this ends and he's waiting for me to catch up. It dredges up memories of standing across another desk, that time staring at my boss and hearing words like 'too controversial' and 'too volatile.'

Even those memories don't stop the heat that curls in my stomach and spreads slow and treacherous when Connor Rives strips off his jacket and tosses it on the desk. My grip loosens on the chair before I drag myself back to my senses. Some reckless part of me whispers it's safe to let go here and I slam that door so hard it echoes. That kind of safety is a lie I've heard before.

"I got it from Davis Prescott. It was on a private forum within an hour of the seminar's end. He's worried his name will get dragged into this."

My stomach lurches. Davis trusted me enough to walk through that door. This isn't just bad. This is the sort of thing that ruins people. That lets truth drown under sensationalism and self-righteousness.

"I've never..." The words falter on my tongue and I can't finish the statement. It's not true. Not entirely.

One eyebrow lifts a fraction. "Haven't you?"

There's nothing cruel in his expression. It's a precise single cut that makes his point. The tiny me on the screen holds up her fingers. Again. Why do these things have to loop?

"Not like this." My voice is shaky and the correction tastes bitter. This video shouldn't exist. The other one, the one from New York, wasn't the problem. There were no rules against filming that panel, no lines crossed. The problem was that it went viral and it made the wrong people uncomfortable.

My employer started by calling it unprofessional and escalated from there. The internet called it indecent. And the wife of the man I was stupid enough to trust called me worse. Then hired help to mount a public smear campaign.

"I know." His tone softens, unexpected. He doesn't move, but the air shifts. He doesn't need to explain how he knows. Of course he does. Any PR fixer worth his retainer digs deep before lifting a finger. Men like him don't solve problems; they bury them under polish and call it protection.

For a heartbeat, the video looping on the iPad blurs into the red dress I wore in that other clip. The video turned my career, and my life, upside down and still follows me like smoke from the fire that made me. I choke down the memories, unwilling to continue down that path. If Connor Rives found that, it's safe to assume he found everything else. Maybe even the name of the fixer who helped crucify me.

"I have never before had a breach at an event I managed." My tone is sharper than I intended but I don't care. I need footing, something to claw back control. "I've rebuilt my career on honesty and my reputation rests on trust and confidentiality."

Something flickers across his face. Maybe empathy, but it's gone before I can be sure. He exhales once, slow and controlled, a measured breath that speaks of habit. There's no judgement, just recognition. It's a quiet 'I see you.'

His gaze slides to my mouth before snapping back to my eyes. I recognize that trick. He's reading me the same way I read others. He's almost predatory in his precision. Part of me hates it. Another part wants to see what he'll do if I push back, and that's the most dangerous part of all.

"Well, it's happened." He nods toward the iPad, where the clip continues to loop. "I told Davis not to go, but he did, and now it's my job to protect him. While this makes the rounds like a celebrity sex tape."

His words hit like a slap. Celebrity sex tape. Every professional woman's nightmare. Maybe he intended it as a dig and maybe not. But it sounds like something a fixer would say. A man who's already figured out where I fit into the approved narrative.

Still, heat rushes up my neck until my ears burn with humiliation and panic. Then defiance rises beneath the shame.

I made mistakes in New York, mostly in how I agreed to take the hit and keep silent. That's not happening here. I've spent too much time and effort dragging myself out of the ashes.

"I'll call my team and go through the attendee list. Phones were locked up, but..." I nod toward the video.

"Figure it out." His tone could cut glass. "Because if you don't, someone else will, and they won't care who gets hurt. They sure as hell won't think about protecting you."

Protecting me. Not my reputation. Not my career. Me. It

echoes in my head louder than it should. I can't tell if that's a threat or a promise.

"Turn that off." I jab a finger toward the iPad and force the rest of my fingers to uncurl from the chair.

He waits one beat before silencing the damn thing. Then those hypnotic eyes pin me again. "This isn't going away. Decide how you want to handle it. The video is bad enough, but Davis recently announced he's running for the House in a district that swings on family values. Even a hint of his name at this event could kill his campaign before it launches. My first order of business is to protect my client."

Our client, thank you very much. Davis Prescott isn't just an attendee at a seminar. He and his wife have been therapy clients for years. I knew about the campaign announcement before it happened. Connor Rives might be a PR mastermind and expert fixer, but I'm not new to this game. I happen to prefer a fresh set of rules.

"Don't make the mistake of underestimating me."

Something in his eyes tightens. The ghost of a smile, half challenge, half respect, and a hint of heat that makes me catch my breath. I adjust my bag and start for the door, each click of my heels a minor victory.

But I glance back. Not because I want the last word. Because Connor Rives looks like walking temptation, and I hate that my pulse skips.

He's watching me, unreadable. I hold his gaze long enough to prove I'm not cowed and maybe long enough to show I feel the pull between us. His mouth tilts. Not quite a smirk, but enough to spark heat low in my belly.

In any other circumstance, I'd be intrigued. Cautious for sure, but intrigued. But I know better than to be curious about men who make careers out of manipulating the truth.

BEHIND CLOSED DOORS—CONNOR

The hourly rental office is impersonal and as forgettable as a cheap hotel room. A space that exists to be forgotten. Which works in my favor. It provides discretion. My clients aren't seen walking into the office of a fixer. When there's nothing to focus on, they focus on me, and they talk. In this city, silence is currency, and I know how to make the most of it. This woman, however? She's a flashing billboard of outspoken honesty, and that makes her dangerous.

Like the look she gives me as she's walking out. There's nothing professional about it. Not that I'm one to judge.

On the video, she's a goddamn pinup in blond curls and red lipstick. The pencil skirt, the seamed hose, and a confident smile add to the sense that she knows exactly how much control she has and dares you to test it. It's a curated image, perfect for the classes she presents. She knows the effect. I've watched enough times to catch the details, and her tells. The way her chin tips before she lands a point. The slow drag of her fingertip along the margin of her notes. Every gesture deliberate and meant to hold a room.

The Prescotts called me the moment they saw the clip. I took a few minutes to dig into Dr. Emery Nicole before reaching out. It didn't take long to find the history. Seven months isn't that long, even in internet time. She was wearing a red dress in that video.

Then came the fallout. One comment that led to a devastating avalanche. The wronged wife. The contrite husband. Careful messaging designed to shift blame. The result? A woman burned alive in the court of public opinion. I recognize spin when I see it.

Her public response? Measured and careful, but her eyes were dead. She made one statement, then shut down and went dark. A move that suggests she had no choice. Now that I've met her, I can't imagine her being silenced and I can see the damage between the lines.

Years of performing, of learning how to read an audience in order to feed their hunger, without ever letting them see yours, gave me some finely honed instincts. Now I sell image control instead of skin, but the principle's the same. Make them look where you want, believe what you need them to. It's how I thrive in a city, and a career, built on manipulation.

Dr. Emery Nicole walked into my rented office wearing the same clothes from the video. Her lipstick as perfect as her composure, but there are micro-fractures in her facade. They show in the pulse at her throat, the way her fingers tighten around her bag, the shallow breaths.

The overhead light catches in her hair, a halo that doesn't fit the situation. It throws me off balance more than it should, stirring the part of me I keep caged. The one that likes to test limits and see what breaks first, control, or the person holding it.

The screen doesn't do her justice. On camera, she's beautiful. In person, she's magnetic, exuding a heat that slides beneath your guard before you realize you've been marked. I shouldn't notice, but I do.

I'm used to clients walking in wary. She walked in armed. Not with fear, but with caution and a blade honed by experience. She doesn't trust me, or what I represent. I can't blame her. She's been on the receiving end of spin before and she's still bleeding from it.

She looked at me like she already knew what I'd say. As if I'd spoken those words before, in someone else's mouth. And maybe I have.

Her stopping at the door feels intentional. One second

she's leaving and the next she's standing there staring at me. It feels like a test. Like she's gauging me. Seeing who blinks first.

Most people fold when I push. She didn't. She bristled and held her ground. Smart or reckless, I can't tell yet. Either way, I respect it, and it somehow makes her even sexier. Which is inconvenient as fuck. I'm here to contain the explosion, not start another one.

Her chest rises and falls in a measured rhythm, like she's pretending the air between us isn't sparking. It hit me the second she walked in; there's no way she didn't feel it too. Hell, that look back was either a confirmation or a challenge. Maybe both.

"One more thing." I take a slow breath, watch her shoulders tighten.

It doesn't help that my brain has drifted from the crisis at hand to cataloguing all her little signs of interest. Like the way her pupils widen, or the little hitch in her breathing when our eyes lock. In any other situation, we'd be halfway to getting horizontal. But right now? My client comes first.

"Don't go to the press. Don't post a statement. Don't give anyone a soundbite they can twist."

Her chin tips up and her eyes narrow. "And if I already have?"

"You haven't." The timing makes it a safe gamble and the tiny roll of her eyes tells me all I need to know. Still, I push harder, checking to see how far she'll bend. "If you did, start praying it's as boring as you think it is."

She takes two steps away from the door. Close enough for heat to carry. "Nothing I do is boring. And I don't scare easily, Mr. Rives."

Challenge it is. God, I love a challenge. The energy between us spikes, sharp and alive. She may as well have thrown down a gauntlet. The urge to pick it up is strong, but it'll have to wait. I've got bigger problems. Like my client, and how fast this whole mess could spiral if I let it.

"Good. Then you'll be smart enough to realize this isn't about scaring you. It's about not giving your enemies ammunition. If we're going to fix this, we move fast, and together. Starting with where this came from."

I keep my voice cool, professional. It should douse the spark. It doesn't. The air between us only tightens, sharp as static. Her smile is pure defiance wrapped in restraint, the kind that dares me to lose my composure first.

"You're preaching to the choir. I will not get anything done while standing here verbally sparring with you. I'll text when we find something."

She holds my eyes for a beat that stretches too long before she turns for the door and leaves without another glance back. The room feels emptier than it should.

I tell myself the interest is professional. She's a variable I need to understand and manage. This mess could reach far beyond one client. It could dismantle everything I've spent years building.

When I came to DC, I was a hotshot PR guy with a handful of personal clients. A little luck and a lot of hard work landed me a few bigger deals. The suits and polished image are a far cry from the young man with a stage name and a G-string stuffed with sweaty bills at the end of the night.

She looks at me like she already sees through it all.

The truth? I'd stake everything on my read. Dr. Emery Nicole, psychologist, sex therapist, podcaster, educator, is fierce and defiant on the surface. Beneath the sparring, though, is heat. The kind that hums between two people who recognize something dangerous in each other.

She likes control in public; I'd bet she's nothing like that in private. I felt it the way I read leverage in a room. By pulse and instinct, long before anyone realizes they've given it away. She walks a razor's edge between resistance and surrender. And that? That's what I live for.

Emery Nicole isn't just a problem to manage. She's a test of discipline. She makes me want to close the distance, take up the fight and see how far she'll let me go. What unsettles me is how she got under my skin, and how I can't tell whether she wants to bite or bleed, but I want to find out. The dangerous part isn't the impulse. It's how fast she brought it out of me.

DAMAGE CONTROL—EMERY

Bless my team for coming in on a Sunday evening. The second I left Connor Rives' office, I called Alex. They gasped in horror, then pivoted straight into battle mode with a categorized plan of attack. Because that's Alex. My spreadsheet-powered calm in any storm.

The office lights hum overhead, too bright and casting garish light on the stacks of client files scattering the conference table. I can still feel the tension from Connor Rives' stare threaded under my skin, but Alex, steady, efficient, unflappable, cuts through it. They don't need to ask if I'm okay; they already know I'm not. They dig in and help figure out how to make it better.

"Got the security footage from the Honey Pot," Alex says, tablet glowing, legal pad beside them layered in color-coded sticky notes. Their version of triage.

I stretch and roll my neck. It's been a long day and it's not likely to end soon. My pulse hasn't settled after learning of this blowup, but I push that aside so I can focus.

"What did you tell Glenda?" The venue manager's a longtime listener, quick to help, but this was our first collaboration. Trust without oversharing is the line I walk daily. Never mind that it chafes me to have to think that way. Life's handed me enough hard lessons that even I can't cling to that level of naivety.

"Just that there was an issue and we need access to every feed. Interior, exterior, loading dock, entry to the classroom space. Everything. She's on board."

Translated into Alex speak, that means they'd scared the poor woman half to death with precision politeness. Excellent.

It's comforting, that efficiency. Predictable. Alex doesn't need to raise their voice to take control. They rearrange the chaos until it obeys.

Dee sets a tray of steaming mugs in front of us, then slides one my way, one to Alex, and cradles his own before popping open his laptop.

"Triple shot. Figured we'd all need emotional support in liquid form." Leave it to Dee to understand my need for caffeine. The smell of roasted beans brings a smile to my face. Warm comfort in ceramic cups.

Alex lifts a brow. "At this hour? We'll be vibrating."

I wrap both hands around the mug and inhale like it's oxygen. Which, right now, it might as well be. "Caffeine now, survival later. Don't knock it unless you want me passing out on you."

Steam fogs my reading glasses as I take the first sip, dark and grounding. The taste jolts me back into focus, into the part of myself that knows how to handle chaos.

"I've been tracking the video." Dee's tone is grim. "It's spreading. Fast."

The words land heavier than the caffeine ever could. My heart gives a slow, deliberate beat. It's the sound of crisis taking shape. Even Alex goes still, their pen hovering midair, the hum of the laptop fan the only sound in the room.

Dee is a realist and not prone to the dramatic, so his tone

sends a chill down my spine. I want to email every attendee right now, warn them, and offer apologies. My fingers twitch toward the keyboard, muscle memory ready to move before thought catches up.

The text Connor Rives sent after I left his office holds me back.

'Don't offer any response until we talk again.'

I hate that he's right. Never mind that the idea of pushing something under the rug turns my stomach. The idea of hiring him isn't any better, but even I have to admit there may be no choice. In this situation, I need all the help I can get.

I've danced this dance before, and it nearly cost me everything. The difference now is I know how it ends if I get it wrong.

"I think I found something. Most of their cameras are old or low-res, so the quality isn't great." Alex taps their screen and the big monitor on the wall comes to life. "Watch the guy near the shop door."

They freeze the frame. The Honey Pot's entryway glows under the security cam's eye. The man stays at the edge of the light, face turned away from the camera as if he knew where it was. Another tap and the view shifts, showing the man turn into the alley.

"Glenda confirmed there's no camera coverage in the alley itself," Alex adds and clicks again. "But this guy shows up again by the loading dock."

My stomach tightens. Whoever this guy is, he understands angles and visibility.

Dee squints at the new image then sits back. "Front entrance and loading dock. That's it? Wasn't there a side door around there?"

"I sent a note to Glenda but haven't heard back yet." Alex

glides their thumb along the tablet and taps, sending another image to the screen. "What do you think?"

I lean in, trying to pick out features in the fuzzy footage. The man is half turned, but there's enough of his face to make out a smirk. Not the expression of someone casually standing around.

"Can you roll this section?" I stand and get closer to the screen as Alex plays the segment. The man's body language seems natural. "I don't recognize him. Could he be an employee? He seems very comfortable."

"No connection to the venue, or anyone there that we know of yet." Alex advanced to a new frame. "Caught him lighting up."

"Strange spot for some rando to smoke." Dee scowls at the image then back at his laptop. "He doesn't match any of the attendee profiles, nor any of the volunteers on Glenda's list."

"There are innocent reasons to be near the dock." My mouth forms the words but my brain and my gut tell me they're garbage. There could be innocent reasons, but odds are, that's not the case. "Deliveries, maintenance..."

"On a Sunday," Dee counters.

He's right. While possible, it was unlikely. My stomach knots. "Inside cameras?"

Alex taps their tablet. "They're pretty limited. Just the cash register, shop floor, and inside the office. Nothing inside the loading area, the classroom or on the stairs."

So we're stuck. I want something actionable, something to chase. What I get is uncertainty. The Prescotts trusted me and now their fixer is breathing down my neck. It's no surprise they hired someone like Connor Rives. Davis Prescott is a moderate from New York with the added stress of an election cycle. He has a lot at stake.

As for the professional fixer, he might be infuriating, but

there is no denying he's competent. And unsettling in ways I haven't yet unpacked.

The thought irritates me more than anything. I can still see the steadiness in his eyes, the measured way he took up space. A man used to stepping into fire and controlling which direction it spreads.

Something about him hums in my bloodstream. Even the devastating news of a security breach didn't stop my brain from clocking that underneath all that polish, the man has a coiled energy that pulls at me.

It's a hunger I've kept to myself, sharing tiny pieces with select past partners, but never fully explored. And certainly not with men who know how to manipulate a narrative.

Which is exactly why I should keep my distance and exactly why I know I won't.

I dig my phone out and type a message before I can overthink it.

> Possible face identified. Come to my office. We'll brief you. Call when you get here and someone will let you in.

I add the address even though I'm sure he already knows it. Whether from his own digging or from the Prescotts.

Alex's gaze flicks to my phone. "Connor Rives?"

"He's our client's crisis manager. Like it or not, we'll need to work together." My tone says begrudgingly. My pulse says god help me.

Alex crosses their arms and leans back in the chair. "Usually the idea of spin causes you to break out in hives."

They're not wrong.

"I can't risk it." If mine were the only reputation on the line, I'd take the hit. Been there and done that. I don't mind stepping up and being loud. That's my choice. My clients? Different story.

Alex's laugh doesn't surprise me. Dee's does. He shakes his head and braces his elbows on the table. "Play nice, but play smart."

"You know I will." These two have walked through the fire with me. Chalk up another reason I love my team so much. They know the memories this situation drags up, and how much I dislike people who make a living hiding and manipulating truths. Hiding isn't the same as lying, but unless I'm very wrong, Connor Rives is far too good at both.

I consider changing. I even glance toward the small closet where I keep a few outfits for videos. But no, he gets me like this. The classy and sassy, not quite edging into sexpot and still in the stiletto heels the online world's been judging.

I've been burned before, by the wife of a man who looked at me like I was a weapon, then painted me as the villain. And by the man I loved, who was content to play the victim to save a marriage I didn't know existed. I don't trust easily. Not with hearts, and especially not with headlines.

Still, there's no hiding the chemistry that simmered beneath the surface in that tiny office.

Which is just what I don't need on top of everything else.

But need has never factored much into what the body wants.

THE FIXER ON THE DOORSTEP—CONNOR

The rowhouse is the kind you could walk past a hundred times without noticing. There's no signage beyond simple brass numbers and a heavy wooden door polished by time. The man who answers could model for an editorial spread, but the faint disgust in his expression tells me he knows who I am and doesn't like it.

He doesn't have to like me; in fact, I'd be worried if he did. After what happened to Dr. Nicole in New York, anyone in her inner circle should hate fixers on sight. From what I've read, I'd guess he's her assistant, which means he was in the blast zone.

He leads me through a darkened lobby, past the elevator and to the stairs. A little cardio is always a good plan. The place smells like clean wood and old paper. I love it and hate it. It smells like history dressed up as reverence and power wrapped in calm, pretending it's never hurt anyone. Like every place that tells a story but conveniently leaves out the blood; it reminds me of quiet offices where secrets get traded for absolution and appearances hide sins long enough to sell the next version of the truth. My stock in trade.

Upstairs, he opens a door into a space that surprises me. The room whispers welcome in soft colors, curved furniture, and light that flatters everyone. It's not the pinup vibe I expected from Emery Nicole, public provocateur. I'd expected bold colors and sex appeal turned up to eleven. Instead, it's quiet command in cashmere tones. While the aesthetics are nice, I recognize the tactic. Create a soothing space with soft landings that encourage someone to exhale and relax, then open up. It's the same principle I use, different weapon.

A stack of framed art propped in a corner says she's not yet settled in, but I knew that from my research. Dr. Emery Nicole. Impressive credentials, sharp instincts, and enough grit to take a scandal and turn it into opportunity. She's not reckless; she's intentional. That's a difference I respect.

I scroll through the details I memorized earlier. Press quotes, speaking topics, the phrasing she uses when she's on camera. People reveal more in repetition than they realize. She always circles back to trust. Most people mean approval when they use that word. She means disclosure.

The cynic in me wondered if she manufactured the whole New York mess to gain more fame, but she posted one response when the story was hot, then went silent. She waited nearly five months before putting out a podcast and video that were emotionally raw and tactically brilliant.

One look at her world since she moved to DC put any lingering doubts to bed. Grit I respect; it's her brand of honesty that worries me. Especially with our mutual client. Honesty sells until it exposes the wrong name, or an uncomfortable truth.

There's a fine line between transparency and exposure. She seems determined to walk it barefoot. Bloody feet don't slow a woman like Emery Nicole. The footprints just mark the path where she's been.

I told myself the deep dive was strictly professional, but walking into this space, catching the clean, sharp scent that reminds me of our brief meeting earlier? My interest isn't nearly as professional as I'd like. It lingers, sharp and pressing on the caution I wear like armor, making it feel tight. Or worse, threatening to cut right through it. She's part of my job, nothing more. That's the line I draw, even though I suspect it won't hold.

The young man pushes through an interior door and leads me into a more functional workspace. Here, the newness is more obvious. There are no desks, just two long worktables, and boxes still line one wall. The faint scent of cardboard and coffee hangs in the air. New beginnings and unfinished business. A giant of a man sits at one end of the table, his bald head bent over a laptop, while she sits at the other, one hand gripping a coffee cup so hard her knuckles show white. She's wound tight, but only where she allows it. The coffee grip's intentional, a permission slip to crack, just a little, without anyone thinking she's not in control. They both look up as I step closer.

"You said you have something?"

She nods, her face a mask of frustration. The lipstick is gone, but the rest? Still the same. The fitted black pencil skirt. The red heels. That deep red wrap top that hugs every inch of confidence. She wore this for a room full of people eager to hear about pegging, and she's still in it now, hours later, holding court in her own office. Everything about it says it's an intentional choice. She's sitting in the wreckage wearing provocation like armor she has no reason to remove.

Any other client in this kind of chaos would've softened the message, thrown on a blazer, changed the conversation by changing the visuals. She's not backing down or trying to alter her image. The signal's clear: she owns the message and the fallout. My pulse kicks once. Hard. That red top isn't just bold; it's calculated. A line drawn in silk and confidence. My brain offers an image I didn't ask for: that same fabric looped between my fingers. The shape of control, coiled and waiting. I shut it down fast. Discipline is muscle memory by now, but some reflexes remember what it's like to answer power with power.

"Mr. Rives." Her voice is cool and even, but there's something in it. The same resonance I'd felt earlier. Even in the tension and stress, she's thinking three moves ahead and I'd bet money she researched me as thoroughly as I researched her. She nods at the conference table. "Have a seat."

"You don't have to summon me like a misbehaving teenager, you know. A simple 'please' works."

"Please." Her arched eyebrow and the crisp gesture to the table are moves that conjure images of strict schoolteachers or prissy librarians. The exact kind of prim and proper I delight in undoing. My mind betrays me again, sketching the smallest details like the tilt of her wrist, the clean line of her neck. "And try to keep up."

Instead of irritating me, her calm sends a slow, deep heat through my chest. Rattling the cage bars again, waking the part of me that lives for a challenge and knows exactly what to do with defiance. Banter like this is usually a signal that says, 'game on.' The question is whether her interest is real or a device to disarm.

She introduces her team quickly.

"This is Alex, my assistant. Pronouns are they/them."

I nod, filing it away. Model-perfect veneer, but the eyes tell a story. Alex is the calm, calculating one who catches everything you don't say out loud. They already have me assessed and categorized. Efficient. A mirror I don't mind looking into.

"And Dee. He handles tech and security."

Built like muscle hired for intimidation, but the handshake and tone are steady. He's quiet, reliable, and easy to underestimate until it's too late. A good asset if you know how to use him. She clearly does.

"Since we're going to be working together, I prefer a first-name basis if you're comfortable."

She sets the ground rule in a tone that sounds like a dare, smooth and deliberate, and damned if I don't feel it low in my gut. I know how easily control can shift when someone willing meets someone who knows how to take it, and I like the sound of surrender too much for my own good.

I give a slow nod. "Works for me."

Not because it levels the playing field, but because I want to hear what my name sounds like on her lips.

She nods to Dee and he sits back, pushes a button on a

remote, then points to the screen on the wall. The still image that comes up makes me suck in a breath.

"That's your suspect?" I already know the face. It's clear she doesn't, but she's bound to know the name. "Bronson Drake. Freelance 'journalist' and professional troll. This guy feeds on scandal."

Her assistant frowns. "Why does that name sound..."

"Because he's behind at least three exposés in the last year. Including one about..." She waves her hand in a dismissive gesture and Alex's eyes go wide. Emery sits back, arms folded, glaring at the image. "He never uses real photos. He was definitely not on our approved list."

"Not on Glenda's either," Dee adds. "He got in with a fake name or inside help."

Emery's jaw tightens. "We'll find the breach. But first, we stop the bleeding before he posts more about the event. I want him neutralized without collateral damage to our mutual client, or anyone else."

She says 'anyone else' like a vow, not a footnote. Her focus is impressive. Hearing Drake's name had to send her pulse skyrocketing, but her surface is calm. She's still too idealistic, thinking there's a way for a clean fix, but I can't fault her instincts. Drake isn't the type to respond to scare tactics. I take a deep breath while trying to decide how much I need to say to Emery and her crew. Since she's big on radical honesty, I settle for my version of it.

"I want him buried so deep he has to dig himself out before he can click the 'send' button to publish his bullshit."

Her gaze sharpens, and for a fraction of a second, something in it matches the tightness in my body. There's an electric feeling, as if we'd both taken a step toward something big. The air seems thinner and every sound in the room has an edge. Recognition can be louder and more powerful than simple attraction. It carries further and it's harder to ignore.

"You're about secrets. I'm about truth. That's going to be interesting."

"Not as interesting as watching you try to make truth survivable." I don't have to remind her she nearly lost everything because someone else decided which version of the truth to tell. She knows.

Our eyes lock and it's like the first pull of a riptide. Subtle and easy to miss until it's too late. Then she breaks eye contact and slides a single sheet of paper across the table to me.

"I understand discretion and privacy. Those are very different from secrecy. This isn't my first rodeo."

The page is an itemized summary of a plan, and it's a good one. It just doesn't go far enough. She's protecting principles and I'm protecting outcomes.

"This is a good start." I tap the page and fix my best encouraging smile on my face. Time to treat the good doctor as if she's a client and not an adversary. If nothing else, it's clear we have a mutual concern for damage control here.

"Why do you think you're here?" Her smile is sweet and smooth, and I've played right into her hands. "You insisted I not do anything right away, and that we need to work together and quickly. I agree."

She braces her elbows on the table and her smile brightens. "Do you want to draw up a contract for us working together, or shall I? I assume you work with confidentiality agreements and a whole variety of other things."

It's not often I'm surprised in business, but she's done it. She doesn't spar to win; she plays for balance, and I can't decide if that's mercy or strategy. Either way, it's leverage.

"I'll modify my standard contract and send it to you. Feel free to edit and we can discuss what works." Not something I normally offer, but there is nothing normal about this situation. I extend my hand to shake and she takes it slowly. Her hand is smooth and warm, sliding into mine with deceptive calm. Heat arcs up my arm; discipline keeps me still.

Her eyes lift to meet mine. Whatever spark caught earlier roars quietly back to life, sharp and unmistakable. It's also very mutual. The proof isn't in her smile or her touch. It's in the stillness that follows, in the space neither of us steps out of. It's in the way she looks at me and dares me to be different from every man who's burned her. On the outside, I'm steady. On the inside, I'm bracing for the storm she brings with her.

"Agreed."

For the first time in my career, I'm not sure who is hiring whom. The look in her eyes stops me cold. She is heat and danger personified, equal parts warning and invitation. It's a risk I shouldn't even consider, and a door I already know I'll open.

MONDAY, MARCH 23

STILL IN MY HEAD—EMERY

There's not enough coffee in DC for me today. I wave at the receptionist and take the stairs at a brisk pace, hoping the exercise will jump-start my brain. My legs protest, my shoulder twinges, and my nerves hum like a power line that never shut down last night.

Waking up after far too little sleep to discover the video had gone viral is not my idea of the way to start a week. Dee greets me in the shared kitchen with a steaming mug of coffee, my third of the morning, and the faint, pitying smile of someone who already knows the headlines. I accept the cup then push through to the workroom and settle at the table where Alex has laid out a tidy summary of the situation.

Social media comments range from juvenile jokes to think pieces about sex-positivity and professionalism. More than a few lurid headlines paint the whole thing as salacious. Connor would probably call it predictable. I call it a migraine in the making.

'Paging Dr. Hot Takes'
'Sex-Positive or PR Disaster? What the Emery Nicole Clip Really Means'
'Real Men Know It's About Confidence, Not Size But Try Telling That to Dr. Emery 'Size-Queen' Nicole'

The last one makes me chuckle. I've been called worse, and less accurately. I do like bigger; I just don't care whether it's factory installed or aftermarket. There are toys in my drawer that could intimidate an insecure man, and I don't buy them for the aesthetic.

Dee clicks on the last link and the teaser line blares through the speakers:

> "These so-called experts keep moving the goalposts, man. First it was personality, then came performance, and now it's inches. Regular guys can't win anymore!"

Alex rolls their eyes and waves a dismissive hand. "Gross. It's giving incel vibes. He probably swears he's a nice guy and wonders why no one swipes right."

Dee snorts into his coffee. I almost choke on mine. For three seconds, the whole mess feels ridiculous enough to laugh at and it feels good. Then the weight of it settles back in.

This isn't something I can ignore or hope blows over, and no matter how much I want to come out swinging, I need to temper my response. So far, I'm the only one in the crosshairs, and I'd like to keep it that way.

Which means I need to finalize that contract with Connor.

The idea is infuriating, but faced with the rapid escalation of a potential career-ending mess, I don't have a choice. Worse,

I've got an inbox filled with messages from concerned attendees, and they deserve answers.

"We've got the social tracker up."

Leave it to Alex to steer things back to the task at hand. Dee settles at the table with us and I look to the fourth chair. Empty.

"Erin coming in?" The moment we got settled in DC, we realized without a corporate office to provide administrative support, we needed to expand the team. Enter Erin, a final year grad student who I hoped to groom into an assistant role and free Alex for bigger things.

"After lunch." The eye roll Alex delivers is epic.

Fine. We'll manage. "Order breakfast?"

The look they give me says it all. Of course Alex is on top of that. Probably pulled up the delivery app the moment I walked in the door. My phone buzzes, pulling a groan out of me. I'd like to shut it all off and spend the day in bed, but that won't fix any of this. Instead, I tap the screen.

At Shea's. What does everyone want?

I exhale. Of course he's picking up food. I send him our usual orders. "Cancel delivery. Connor is bringing food."

Alex makes a face but nods. I can't disagree with their sentiment. I'm picky about expanding my team, and Connor Rives would not make the cut in a normal world. Nothing about this is normal.

Twenty minutes later, the man strolls in, all cuffed-up sleeves and impressive forearms. He sets the trademark bright teal bags on the table.

"Who got double bacon and American cheese?" He holds out a sandwich wrapped in teal and white stripes with 'HQ-Bx2' scrawled across the neat fold.

Alex snatches it with mock reverence. "You're forgiven for doubting the perfect egg sandwich. Sadly, Shea's doesn't do rolls, so a bagel has to do."

If Connor gets the subtle reference to Harley Quinn, he keeps it to himself.

"I'm thinking the turkey, spinach, and egg whites is yours." He slides the sandwich across the table to Dee. I'm surprised Connor guessed right. Most people assume that one's mine. He drops a sandwich into my hands and the smell is heaven on earth. "Eggs, kimchi, greens, and sriracha mayo. You like it spicy."

His tone matches his smirk and the air between us sharpens, charged in ways caffeine can't explain. I unwrap my breakfast and take a hurried bite instead of answering.

He pulls out a second one and my eyebrows go up. I swallow fast and give him a look of shock. Maybe dialing up the snark will keep my inconvenient interest in him from growing.

"What? Not doing the healthy thing?"

Connor shrugs. "Once you say 'bagel,' healthy is relative. This sounded good, so I figured I'd try it."

Silence descends as we all get much-needed food. I'm halfway through my sandwich before Alex wipes their hands and taps the tablet.

"We've hit half the media outlets for takedowns."

Connor nods, sipping coffee. "Keep pushing. The biggest concern is containment. Finding out how Drake got in is a close second."

Dee doesn't look up. "I've checked all the footage. No front or dock entry. Still waiting on Glenda about the rest. I'm damn certain there's another door, but it's not on any of the cameras."

"Good plan." Connor's approval lands heavy. "When you

contact editors and site admins, mention attendee NDAs. Make it about their privacy, not Emery's or even the venue's. Fear of liability shuts things down faster than ethics."

He's right. Damn him, he's right.

I nod. "We'll frame it that way."

He relaxes slightly. "Discretion keeps truth alive, Emery. Sometimes you protect honesty by slowing it down."

"Or by refusing to bury it," I counter. "We can do both."

We trade looks and he doesn't argue. Which, as far as I'm concerned, is progress.

"I'm stuck on access until Glenda gets back to me. I've also reached out to the neighboring shop. They may have exterior cameras and other angles." Dee hauls in a slow breath and swipes a hand over his face. "I'm cross-referencing all staff, volunteers, and even our team with Drake's aliases and the sites where he commonly posts. I doubt anyone is that openly connected, but no stone unturned."

The idea that someone I know and trust could have let Drake in turns my stomach. I push my empty cup aside. "I want to draft an email to attendees. They deserve to hear about this from me."

Connor's jaw flexes. "Bad idea."

"It's the right one." I knew he'd disagree, but I won't budge on this one.

"The video went viral. They know. You risk making it a bigger problem."

The tightening around his eyes is subtle, but I catch it. That and the flare of his nostrils as he inhales. I can almost imagine him counting to ten. I don't wait.

"These people trusted me enough to walk into that room. I'm not hiding from them."

His silence is taut as a wire. Finally he exhales, slow and

measured, then pins his gaze on my face. "Fine. But keep it tight. No adjectives. No loaded language."

I can't tear my eyes away from Connor's. The clack of fingers on a keyboard tells me Alex is doing what they do best. I don't need to hear their firm 'on it' to know it's being taken care of.

Connor doesn't blink. "Show me before it goes out."

"Of course." I hold his stare like we're locked in some epic battle, and maybe we are. There's not a chance in hell I'll let him spin the way I talk to my clients.

His mouth twitches, like he knows. "Good."

We go back to work, silent but buzzing with unspoken tension. For now, at least, the war has a truce.

THE BACKLASH BEGINS—EMERY

By the time the clock hits eleven, caffeine is the only thing keeping my spine upright. The office hums with a steady mix of typing and controlled panic. Dee's got three monitors lit up, Alex is fielding calls, and Connor's commandeered half my whiteboard with a grid of names and arrows that would make a conspiracy theorist proud.

He's good, disturbingly good. He moves with quiet certainty, every line he draws deliberate, each arrow like a scalpel dissecting my chaos into something manageable. It's the same surgical precision the last fixer used when he carved my life into headline fodder. Watching Connor work is both infuriating and magnetic.

"Do you always take over your client's offices?"

"Call this a demonstration to encourage you to sign that contract."

Alex's phone buzzes and they pale. "Drake posted a teaser link. He's calling it Political Sex Education."

My stomach plummets. "Is it live?"

"Not yet. It's a teaser."

Sounds blur into the background and I swallow hard. A low hum builds in my chest. It's a familiar sensation I'd hoped never to experience again. The last time this started, it ended in scorched-earth betrayal and a social media firestorm. This feels the same. Maybe worse. It's like the universe decided I hadn't been through enough and needed a repeat. What lesson am I supposed to be learning here? I want to scream. I want to find Bronson Drake and discover what drives someone to be like this.

Connor's head is bent over his laptop, expression carved from granite. "He's baiting you. Don't give him free advertising. Not even in your head. Especially not in your head."

"I'm not..." I stop myself. He's right. Again. That somehow makes it worse. He sees the play unfolding like he's been here, done this before, and maybe he has.

"Got something." Dee sits back; his features painted with shock. "I knew there was another door. Glenda says the side door near the dock was unlocked from the inside at 1:45. Fifteen minutes before the class started."

The sounds of the city, of the office, all come roaring back loud and clear as everyone goes silent. Alex's fingers still on their keyboard and their gasp echoes in the sudden quiet.

"And there's no security footage?" Connor stands in a rush and looks over Dee's shoulder. He radiates command like heat, and it'd be a lie to say I don't find that hot as hell.

"Not of that door, no."

Cold dread coils in the pit of my stomach and I wrap my arms around my middle. "We loaded in from the dock. Never used that door."

Dee lifted his gaze from the screen. "She's right. We loaded in. I checked with Glenda and their staff to go over the attendee list. All the staff were either in the shop or upstairs. Alex and Emery went up to the classroom and Erin set up a merch table in the shop."

Connor's gaze lifts, sharp. "Erin is your intern?"

"Assistant in training," I correct automatically, even as my pulse stutters. The cold spreads to my fingers and toes. "She's twenty-two. Finishing her degree. She's..."

"Eager. Tech-savvy. Idealistic," he finishes for me. "Perfect profile for someone to exploit."

I glare at him before I can stop myself. "Maybe she went out to the van for something and forgot to lock back up. People make mistakes. New staff aren't as familiar with security protocols."

"Sure." His tone is mild, but I catch the undercurrent. Trust but verify. That corporate, careful way of saying he doesn't trust anyone, me included. There's no doubt he's done more digging since yesterday and he knows what a fixer did to me, but still thinks he can manage me.

I pull in a breath. "Let's finish triage first. Drake's countdown comes first."

Connor studies me a second longer before nodding. "Fine. But you're blind if you don't look inward, too."

The words sting because they echo my own private fears. Because he's right again and it all feels too close to wounds I don't let people see. Especially not men who talk like they know better. Especially not fixers.

A big hand lands on my shoulder a second before Connor squats next to my chair, bringing those whiskey-hued eyes level with mine.

"You care too much, Emery." His voice drops low enough that it's almost private, a frequency that slides under my guard as his fingers tighten for a beat, then he takes his hand away. "That's both a blessing and a curse."

It's a line that should sound patronizing, but it doesn't. My breath catches before I can stop it. He's too close, too steady, too unflinchingly calm when everything in me feels like static. It's unfair that someone who represents so many of my worst memories also makes my body lean in, just a fraction, before I remember to resist.

He straightens, reclaiming his space and the authority that comes with it. I should be grateful for the distance. Instead, I feel the echo of his touch ghosting across my skin.

He's right about me caring too much, but he doesn't understand that caring is what makes me good at what I do, and keeps me from becoming something I'd hate. And God help me, much as I'd like to hate him on principle, that is not the word that comes to mind right now.

His gaze flicks to the contract still sitting on the corner of the table, edges slightly curled from when I bent the page during edits. He doesn't touch it. Just looks at me, expression unreadable.

"This isn't slowing down," he says quietly. "You shouldn't have to do this alone."

"I've done worse." I keep my voice neutral. "And I'm not alone." I nod toward Alex and Dee, both still buried in their screens and headsets. "I've got them."

"And now you've got me."

I huff. "Is that part of the sales pitch?"

"It's part of the contract. Which you started editing. Which means, whether you'll admit it or not, you're considering it."

He's not wrong. Maybe I need to accept that he knows what he's doing and, for now at least, we're on the same side. I reach for the contract, flipping through it quickly. "I only did a first pass. There's still language I need to look at more closely."

He steps in closer, not touching, but radiating heat. He scans the margin notes in seconds. "All of this is reasonable. I'll accept every change."

"Of course you will," I say, drier than intended. "They're basic. I should never have had to write them in."

His smile is almost gentle. "But you did. Because someone made you need to."

The truth of that hits harder than it should. I don't want him to be the kind of man who sees that quickly. It takes him minutes to make the changes and send the new document for a digital signature.

My computer pings with an email notification and I open the link and give the new contract a quick scan.

"Fine. Fuck it." Another click, a digital signature, and it's done.

His jaw tics once, but there's no victory in it. Just understanding. He taps a few keys on his laptop and my email pings again with his acceptance.

"Done. We'll make it count."

I can't decide if his level of efficient competence is maddening, or stoking the flames of arousal I've been trying, and failing, to stamp out.

OUT OF CONTEXT—EMERY

Another teaser goes live at one. Fifteen seconds, cropped from my introduction, paired with a clickbait headline: Therapist Teaches Sex Class for Politicians?

The caption doesn't name Davis Prescott, but it might as well.

Dee swears under his breath. "We flagged that account for takedown twenty minutes ago."

"It's mirrored," Connor says. "Hundreds of reposts by now. You can't chase them all. You starve them."

He's calm. Infuriatingly calm. The kind that looks effortless until you realize it's armor forged from experience and built for detachment. I want to match it, but fury tastes sharp in my throat.

"Then we feed truth instead. A statement, or even a podcast note."

Connor shakes his head. "Too soon. Every word you say right now gets weaponized."

"And silence screams guilt." One of my few regrets is agreeing to stay quiet for so long when things blew up in New York. It allowed others to sell their version as the truth. I hate feeling powerless. I hate being reduced to waiting for the shoe to drop.

"Public reaction looks like guilt confirmation." His voice is level and firm. Everything he says is logical and devoid of emotion. This is what he does. It's why I agreed to work together. Why I signed his client contract with minimal changes. It's not his life on the line, so he has no problem keeping feelings out of it, and that can be helpful right now.

Still, I hate that he's right. I hate it even more that some part of me finds comfort in his control. It doesn't help that he's close enough I can smell a faint trace of his cologne. Clean and restrained and threaded with danger. It suits him. He's a man who builds walls out of reason and pretends he can live inside them forever, but that stillness is confined to the surface.

He is everything I should avoid. Reminder and temptation, structure and heat, and my body doesn't care.

Doesn't care about optics, or timing, or danger, or even ethics. It buzzes like I swallowed a current.

Betrayed by my own body.

Alex breaks the tension. "I got a response from The Herald. Editor says if Drake posts, they'll 'contextualize' it."

Connor's phone pings. He checks, mutters something sharp, then looks up. "That editor's full of it. I know someone higher up. It'll take one phone call to fix this."

I should thank him, but gratitude feels too much like surrender. Especially when every favor comes with fine print. Especially when the last time this sort of thing happened, I got blindsided by a fixer and a wedding ring I didn't know existed.

Connor steps aside to make the call and the side door opens. Erin slips in, quiet and flustered, scarf in a messy loop and her face flushed.

"Sorry I'm late. Dentist. One of those don't cancel or you'll wait six months for another appointment things."

"Fine." My response is automatic, but my mind is still on the door that got unlocked and the escalating catastrophe tearing apart my world. My nerves hum the way they did in New York, right before everything caught fire.

She sets her bag down; tablet hugged to her chest. "What did I miss?"

"Containment plan," Dee says without looking up. "Drake's teasing about a big post."

Erin winces and settles into her usual spot at the long table. "I saw. It's already got a hashtag. #EmeryGate."

Another stone of dread drops, pushing my breath out and sending ripples of cold shivers through my body. "Where?"

Erin blinks, then shrugs. A gesture I dislike but can ignore on a good day. Today isn't a good day.

"Where did you see it?"

Another shrug, but this time it has the air of feigned

indifference. Like she's excited by all this. I shake my head and push the thoughts away. The last thing I need is to let doubt and suspicion tear us apart from the inside. I need to trust my team.

"Uh… someone texted me a screenshot?"

Alex's head jerks up. "From whom?"

"I don't know. It's in a group chat. Classmates talking."

The explanation rings sort of right. Erin is perpetually online and deeply invested in social media. It makes sense that she'd see things first. Still, the timing feels off. Too fast and plugged in. Too convenient. A small part of me whispers that if it were as widespread as she claims, we should have seen it.

Another part of me files away her too-eager look and remembers how fast betrayal can happen. How trusting too easily can cost everything. Maybe I won't shove the suspicion too far from the surface.

"Focus on emails. If there are questions from attendees, I need to deal with those first. Sort and compile. No canned responses."

She nods as if eager to get to work. Or more likely, eager to change the subject. "On it."

Connor ends his call, slides his phone back into his pocket, and looks from me to Erin. "Everything okay here?"

"Fine." I say it too fast and his gaze lingers on me a second longer. Like he knows something's off. He probably does, and I can't decide if that's comforting or terrifying.

There's no way he hasn't read every headline by now. Probably knows more about my public scandal than I do. That should feel invasive but somehow doesn't.

"Good." He pulls a chair over and sits next to me. I do not need another dose of whatever chemistry is brewing between us. Connor is a good-looking man, and his tailored dress clothes show off a body that says he works out, but I can ignore looks. It's the quiet intensity of him and the sense that there's so much more hiding behind his smooth exterior that gets to me.

On the surface, he's too controlled. Does he ever let go? I think he does. That's what has me intrigued. I want to know what he's like when he drops the mask, and what it would be like if he did it with me.

The chair creaks as he leans forward, forearms braced on his knees, close enough that I can feel the warmth radiating off him. He doesn't touch me, but the proximity alone feels like a test. A reminder of how easily control can shift, and awareness can turn into something else entirely.

"We've done what we can for now, and we'll keep working on containment. Stop trying to be a rock in all of this."

I open my mouth to protest, then snap it shut. It would be easy to claim I've got all the support in the world, because I do. I could point to Dee and Alex. Two people who stood with me through ugliness before.

For most people, that would work, but Connor Rives isn't most people. He'd know. Somehow, he'd know.

"You're not doing this alone."

He's said some form of that before. It's the same thing both Alex and Dee said to me in New York. It sounds different coming from Connor. From Alex and Dee, it's a promise. Connor makes it both a promise and a warning. It's not that I don't have to do it alone; it's that he won't let me.

That should scare me more than it does. That should remind me of everything I lost when I trusted the wrong man.

The last thing I need is to let someone like Connor get too close.

The air between us hums. Across the room, Erin has her head down, typing vigorously. Alex and Dee are both buried in their own work.

And I can't shake the feeling that too close with Connor might have already happened.

THE DISTANCE BETWEEN US—CONNOR

I leave Emery's office at four, the air between us still tense with all the things we haven't said. She's brilliant, relentless, and infuriating. She's also blinding herself on purpose. That combination shouldn't fascinate me. Every time she digs in her heels, I see a flash of something I haven't seen in years. Emery still believes truth can survive without armor.

Erin might not be malicious, but she's sloppy. Idealists often are. And sloppy people are dangerous. They're the ones who think intent outweighs impact.

Outside, the street's loud with afternoon traffic. I stop under a lamppost, thumb open my phone, and send a message to my analyst.

> Create a mock internal memo about a "Tuesday night follow-up Q&A for attendees." Send only to Emery's office emails and mark it confidential. Nothing sensitive. Just bait.

If that fake detail leaks, I'll know where to look. It's not paranoia. It's proof. In my world, proof is the only thing worth believing in.

The reply comes quickly.

> Understood. Want us to go deeper? Her devices? The intern's?

I pause at the corner and consider. Emery already granted access to any work equipment her office provides. She's not hiding anything. She saw the contract addendum and offered the permissions. But prying into her personal history? Or her staff's? That feels different. Not yet.

Keep it to office accounts and devices for now. Nothing personal. I want a clean paper trail.

Got it. Want to game out more of these little tests?

Yes. One's not enough. We'll start simple and build. First one's bait. Rest, we plan tomorrow.

The afternoon air is cool and damp, typical spring in DC. Emery's insistence on transparency is noble. It's also naive. Truth without protection isn't bravery, it's exposure. And yet, when she argues, when she leans over that table with fire in her eyes, I want to believe she's right. She speaks like someone who hasn't been broken. Or more like someone who survived, but refused to let it turn her bitter. Exposure is how people get destroyed. Careers get gutted, reputations shredded, and lives are ruined because someone thought honesty was a shield instead of a spotlight.

Emery sees people as fixable. I see them as fallible. That's our difference. It's also a big part of what I find so attractive about her. She still fights for redemption; I fight to make sure the damage doesn't make the news. Somewhere between those philosophies, we're circling each other like predators who forgot which of us started the hunt. Except the danger isn't in the teeth; it's in how much we want to be caught.

I stop at the crosswalk, watching the traffic blur past. Drake has been trickling out teasers all day. A brilliant strategy that keeps the story fresh in people's minds and makes it harder to contain the fallout. He's playing the long game, bleeding the narrative one drop at a time. It's the same trick I'd use in his shoes. I don't have to like it, but I'd be a fool not to recognize it and even respect it in a way.

Whatever happens next, we'll either win together or go down fighting.

My phone buzzes again.

Canary set.

Good. Now I wait. Every leak tells a story. Every betrayal leaves a fingerprint. You have to set the right trap and give people enough time to reveal themselves.

If the fake Q&A shows up anywhere online, it'll be easy to track the source. I'm certain Emery isn't doing this to herself and have no reason to suspect Dee or Alex. Both are loyal, competent, and too experienced to make rookie mistakes. That leaves the weakest link. The one with the nervous hands and the too-bright eagerness.

It's the intern, no, assistant in training, I'm not sure about. Emery's trust is unexpected, considering what she's been through. Then again, her dynamic duo of a team has given her reason to believe. Or at least hope.

I can't imagine trusting anyone the way she trusts them. But in less than twenty-four hours of knowing Emery, she's made me feel like anything is possible.

Hope is dangerous, and maybe that's why I can't look away from her.

Whatever happens, the clock is ticking, and I've got a job to do—protecting my client. Sure, Emery's my client now, on paper, but I've been around long enough to know there are always layers beneath the contract. The real question is, when this blows up, and it will, am I protecting the Prescotts, or risking everything to protect her?

And if I choose her, what does that say about me?

CONTAINMENT MEASURES—EMERY

By the time the sky turns violet behind the rowhouse windows, I've lost track of how many notifications I've silenced. Drake's exposé dropped around dinner time, complete with screenshots, pulled quotes, and a blurred still from the video that's everywhere.

The pings from incoming messages got so frequent I silenced my notifications. It's death by polite email. A thousand tiny cuts wrapped in professionalism.

Erin left hours ago. Alex and Dee hover, waiting for orders I can't give.

"Go home. Have a good dinner. Get some sleep." There's nothing we can do at this hour. No amount of strategizing is going to change what's already out there. From here on, it's damage control.

Dee looks like he wants to argue, but Alex lays a hand on his arm.

"Text if anything changes."

When the door clicks shut behind them, the solitude hits hard. I sink into the couch in the front office, arms wrapped tight around myself. I let the silence stretch until it's heavy enough to feel like a second heartbeat. This is the part no one warns you about, the ache that comes after the adrenaline fades. The not-quite-panic that settles behind your ribs when you survey the devastation. They don't talk about the shock after the blowup, when you realize you're the only one left to sweep up the debris.

I've learned to embrace that quiet space.

A sharp knock rattles the office door.

There's only one person that could be. I thumb the access control on my phone. Connor steps through the moment the lock turns. He's ditched the tie, and I swear he rolled his sleeves up higher. Damn him and those forearms. An almost eerie calm radiates off him like a shield. His presence is its own gravity. He brings a measured and contained stillness that suggests power more than peace. He's too composed and it makes me wonder if anything ever gets under that skin.

"If you came to tell me it's out, congratulations, you're late."

He settles on the couch, his eyes traveling over me as if checking for damage. Joke's on him; it's all internal. It doesn't show up on cameras. Only in the places where stillness allows doubts to seep in.

"I came to make sure you didn't try to fix it alone."

Maybe he's forgetting I've been down this road once before.

"I'm not your responsibility."

He laughs and spreads his arms over the couch back. "We have a contract that says otherwise. I'm in this at least until the fire's out."

Because he's a fixer. He's focused on the problem.

"That's where we differ. You see a fire. I see people."

"And people burn." His voice is low and gentle. He's not being cruel, just honest. It's terrifying how calm he sounds while saying it. Like a man who has no fear of getting singed.

I sink deeper into the corner, hugging a cushion to my chest. "Half my week is canceled. A national conference pulled my panel. I'm fine, though."

He sits up and places a folder on the coffee table, then braces his elbows on his knees. "You're not fine. But you're still standing, and that's more than most."

The folder feels important. Why else would he come back here tonight? "What's that?"

"Damage assessment. Outlets that matter, ones we can still reach. And—" he leans forward and flips to a page "—a list of events you should keep. The ones that show strength instead of retreat."

My pulse stumbles when I see the title at the top of the list. Tuned In and Turned On: Flirt Like You Mean It.

"That event is Wednesday." I can't imagine going to any event so soon, much less one that's meant to be sparkly, lighthearted fun.

"Keep it." There's no arguing with his tone. Still, I have to try.

"It's a singles event, not a press statement."

He leans back and spreads out again. "Exactly. You being visible tells people you're not hiding. Optics of resilience. Besides"—his mouth tilts—"it's an opportunity to redirect the narrative. The unflappable expert educator."

Oh, I'm flappable. The way his shirt stretches across his chest is a solid distraction from everything else. I won't let myself look down. I already know he's got a very fine ass; I do not need to check out the front view. Not tonight. Not when every nerve in my body already feels wired wrong.

This is not simple attraction. This is full-on disruption that threatens to make me question what would happen if I let him in.

The way he carries himself, he knows what he looks like, and I'm damn certain the image he presents is one hundred percent intentional.

"And you'll be there to manage optics, I suppose?" Pulling up snarky humor is a far safer path than where my brain, or, more accurately, my body, seems determined to go.

"Absolutely." Again with the half grin. It lifts one corner of his mouth and makes him look cocky as hell. It's a dangerous smile. I get the sense he's thought three steps ahead, and one of those steps is me.

"Front row, I bet." Was this arguing or flirting? Or both?

"If that's what it takes." He looks calm. Like nothing could ruffle or rattle him.

I should tell him no. Instead, I nod, because something about the certainty in his tone steadies me. It's infuriating how easily he can take control of a situation I've built an entire career on owning.

He stands, slides his hands into his pockets, and damn if that doesn't pull my attention south. I snap my eyes back to his face in time to catch the smirk that says he caught me looking.

"You'll get through this, Emery. Drake wants chaos. You give him calm."

"Easy for you to say." It was different in New York. I was fighting corporate attitudes and a vindictive, wronged spouse. Plus, no one else's reputation was at stake. I was only calm because I had no choice, and as soon as I realized there would be no escaping the picture that had been painted of me, I turned tail and ran.

This isn't the same. Other people's reputations are on the line, and I'm not going to walk away and lick my wounds this time.

"It's not easy, but it is necessary." He moves closer and my eyes slide down his body. I stop at his belt buckle, matte silver, and stand in a rush before I can focus on more. The motion is instinctive. If I don't move, I might do something stupid, like believe him. Or succumb to the desire to find out if he's always so controlled.

For a second we look at each other. The air vibrates with everything we won't name. It's exhaustion, defiance, and the heat that keeps threading between our arguments all pressed into a wild cocktail. He's mesmerizing and dangerous, and impossible to turn away from. I feel like the proverbial moth drawn to a flame.

"Go home. You're off the clock." Earlier, the solitude weighed heavy, but I welcomed it. Now, it's the last thing that I want, but for very different reasons.

"Not yet." He hesitates at the door. "Stay on top of your emails this week. I'm running a test."

That little dose of reality snaps me to my senses and douses the fire that had been trying to flare up. "Trust issues?"

"Verification." He gives a faint smile. "Trust comes after."

When he's gone, I drop my face into my hands and let out a shaky laugh that almost sounds like a sob. I'm still standing. It may be shaky but it's better than the alternative. Still standing, still fighting, even when everything feels like ash.

Wednesday's class is staying on the calendar.

If I'm going down, I'm going down doing what I do best. Talking about connection, desire, and the mess we make trying to be human.

If Connor Rives thinks he's going to be a passive observer, quietly working behind the scenes to manage optics? He's wrong.

Oh so wrong. Somewhere between the damage and desire, I have to admit, Connor's not the only one testing boundaries.

And I'm not sure which one of us I should be more afraid of.

TUESDAY, MARCH 24

BACK ON RECORD—EMERY

"This'll solve the street noise," Dee says, tugging the last acoustic panel into place and smoothing the thick curtain closed over the biggest window. "Not studio-quality, but sound-friendlier than it was."

"Is that a technical term? Sound-friendlier?" I navigate the cables snaking next to the couch.

"I'm a man of many talents." He grins and straightens. "Cables are routed, gain is clean, and the last of the reverb's under control. Oh, I replaced the intro track in your template folder."

"Legend," I murmur, pulling up my rundown and setting my phone to do-not-disturb. "Hey, Alex, we still doing the lipstick red on the promo?"

"Unless you want to switch it to flamingo pink," Alex deadpans from across the room, turning their screen so I can see the episode title art. "You wanted to get this up tomorrow. Final call?"

I glance at the mockup. Perfect as expected.

"Love it. Keep the red."

Alex gives me a thumbs up, hits a key on their laptop, then settles at the makeshift control table Dee's arranged.

"We're taping video as well for social snippets. I set you up on the end of the couch. Better lighting and sound, and I think it looks more inviting and less clinical than you sitting in a chair." Dee has a light sensor in his hand, holding it near one end of the couch.

The front office is warm and welcoming, meant to feel safe and inviting. The space is my therapy room and doubles as a podcast set on recording days, and it works better than it should thanks to the second-floor location that helps muffle some of the city noise, and the drapes, plus Dee's setup, take care of most of the rest.

I take a seat and look around while he checks levels. We've only been in this space a few months, but it's already starting to feel like ours. The office was a balance of needs against cost. We splurged on a good location, secure entry, a building receptionist downstairs. All things that would help clients and patients feel safe. Then we had to make the two rooms plus a shared kitchen serve a variety of roles.

The space isn't perfect, but budgets only stretch so far and I'm not complaining about the lack of a recording booth. I've got Dee and Alex, and together, we make it work.

"Let's do a test of audio."

Normally, I use a table microphone, but when we're also shooting video, I switch to the lavalier. Dee fusses with getting it in the right spot, then joins Alex at the table. I chatter for thirty seconds, enough for them to get the sound levels dialed in.

Alex nods. "Want ambiance from the start or drop it in later?"

"Layer it in after." I glance at the notes on the big monitor in front of me, out of the camera's view. "I want the voice to land first."

Alex nods and I see the notes change on the screen. "Looks like you moved the desire hook?"

"Yes. I'm closing with that. I'm opening with performance versus connection—how we signal, what we hide. Then take that into connection. It'll be a natural segue."

I square my shoulders and brush my hair off my face. Dee gives a thumbs up and the text on the screen scrolls to the opening script.

I take a breath. Settle my voice. And begin.

"Welcome to Let's Talk About Sex—where we explore pleasure, power, and the spaces between."

By the third line, I'm locked in and hitting the perfect balance of calm curiosity with a hint of wicked. I talk about the performance of politeness, the theater of email signoffs, the intimacy of a look held too long. I draw parallels between sexual scripts and everyday interactions; how the lines blur when we stop paying attention. How authentic connection that's real, raw, and mutual isn't a given. It's a skill.

The podcast has always felt like home. I don't mention Connor, but I'm thinking about him when I say you can touch someone with your voice. His voice lingers in my head longer than it should. He doesn't flirt. He commands attention. My words flow smooth and sure, like my entire life isn't spinning out of control for all the world to see.

The script rolls and I nearly fumble over the next sentence as my breath catches. I clear my throat and keep going, knowing Alex can take care of a little slip.

"When I say restraint, I don't just mean physical. I mean holding space. Holding tension. Choosing not to act, even when you want to. Especially when you want to. When practiced with intent, restraint can be every bit as intimate as surrender. Sometimes more."

There's no denying it. Connor is everywhere in this episode. His critiques, his silence, the way he looked at me before he left like he could read things I hadn't said out loud.

"Desire isn't a finish line. It's a conversation. Desire is a dialogue, not a destination. It's something you build, exchange, shape together. The best kind of heat doesn't come from racing toward the end. It comes from listening while you're getting there."

Yeah, there it is again. I drafted this podcast late last night, well after he left. Alex and I refined it this morning before I made final edits, and somehow I'd missed the connection until the words came out of my mouth.

I make it through the close of the episode and look to Alex and Dee before I move. They both give strong nods, so I unclip the lavalier and stand. Thoughts of Connor linger, teasing the edges of my brain. I don't want to admit the level of attraction I feel to him. I don't want to examine that too closely.

Especially now. Doing something other than damage control restored some sense of normal. Like maybe we can all get through this, again, and move on.

Dee snags the mic from me. "You were on."

"There's one tiny bobble I can smooth over, but that's the only edit." Alex is typing away, and I know what bobble they mean. Connor is a walking, talking example of restraint, and no matter how much I want to deny it, I want to figure out how to crack it open.

"Also, you dropped the best line of the quarter."

I raise an eyebrow. "Which one?"

"Desire is a dialogue," they quote, tapping the keyboard like a gavel. "Clip it. Print it. Put it on a tote."

I laugh, and this time, it lands somewhere clear and feels good.

"I'll cut the teaser later," Dee adds. "Want me to include the bit about curiosity over conquest?"

"Yes. And since we're running this tomorrow, add in the workshop promo."

Dee nods and Alex fixes me with a sly grin. "You were on fire last night. I looked at the outline for the next recording. Your favorite topic. Power dynamics in the wild."

I roll my eyes, but they're not wrong. We've got three episodes to record today, and I can thank Connor Rives for the inspiration for all of them. Tomorrow night, I'll be onstage again and talking to a room full of strangers about how to make flirting a conversation instead of a game of win or lose.

Connor will be right there with me. I've known him less than two days, but my body doesn't care, and my instincts are worse. I should be focused on regaining control. But I keep wondering what it would feel like to stop performing and just say yes.

UNDER SURVEILLANCE—CONNOR

Four monitors glow in front of me. One scrolls with encrypted chat from the Prescott team's lead counsel. Another streams a news segment I asked my media analyst to flag. A third holds client files, secure behind layers of encryption. The fourth hosts my daily dashboard—new requests, current projects, threat updates, and timelines. All of it running smoothly. All of it under control.

As it should be.

It's a good day. Quiet, relatively speaking. No one caught with their pants down, literally or figuratively, no leaks, no press calls, no wild accusations. Just the usual: keeping optics clean, threat vectors low, and egos stroked in the right places.

Exactly the way I like it.

I toggle over to the Prescott files to double-check the projected media timeline. Still holding strong. So far, the majority of the fallout is on Emery, and I know she'll be fine. She handled the first wave like a pro.

My earpiece clicks once—an internal cue. Grace.

"Go," I say, not looking up.

"I've got a maybe-client for you. From California. A rep called the inquiry line about an hour ago and flagged it priority. Entertainment-adjacent. Not political, but apparently big." Grace's tone is measured but curious. "They didn't drop a name. Just said it was time sensitive."

California. Jesus. I haven't thought about home in years.

I lean back in my chair and let the tension settle across my shoulders. Entertainment, though? Fuck no.

I burned that bridge. Then buried the ashes.

I keep my voice even. "Tell them no."

"You sure? They said they'd call again."

"Let them. The answer's still no. I don't do entertainment. And I don't work in L.A."

"Copy." She disconnects.

I stare at the screen for another moment, jaw tight. There's no reason that request should've gotten under my skin, but it did.

California means baggage. Entertainment means exposure. Both mean a part of my life I locked down hard and don't plan to revisit. I didn't claw my way out of that life just to stroll back in through the front door, dressed in a suit and pretending like I'm not still carrying the heat of that spotlight on my skin.

Strip clubs can leave scars. Most of mine are internal. The rest? I walked away with muscle memory. My body still remembers the rhythm. And the instincts I honed on that stage? I've sharpened them into weapons. They're the reason I see what others miss. The reason I'm the one people call when everything's on fire.

I click back to the Prescott dashboard.

Emery's name is right there in the side thread and I click over to her feed. Still chaos. Posts promoting tomorrow's flirting class have a mixed bag of comments. I'm glad I'll be there tomorrow, in case people get intrusive. Mostly, it's because she's on my mind more than I care to admit even to myself. And tomorrow night, I get to see her in her element. In person instead of on video. The thought of it sends pressure coiling low and hot in my gut, looking for a crack in the discipline.

God help me.

I haven't heard from her today. Not that I expected to. She doesn't owe me shit. I'm not her keeper. I'm not even her real consultant. Ours is more of a partnership of convenience. Carefully contained and situational. Nothing to spill over into our lives outside of work. I keep telling myself that and hoping the lie will stick.

Tomorrow night may test my restraint. There's nothing I find more attractive than a woman who knows her worth and pushes back without a flinch when others question it.

And Emery Nicole?

She doesn't flinch.

She shines.

That dark, dangerous part of me I keep locked up and buried deep wants to drag her behind that spotlight and see what she'd do if I gave her the space to fall apart. And more importantly, if she'd trust me to put her back together.

But that's not tomorrow's job. Tomorrow, I behave. I keep my hands to myself and stay in my lane.

Even if every damn instinct in my body is already veering off course.

Even if I know, deep down, that the second I hear her voice, I'll start counting the beats until I can take it from smooth and steady to raw and real.

WEDNESDAY, MARCH 25

TUNED IN/TURNED ON—EMERY

The Gilded Raven is a bar that lives for golden hours—brass fixtures, a jungle of hanging plants, and a backlit wall of bottles that looks like a stained-glass window for sinners. It hums with the pre-game pulse of a single's happy hour: low thrum of bass, the soft clatter of glassware, laughter that spikes, flares, then settles. The whole place smells like lime, cedar, and the faint electricity of a room ready to spark. A neon script sign coils over the bar like a dare; the room feels primed to say yes.

They've cleared a corner for my workshop—thirty chairs, a small riser, a whiteboard. Beyond the velvet rope, bartenders build complex drinks with torched citrus while a cluster of singles negotiate finding a seat. I don't do reserved seating for this very reason. I watch the crowd, looking for who's likely to participate, where the shy ones are, and who's the possible troublemaker.

Except I already know where my most dangerous one is sitting.

Front row, aisle seat: Connor Rives. Impossible to miss.

He picked the spot like a bodyguard and a tactician, not a man looking to mingle. Dark shirt, sleeves rolled enough to show forearms lined with veins and control. No tie. No smile. Just that steady, fire-warm gaze tracking me from the second I stepped onto the little riser. It's like a hand placed at the small of my back. Possessive, even if he doesn't touch me. It shouldn't make heat lick at my skin, but it does.

If he thinks sitting there will rattle me, he's underestimating both my love of a stage and how stubborn I get when a man looks at me like a challenge. I smooth my red dress—reclaiming it, not hiding from it—and click the mic on.

"Welcome to Tuned In and Turned On: Flirt Like You Mean It." The room quiets. "You found us between the mezcal and the martinis. Excellent choices all around." A ripple of laughter and the room loosens. The sound lands like a blessing and my tension drops a fraction. I take a deep breath and continue.

"Tonight, we're going to talk a little, and then play some flirty games. House rules: curiosity over judgment, yes means yes, no means no, and if you bump into a boundary, you back off. If you think you're the exception to basic courtesy, I have news: you're not."

Another chorus of laughter, this time heartier. Heads tip forward. Shoulders lower. And it begins.

"Tonight isn't about lines. It's about attention and noticing." I launch into the three pillars: eyes, body, voice, then add consent. This class was originally a half-day workshop, but I've pared it down to the bare basics, and it's become a popular icebreaker for things like this singles meet and greet.

I get through the eyes. A two-beat gaze, flick to the lips,

then back to the eyes for a beat, then away. Setting the stage for invitation.

I feel lighter. This is my lane. This I can do with half my neurons asleep and the other half in crisis triage. The video and the threat are still out there, still gnawing at the edges of everything, still waiting to be weaponized. But inside this room, for the next ninety minutes, I get to be the thermostat.

We get through the talking part and the room is lively. Time to move on.

"We're going to have some fun. I'll demonstrate first so you can get a feel for it. Since we're playing, we'll use some code words."

I go through the stoplight system: green for good to go, yellow for slow down, and red for stop. "When you meet someone at a bar in real life, you don't share that language. That's what paying attention and noticing are about. If you pick up someone's red signals, you stop. If you pick up yellow, you back up and check in. Now, I need a demo partner."

A cold ask is always a gamble. There's always a chance no one steps up. Or of making the wrong choice for which volunteer. A small movement catches my eye.

Connor.

His hand is raised, not high. A small shift. Like a man who never has to try twice and is used to being noticed.

It's a terrible idea. It's a terrific idea. My brain says turn away; desire says run with it. My pulse kicks up and desire wins.

"Front and center?" I say, pinning lightness to my tone, despite the way my stomach is clenching. He stands with unhurried grace, then steps onto the riser, smooth and easy. Effortless in a way that sets off warning bells. A ripple of appreciative sounds travels through the room. I can't blame them. Connor Rives is an amazing specimen of a man.

He doesn't crowd me, a tough task in the small space. He stops two or three steps away. Like you might if you were approaching someone at a party or club. It's measured, polite, and absolutely calculated. The crackle of energy that always seems to exist between us turns into the sharp snap of lightning about to strike. The room lowers its volume, like everyone knows something is about to happen.

I click the second mic on and hand it to him while the internal debate rages. Do I pretend I don't know him? That feels wrong. The calm of moments before threatens to crumble. I choose my brand. Honesty.

He shifts slightly, turning away from the room, then winks. His eyes cut to the mic in my hand and I shake myself. I have a job to do, and for better or worse, Connor is part of it now.

"I usually work with strangers for this, but Connor here was good enough to step up. Hi, Connor."

"Hi, Emery." That smooth baritone wraps around my name and pulls at something deep inside me. It doesn't help that he's arranged his face in an angelic smile that promises there's a devil underneath. The crowd hears charm, but I hear warning sirens.

I wonder what the audience sees when they look at us and if they sense the undercurrent. I turn to the crowd and force myself back to the presentation. "Remember, either person can say stop at any time and it will be respected. Let's start with eye contact."

I turn to Connor. Meet his gaze. His lips curl a bit to one side. I count the beats—eyes, mouth, eyes, then look away. I can teach this with anyone and have countless times, but this is different. It's not just connection; it's combustion held at bay. There's a tension like a violin string being tuned almost to the point of breaking.

Another glance at Connor. His gaze doesn't waver. A slight lift of his eyebrows offers an invitation. Challenge me, it says. Show me what you've got.

"Anyone catch that?" If I don't say something, don't return to the rhythm of the class, I'll get lost in those whiskey-colored eyes. "Eye contact is a conversation. It's not staring someone down. It's a silent hello, and waiting to see what they do with it."

There are a few laughs. Still relaxed and engaged, but the tension between us has spilled into the room. Connor hasn't moved and the next step feels like playing with a lit match near a tinderbox, and I'm the one holding the flame.

I pull two barstools to the center and gesture for Connor to sit. He angles his body slightly toward me, as if tracking my every move. Despite the civilized posture, he's a predator on the hunt. There is nothing passive about his calm exterior. It's focused and controlled.

"Personal space is cultural and contextual, so take it slow and look for cues in body language like we learned earlier. Flirting is asking permission to keep going. Can I come closer?"

I turn to Connor, take a step closer, and make eye contact, then look at the empty stool before back to his eyes. His nod is almost imperceptible, but his body speaks volumes. He shifts, making room for me, while also keeping himself open.

"Notice his feet." I call everyone's attention to Connor. The foot closest to me is on the floor, the other heel rests on the stool's crossbar. Open. Friendly. "And arms. The hand closest to me is on his thigh and he's turned on the stool so he's almost facing me. That's an invitation."

I take the other stool, arranging myself subtly toward him. "If someone mirrors your body language, it's a good sign they're tuning in to you."

"Noted." Connor drops another wink, this time so the crowd can see it, and the laughter is warm and instant.

"You'll get your turn." I try to keep my voice light, but sitting this close to him has my pulse racing. He radiates heat and poise. I'm so aware of him it's like my skin's got its own radar.

"I doubt it." His smile is small, but welcoming. I can practically hear the sighs in the audience. I hadn't planned on covering banter, but this was too good to ignore.

"Oh? Are you incapable of following instructions?" Tone is everything, and I make sure mine says I'm teasing.

"On the contrary." His eyes flick to my mouth, then back to mine and the smile cranks up to devastating. "I'm excellent at following instructions."

He leans closer, eyes never leaving mine. "Or giving them."

Jesus. Forget sighs; that was pure pantry-dropping smolder. His voice is a caress along my skin and I clear my throat. "No, I didn't coach him."

I need the humor to regain focus. The room laughs again, and it's the only thing keeping me from combusting on the spot.

There's a fire and intensity in his eyes that tells me if we weren't in this class, we'd be leaving for home. The message is crystal clear and indecent. We wouldn't make it to the bed, and he'd be trying to see how fast he could wreck me.

I swallow hard and force myself to keep going. "When it comes to compliments, defaulting to looks is fine, but focus on things that are their choice, or keep it more general." I breathe slowly and let my eyes trace over him the way I teach people to do. Look with curiosity, not hunger.

"You caught my attention the moment I walked in." I lean closer to Connor and my mouth goes dry. "The second you smiled, I knew I had to introduce myself. Hi, I'm Emery."

I offer my hand and brace myself for the contact. Connor takes my fingers in his and it's every bit as electric as I'd expected. A warm, slow current that travels straight to my spine. I break contact before I want to and dig my heels into the stool's crossbar.

"Your turn."

Connor raises the mic and it catches a soft exhale. I'm not sure if he did that on purpose, but the effect on the crowd is clear. They're hanging on the edge of their seats.

"That dress was made for you. The color and the cut. I haven't been able to take my eyes off of you."

The hush in the room feels personal. Too intimate for a room full of strangers.

"You move like you command the very air, and the rest of us mortals are waiting for your cue to breathe."

Oh. The heat rushing through me is fast and unapologetic. A smattering of 'aws' and a 'damn' from the back land like punctuation. I blow out an exhale and laugh into the mic, intentionally playful.

"Forget the basics. This has turned into an advanced lesson." We run through a few more beats, covering how to break eye contact, or exit gracefully. Then I encourage the room to pair up and remind them of the stoplight system. We start with being silly. Give us your worst pickup lines. Then we work at turning them around.

There's something sacred about this part. Not just watching people flirt, but watching them soften. Open. Choose courage over coolness. No surprise, I see more than a few numbers being exchanged as I wander the space, doing what I do best, making the human mess feel more manageable.

Except there's no managing the six-something feet of controlled trouble hanging off to the side, watching everything. A woman approaches him and he smiles, then shakes his head. He's devastatingly handsome, attentive, polite, and unavailable. A walking contradiction that's catnip to many women. Including me. After a few minutes, I ask everyone to come back to sit.

It's gratifying to see the way the room has rearranged. What were thirty strangers are now colleagues of a sort, and a handful have paired up, at least for now.

When it's almost time to wrap it up, I take a few questions, then settle on the barstool to bring the point I always try to emphasize. If some folks take only one thing from this class, I hope it's this.

"Consent is not something you push your way through. It's not a one and done thing. It's a practice. Every day. Every moment. One of the sexiest things you can ask is, 'do you want this?' and then listen to the answer. Turn off your ego and your libido and pay attention."

Connor is in my peripheral vision as I finish up. Still. Watchful. Something in his expression says he's not listening; he's memorizing.

The room dissolves into happy chatter as the velvet rope unhooks and folks head toward the bar. My pulse slowly returns to earth. I circle the room, shake hands, field a few nervous questions. Out of the corner of my eye, I catch him, hands in pockets, saying nothing, letting people pass like he's a rock in a river.

When there are no more hangers-on, I slip through the side door into the quiet and cool of the corridor. The thrumming bass fades and I lean against the wall, pressing my hands against the rough painted brick. I need a full minute to breathe.

The door creaks open and footsteps, even and unhurried, echo. Even after only a few days' acquaintance, my body knows. Connor.

"Successful optics?" I don't look at him. I don't dare. If I'd had any doubt about the chemistry raging between us, tonight dispelled it. My pulse stutters when he stops an arm's length from me and leans his shoulder against the wall.

"Unflappable." There's a quiet authority that somehow manages to unravel me.

"Look closer. There's flapping." I'm not sure I want him looking closer. I'm very sure I don't want him seeing the source of my current state of very not unflappable. It has nothing to do with the whole viral video and everything to do with him.

"Then it's a good thing I came to stabilize the optics."

"Is that what we're calling it?"

I turn. He's closer than a colleague should be and not nearly as close as I want. The hallway turns us into a frame: him, me, the window. The hum between us is alive, and the crisp hint of his cologne will reroute my memories for weeks. He smells like clean skin and restraint, like a man who never forgets what power feels like but refuses to flaunt it.

"Thank you for helping," I say, because it's easier than admitting I liked it too much. "On stage."

"Anytime." His gaze searches my face, probably collecting tells again. "You did something for them in there."

"For them," I echo. "Not for me." If I let myself admit how much I needed to feel competent again, to feel wanted and seen without judgment, it would undo me right here in this hallway.

His jaw flexes, subtle. "You're allowed to want things for you, too."

"I want my name back." My throat is tight. "I want my clients safe."

"And?" His voice gentles. "What else?"

It's reckless to step into this. It's also honest. My rules. I take a breath that tastes like desire. "I want..."

I can't give voice to the feelings rushing through my head and body. His gaze pins me to the wall, flickering between my eyes and my mouth, then back up. It's too much. Too knowing. He looks at me like he already understands what I'm afraid to name: that I want him. That I've wanted him since the moment he said my name in that low, deliberate tone that doesn't just reach me, it lands.

"Do you want this?" His voice is low and gruff as he tosses my own words back at me.

My brain screams this is a bad idea. My body would rather have this conversation in private. I should pull back, tell him no, remind him, and myself, that this is temporary proximity, professional alignment, not chemistry waiting to ignite.

I take one step closer to him. Connor meets me halfway. I don't know who moves first; maybe both of us.

The first brush of his mouth is careful, the press of someone who knows what it means to cross a line and does it anyway. Heat licks up my spine. I open, just a little, and he answers with a low sound that hits me somewhere I don't have language for. It's restraint meeting hunger, a perfect collision of everything I've told myself I shouldn't want.

My hand lifts to his jaw, rough with end-of-day stubble. He feels solid and steady, like leaning into a doorway you know will hold. His palm finds the small of my back and pulls; the contact short-circuits my brain. There's nothing polite about the way the kiss shifts. I've spent my life content to float and Connor pulled me into the deep end. It's terrifying and exquisite.

The hallway tilts. The window goes soft. This is not the wild shove of lust that swallows judgment. It's worse. It's the kind that builds. That says, 'I see you.' That says I could ruin you, or save you, and neither of us would stop it.

He deepens, not by force but by certainty, coaxing my mouth open like a secret I've forgotten. The world narrows to his kisses, confident and controlled, then suddenly not. It's the break in his control that undoes me. The moment he lets go, just a fraction, I feel something give way inside me.

Without warning, he stops. His eyes seek mine, silently asking permission. He wields restraint like command. I lean in and he answers, pushing me back against the wall. My spine meets cool brick; he's close without caging. When I fist my fingers in his shirt and pull, he gives me his weight, delicious and devastating, and I gasp into his mouth. My nerves spark, every bit of me aware that giving one more inch would mean surrender.

"Oh, there it is. Good girl," he murmurs against my lips, and the words go off in me like a switch. No one has ever said it like that. Possessive and reverent. Wrecked. It hits somewhere deep, the place where control and craving live side by side.

I have had kisses that were like fireworks. Fast explosions that fade without a trace. This is tectonic. A deep shift that forever rearranges the earth under my feet. This is the kind that changes fault lines.

He braces one palm beside my head. With the other, he skims down my ribs and settles at my hip. Not a claim. An anchor. I tip my chin to change the angle and he follows, a quiet sound in his chest that shatters me further. He swallows my little laugh, feral, surprised, and answers with a stroke of tongue that is pure, crafted sin. "Tell me if I should stop," he breathes.

"Absolutely not." I'm mortified and thrilled. His laugh is

low and seductive. It rumbles through me and is a gift I'll never give back.

He exhales like this does something he didn't plan for. His thumb presses gently at my hip and the pressure lights a fuse that sprints through me. He eases off a fraction, a leash pulling taut, then reels me right back in, letting me feel exactly how much power he's not using. It should terrify me; how good it feels to be handled this way, with reverence and command, but all I want is more.

When I finally tear my mouth away, it's not because I want to stop. It's because my knees aren't laws-of-physics compliant. I rest my forehead against his and try to coax air into my lungs. The hallway sways. My pulse is drums and sparkles, my skin too tight for my bones. He waits me out, breathing with me, steady in, slower out. It's a reset and every inhale is a thread pulling me back to sense. Every exhale reminds me what it would cost to stay lost in this.

He smiles and it's not his usual smirk. Not the professional nothing. This is a real smile that's a little stunned and a lot pleased. The look of a man who found the part of the map that says here there be dragons and decided to build a house on the spot. It's devastating. More so because I'm the one who put it there.

"Emery," he says, voice unsteady enough to count as proof. "I am excellent at following instructions. This is me checking in."

The deference is real; the control under it is undeniable. He could take the lead, and it's clear he wants to. He's making me choose it. It's power that offers choice and dares you to take it.

I want to drag him back into the kiss and ruin us both, but I like my job and my integrity. I also like the way he asked.

That moment, that ask, leveled me. Because he could have taken. Most men would have. But he didn't.

I put my palm to his chest, feel the thud that matches mine. "This is a bad idea."

"Undeniably." His thumb strokes once at my waist, a brand through silk. "Tell me no and I'll walk you out and we'll rewrite the narrative with nothing but clean lines."

I picture that safe, competent future. It's clinical and sterile. Then I imagine never kissing him again. I don't like that one.

"Tonight," I say, choosing each word. "We keep it to a kiss. Two professionals who got caught in a moment."

"A moment," he repeats, mouth curving into a smile. "That's not a no."

"You're right. It's not." I search his eyes for any sign of a tell I missed. If I'm wrong about him, I'm risking everything. If I'm right, I'm already in deeper than I should be. "But I can't think about that right now."

He huffs a quiet laugh. "Okay. I did say I could follow instructions." Then softer, his voice low and rough. "Yours."

Heat slides through me again at the echo. I tug him down for one more slow, savoring kiss that tastes like abandon and restraint all at once. He lets me set the pace and then steals it at the end, a clean, sure stroke of his mouth that leaves me dizzy and smiling against him. He takes exactly one breath of victory, then reins himself in. His restraint holds. I hate it. I love it. There's the promise of something more, coiled and waiting.

We separate by inches, both of us breathing like we've been running. He straightens his sleeves, and the motion shouldn't be erotic, but here we are. The man could button a cuff and I'd still feel it behind my knees.

"Happy hour optics." I smooth my dress, as if that will do

anything about my thoroughly kissed lips. His thumb traces under my mouth, threatening to send us both down a path we're sure to regret. "And I'm sure you've ruined my lipstick."

There's nothing angelic about the smile that curls his lips and lights his eyes. "I'll spend the rest of the night thinking about what else I'd like to ruin."

The implications send delicious shivers through my body. "Good. Suffer."

He huffs a helpless laugh and steps back an inch, then another. We look at each other like we both know we've stepped off the map and are pretending to navigate anyway. There's no pretending. We're lost, and the compass needle spins every time he looks at me like that.

"Call a ride and go out through the front," he says, practical sliding back over his features like a suit jacket. "No statements, only smiles. I'll go out the other way."

The fixer reasserts himself, but there's a crack in his voice. I nod, pull my phone out and check my makeup before I do anything else. It's not as bad as I feared; nothing a quick swipe of powder and fresh lipstick won't fix. Not bad for having been kissed into chaos.

"Emery. Are you okay?"

I should say I'm fine, except I'm not. I've been kissed senseless in a hallway before, but this time was different and I will never be the same kind of fine again. This wasn't just heat. It was pure inferno.

"I'm...I will be." It's the best I can do.

"Resisting you may be impossible."

His admission hands me a hard truth and echoes everything swirling around in my body and brain. My rules don't account for him. My body doesn't care.

"Then we need to be very, very careful. For now." I don't

know why I added that last. I should run from this at full speed, not set the stage for escalation.

"For now." He means it. Then he's gone, a shadow sliding toward the exit sign's red glow.

I stand alone for three slow breaths, press my fingers to my lips, and bite back a laugh that wants to dissolve into a prayer. I fix my makeup, call for a ride, then step back into the soft tumult of the bar. My smile is my armor. No one needs to see that my entire world is off its axis.

Connor and I crossed a line. Maybe it's just toes over, but the spark between us isn't theoretical anymore. It's real and bright and hums under my skin in a way I've never experienced before. There's still a crisis to face and the internet is still out there and hungry for scandal, but for a handful of minutes, I fed something within myself. And now that I've tasted what it's like to be seen and wanted, not for my work or my name but for who I am, I don't know how to go back to starving.

COMPROMISED–CONNOR

I shouldn't still taste her.

But I do.

The smart thing would be to walk away after the kiss. To create some distance between us.

Instead, I pace the back of the building, letting the night air scrape some sense back into me. The bass from inside the Gilded Raven pulses through the pavement, but all I can hear is her breath from a few minutes ago. The small, surprised sound she made when she stopped pretending she didn't want me to touch her.

It's been years since I've lost that kind of control. Since

I've had to pull the leash that hard to keep from taking what was freely being offered. And fuck, it's still straining.

I take my time walking up the block, figuring she'll be gone by the time I get to the front. My luck, the front door opens as I round the corner and she steps into the glow of the streetlights, phone in hand. She's fixed her lipstick, but nothing can hide the puffiness of her lips. Her smile is bright and real, but the armor's cracked enough that I can see underneath.

She spots me and sighs. "You circle back for another round?"

"Tempting." I close the distance, stopping before I want to. Keeping her out of arm's reach. If I touch her again, there won't be any restraint left to salvage. "Just forgot to mention, did you notice folks were filming the class?"

Her mouth tightens. "I saw. We'll be lucky if even half of it stays private."

"I'd rather it didn't."

That gets me a glare. "What?"

Focusing on work, the business of managing optics, is easier than what I'd like to be doing. I need something to keep my mind off the desire to tell her to cancel the car and come with me to my place.

"Most of the public won't know who I am. But Bronson Drake will and he'll put two and two together. It sends a message."

Her eyes flash. "So you want him to see that video?"

"I want him to see what happens when he tries to make you small and you walk straight into the spotlight anyway."

"That's spin," she fires back, crossing her arms. "Manipulation wrapped in strategy."

"It's optics," I counter evenly. "You can't fight narrative with facts. You fight it with image."

"Was that kiss optics as well?" she cuts in, sharp.

"No." The word comes out low and immediate. Too honest. It vibrates through me, cracking my carefully constructed restraint and rattling the cage enough to make me wonder what happens if I ever let it break.

She searches my face, trying to find a lie. "How can I believe that?"

I could say because I don't kiss clients. Because I don't risk reputation for impulse. But what comes out is, "Because I didn't plan it. And I plan everything."

Her expression softens for half a breath before skepticism slides back in. "That's comforting."

"It should be," I say, forcing calm back into my voice. "I plan things to keep people safe. Which reminds me, there's something you need to know."

She arches an eyebrow. "That sounds ominous."

"The reason I told you to keep an eye on your email. Monday, I ran a test."

"Meaning?"

"I sent a fake internal memo—a follow-up Q&A for attendees, marked confidential. Only your office addresses got it. If it shows up anywhere outside, I'll know exactly where the leak is."

She blinks. "You planted bait. A canary in a coal mine."

"Standard procedure," I say. "If there's a breach, we need to know how deep it goes."

Her tone cools. "And you're telling me this because... what? You think I can't handle the truth when it comes wrapped in strategy?"

"I'm telling you because you've earned the right to know," I say simply. "You built something solid with your people. Alex, Dee—they're not yes-men. They challenge you. That's loyalty with a spine, and it's rare. I don't want to blindside that kind of team."

That gets her. The defensive line in her shoulders eases.

"I've watched the way you run your space," I continue. "You lead from honesty, not ego. That's why they trust you, and why many of your clients still do, even with half the internet watching. You've got integrity most people couldn't fake if they tried."

She exhales slowly, studying me. "You're serious."

"I'm a lot of things. But when it comes to your team? Yeah. Dead serious."

Her gaze flicks over me like she's trying to recalibrate her read. "So you trust me."

"I trust your integrity," I say. "I trust that, when the choice comes down to optics or ethics, you'll make the one that lets you sleep at night. I don't see that often."

She looks away, the tension between us turning quiet instead of sharp. "And if your little canary sings?"

"Then we fix it."

"We," she repeats, softer this time. "Because of a contract. Because I hired you."

"Yes, we have a contract, but that's not why I said we. You've brought me on as part of your team. As remarkable as you are, you have blind spots. Everyone does. And I see yours."

It's tempting to reach out. Touch her again. But I don't need a class in body language basics to know that Emery is on the fence. Which is better. Everything about her unhinges my control and triggers desires I keep tightly restrained. Not a good combination.

"That's why I said we. We work together on this."

The words hang there between us, heavier than they should be.

She tips her head to the side, then squares up with me,

hands on her hips. "Next time you run one of your tests. maybe give me a heads-up before you start manipulating optics."

I can't help it, my mouth curves. "If I'd asked, you'd have said no."

"Exactly."

Her smile is faint but real, and that undoes me more than the kiss. Her car pulls to the curb and Emery doesn't look at me again until she's settling into the backseat.

"I'll see you tomorrow."

"Count on it."

I wait until they drive off, then pull my phone from my pocket. The canary's still silent.

Good.

Because if it chirps, the fallout won't just test her team, it'll test us. And I'm not sure which of us will come out intact.

THURSDAY, MARCH 26

SHAKY GROUND—EMERY

The office feels too bright. The overhead lights sting like a low-grade migraine, and even the glow from my laptop screen seems judgmental. The headlines haven't changed in hours, but I keep refreshing anyway, hoping maybe someone will suddenly decide to be kind.

Alex sits across the table, tablet glowing and their color-coded chaos under perfect control. Dee's in the corner, half-drowned in code and coffee. Erin's at the other end of the table, shoulders tight as she continues to sort through the mess of my emails.

It's exhaustion made visible, and I'm trying to work but keep getting sidelined by the ghost of his mouth on mine. Connor's hands, his voice, that impossible restraint that felt anything but safe. Every time I move, I feel the phantom weight of his palm at my hip, steady and possessive. My body responding to an order he never spoke out loud. I shouldn't be thinking about him, but it's hard not to when clips from the class keep popping up on social media.

"Another sponsor 'regrets to inform us' but they wish you the best in your future endeavors." Alex's use of air quotes almost makes me laugh.

"Translation: we're radioactive." Because of course we are. No amount of spin can fix this mess. As bad as it is for me, I can't imagine what Davis and Melanie Prescott are going through. Luckily, I haven't seen a lot of negative attention turned their way, but that could change in an instant. The fear of waiting is often worse than the thing itself.

"Temporarily radioactive," Dee says without looking up. "It's not as bad as it could have been, and we're starting to see some positive traction."

He's trying to be kind. I love him for it, but I'm too raw to let it land. "Tell that to my inbox."

Erin looks up from her screen. "Do you want me to keep replying to attendees who emailed about refunds?"

"Yes, please. Keep it brief and kind. They trusted us."

"Wouldn't it be good to say more?" She shrinks a little when Alex, Dee, and I all swivel to look at her. "I'm just saying, your brand is all about transparency, but these are all carefully phrased corporate speak."

Alex presses their lips into a thin line before looking back at their tablet. Dee throws his hands in the air and mutters something about an afternoon coffee before stalking toward the kitchen. I dial my patience up a notch and try to recall what it was like to be so idealistic. It might be easier if I didn't agree with Erin, at least a little bit.

"While that's a noble goal, and one I aim to achieve, the reality is much more complicated and nuanced. Whatever choices I might make for myself, I don't have the right to make those choices for others who would be impacted by this as well. Does that make sense?"

I hope it does, because I'm not sure I have it in me to

explain how I'm spending every day weighing the cost to myself and the compromises I'm making, against the guilt I would feel if attendees were harmed by the scandal.

"I guess." She doesn't sound convinced, but she goes back to typing. Her fingers pause once, eyes flicking toward her phone before she keeps going. Whether nerves or habit, it sits wrong. The poor kid's been tiptoeing around me all day, as if terrified she'll make the wrong move. I can't blame her. The fallout has turned me into a live wire.

Alex shifts their focus. "We can draft another round of takedown requests, but most mirrors will respawn. It's a Hydra."

"Might as well keep cutting heads off until the thing stops moving. It's all we can do." I don't want to fight. I'm tired of it, but this is why I do what I do. Because no one should be shamed for their sexuality or desires.

Dee comes back in the room, coffees in hand, and sets one next to me. "That's the Emery I know. Relentless."

I manage a smile, somehow. "Relentless sounds great until it's you."

It's getting late by the time Erin packs up. She pauses at the door, awkward in that way only twenty-somethings with too much empathy can be. "Do you want me to stay? I could help more."

I shake my head. "You've done enough for one day. Go home, get some rest."

Her relief is soft and guilty. "Okay. See you tomorrow."

When the door clicks behind her, the silence stretches. Alex and Dee exchange a look, the kind that says they should tell me to go home too. I beat them to it.

"You both should go. I'm not great company tonight."

Alex closes the tablet. "You're never bad company. But you can be intense company."

"Consider it an occupational hazard." I try for a smile; it almost sticks.

Dee pauses as he's shutting down machines. "You're not the villain in this story, Emery. You never were."

I look up. His voice is low, rough with fatigue but threaded with loyalty.

"I found something today, but had to wait until Erin left."

Dee opens his laptop and clicks a video. The front door of The Honey Pot. "I keep combing through things, figuring we must've missed something. I must've missed something. And I found it."

On his screen, a thin man dressed in jeans and a hoodie walks into the shop. Dee pauses the video. "He doesn't leave until after the class."

He clicks again and scrolls through the footage we all know by memory now. "There."

Dee points to the screen where one of the shop staff is leaving at the end of the night, and the thin hoodie-wearing man is next to her.

"They're holding hands. I checked the staff list. She's Steph Rawlings, and that's her boyfriend Joe Macon. Who happens to be an ex-employee. He was let go because customers complained about him being creepy."

"Define creepy?" Alex leans in and squints at the video.

"Nothing concrete, but from what I gather, he was enthusiastic and maybe a little too direct. Seems like that rubbed people wrong and after multiple tries, they let him go."

"Huh. So what was he doing there?"

I'm with Alex on this one. An unaccounted-for person complicates things for sure, but it's not a smoking gun.

"I contacted Steph this afternoon. She didn't say anything because, according to her, Joe was sleeping in the downstairs stockroom. Which he apparently does on the regular. He gets off work, swings by the shop and naps until she gets off work."

Maybe a little sketchy, but kind of sweet in a way. My brain spins with possibilities. Did Joe let Drake in, thinking he'd get back at the shop by creating a scandal? Or did he go out for a smoke and forget to lock the side door when he came back in? Or was he sleeping the whole time and this is all a big coincidence?

Well, this is what I have a fixer for, right?

"Good find. Can you send that to Connor? The video and everything you know. And then get out of here. Both of you. I'm serious."

I pull up my podcast notes, but I'm not able to focus. Instead, I half watch Alex go through their meticulous end of day routine while Dee makes quick work of emailing Connor then shutting everything down for the night.

Alex waves goodbye and heads out, then Dee lays a hand on my shoulder.

"I wasn't kidding, Emery. You're always the hero." He heads out through the kitchen door.

The words echo after him. Always the hero.

They shouldn't hurt as much as they do. Maybe because part of me doesn't want to be the hero anymore. Maybe because last night, for one reckless minute, I wanted to be able to let go and let someone else take charge.

When I'm alone in the room, I open my recording app. The red dot blinks, waiting. "We tell clients control is an illusion," I begin, voice quieter than the hum of the computer fan. "But I built my life on the illusion anyway."

Maybe that's why Connor unsettles me. He thrives in shadows, while I built my life dragging things into the light. He covers. I confess. He edits. I expose. And somehow, I keep wanting the safety that kind of secrecy promises.

My throat tightens. I want to say his name but I stop myself. He's been in my head all day: the measured calm, the way he says my name like a secret he intends to keep.

I delete the voice note. This is wrong. My entire career is built on honesty. Not illusion. That's Connor's stock in trade.

I try again. "They say transparency is power. Maybe it is. But right now, it feels like bleeding in public."

Delete. Maybe I'm too raw. It's only been four days.

The screen glows back at me, mercilessly blank. I drop my phone beside the laptop and press my fingers to my eyes.

For a moment, I let myself imagine what it would feel like to have a romantic partner I could trust like I trust Alex and Dee. To be touched by someone who really knows me. To be held in a way that doesn't demand performance, just surrender. To not have to narrate my safety, to simply know it by instinct. The thought of Connor's voice slides through me like heat.

I grab my phone again and tap out a text.

Did you mean it? That I don't have to do this alone?

Delete. Too vulnerable.

Confirming tomorrow's event. Meeting there?

Send.

The bubble vanishes. My reflection stares back from the dark window, fractured by city lights.

I can still hear that even tone wrapping around my thoughts: Don't offer a statement until we talk again. It should sound like control. Instead, it sounds like someone trying to keep me safe. And that's the problem. I don't want to need his version of safety.

"Maybe I'm the story no one wants to tell anymore," I whisper.

The door to the kitchen cracks open and Dee grabs the bag he left sitting in his chair. "Forgot this. And you're still the story worth telling, Doc."

When the door clicks shut behind him, I close my laptop and let the silence have me. For the first time in days, there's no keyboard tapping, no screens glaring, just my heartbeat and the faint whisper of city traffic. And in that quiet, I can admit what I've been avoiding: I don't want to be alone tonight.

In the quiet, soft but ever present, there is the echo of his voice. Connor's promise, steady as a command: You're not doing this alone. And I want to believe him.

THE WEAPON AND THE WANT—CONNOR

I should be working. Instead, I'm watching clips from Wednesday's flirting workshop. I tell myself it's about narrative control and public sentiment. Which is partly true.

The red dress hugs Emery's curves and makes her hair and skin glow. She stands tall, claiming space and creating an environment where it's safe to ask and explore. Most of the comments are positive.

> *"She makes confidence look holy."*
> *"The way she explained consent should be required viewing."*
> *"I'd let her flirt me into therapy."*

Then the creeps edge in:

> *"If a man ran this workshop, it'd be called harassment."*

"Imagine thinking this is professional."
"She's just trying to fuck her way into relevance."

None of it surprises me. I've seen it before. Women like Emery make it look easy to own a room, so people try to take it from them.

My professional brain notes what's working: clarity, boundaries, charisma. She disarms with humor and then hits hard with truth. What's sitting wrong isn't the content. It's her.

A woman unapologetically talking about desire with authority.

The parts of the internet that don't know what to do with her want to tear her down, and I want to torch all of them for it.

I draft a few key phrases and make notes in case we need to address some of the worst comments. Not that I want Emery defending herself to the trolls. Not as the fixer who's supposed to help manage this mess, and definitely not as the man who wants to carry some of the weight so she doesn't have to.

Because the way she looked at me after that kiss? That split second of honesty and heat and want without fear cracked something I thought I'd sealed shut.

Not the kiss itself, though that would be enough. Not the way she tasted, or how she pulled me in like she needed to burn, too. It was the moment after when she looked at me like she didn't regret it. Like she might want more.

That look has me on edge.

Because I did want more. Still do. Badly enough that I'm sitting in the dark, one hand on my mouse, the other curled into a fist on the desk to keep it from reaching for my phone. Or lower.

I can still feel the restraint in my body. The leash pulled

tight. The feel of her against the wall. The smell of her skin. She was fucking gorgeous, and on the edge of tumbling. And I walked away.

Because if I hadn't...

I click to the next clip. Her voice fills the room, confident and bright.

"Flirting isn't about conquest. It's about attention."

She makes it sound so simple.

I shift in my seat and fight the rise of memories. College. The first time a woman asked me for something rough and I didn't understand her version of it. I was careful, but not careful enough. Big guy. Bigger cock. Too much drive in a rhythm I thought was right.

She went quiet. Then cold. Then called me dangerous.

And that word. 'Violent.' That one gutted me.

I know what violence looks like. I remember my mother trying to explain away bruises. The sound of apologies that always came too late. And for a long time, I thought wanting control made me like him.

So I learned.

Not just how to stop. How to listen. How to ask. How to take my own darkness and tame it with method and consent and discipline. And rock-solid, ironclad control.

But there are lines I don't cross. Not fully. I may put a toe on them, but Emery tempts me to leap. When I pressed her to the wall, she melted into it. When I touched her, she arched. When I praised her, she came undone like her body had been waiting for someone to see her.

And fuck, I saw her. I still do.

My phone is already in my hand. Not sure when I picked it up.

I don't text things I don't mean. I don't chase. I don't need.

But my thumb hovers.

Want backup tomorrow? No. Too impersonal.

Can't stop thinking about you. Too much.

I thumb open the keyboard, type one line, then let it sit.

You looked like you belonged on that stage. Like every damn eye in the room should be paying attention.

I stare at it. It's not a line or an attempt at flirting. It's the damn truth.

My thumb hovers over the send button, then I toss my phone to the desk, the message still waiting. If I open this door with her, I won't be able to close it.

She's a client. A strategic partner. And the smartest thing she could do is run.

She won't. Not yet. Because I kissed her like a man who had a right to. Like a man who wasn't built out of secrets and bad history.

She sees things too clearly, and if she looks too close, she'll see the version of me I've kept chained up for years.

The one who liked holding her mouth open with my kiss.

The one who whispered good girl and meant it like a fucking prayer.

The one who got hard when her body begged for more.

I close the laptop. The room goes dark. My cock's hard and aching, pressed uncomfortably against my zipper, and I make no move to deal with it.

This isn't lust. Lust doesn't make me want to come undone in front of her.

I delete the message, down the last of my whiskey and change for the gym. Compression shorts under my sweats, a shirt that hides too much, oversized hoodie. Armor that lets me go past mirrors without flinching.

The hard on? I don't care, but I'm not about to walk into the building's gym with my cock on full display. I need to burn off energy and a hard workout's the safest bet.

I need the weight and repetition. I need the pain. If I can't fuck her out of my system, I'll train her out instead.

FRIDAY, MARCH 27

THE ART OF OPTICS—CONNOR

The rooftop is a carefully curated battlefield of glassware, candlelight, and smiles sharp enough to cut. I slip into the space like I'm stepping onto a stage, reading posture, tone, and looking for potential problems.

Control the tempo. Keep the spotlight steady. Don't think about her.

Which, of course, means I'm already thinking about her.

Then she appears.

Black dress. Red lipstick. A study in reclamation. The air changes. Conversations pause a fraction too long. Heads turn.

She walks like she owns the fallout and everyone here came to pay rent.

Her gaze finds me across the room, skimming my face before lingering a beat too long. That look is gasoline. She knows it. I know it. The corner of her mouth curves in half acknowledgment and half dare and I feel something inside me shift. A click in my chest; the leash goes taut.

Game on.

We move separately but in sync, two sides of the same coin. I redirect the gossip; she redirects the room. When we finally intersect, it's mid-conversation with a podcaster too smug for his own good.

"Quite the week Dr. Nicole," the man says. "Viral fame looks good on you."

Emery smiles like she's sharpening the blade behind it. "Fame isn't the word I'd choose, but education rarely trends without controversy."

"Which," I add, smooth and low, "is why she does it better than anyone else."

The podcaster falters. She glances at me, an electric thrill, brief, and something wordless passes between us. We're in this together.

She laughs, moves on, and I watch her go with a mix of admiration and pure, selfish want. The performer in me recognizes it: chemistry with an audience. Only this time, the only person I want to play to is her.

The night hums. I catch snippets of her laughter, the tilt of her head, the confident flick of her wrist as she gestures mid-sentence. Every instinct says distance. Every nerve says closer. I measure my breath, counting, longer on the exhale. It doesn't help.

When the crowd thickens, she excuses herself, slipping inside, where there are fewer people. I wait a beat, then follow. I'd like to tell myself I'm checking to be sure she's okay, but that's a lie.

Inside, the noise of the party softens. She's standing at the window, city light cutting a line down her back, and I stop because for one second I want to forget who we are.

She's composed on the surface, all polished professional, but I see it.

The slight tremor in her fingers where they rest on the windowsill.

The rise and fall of her shoulders as she inhales is too measured, too careful.

She's still fighting the current.

Still trying to stay upright while the undertow drags her under.

"You were flawless out there," I say, voice low.

She doesn't turn. Just stares out at the city like she's willing it to hold her up.

"You mean strategic."

"Strategic is how you survive."

I close another inch of space. Close enough to feel her tension sharpen. "Flawless is how you win."

She exhales slowly, deliberately, like she knows if she rushes it, she'll unravel.

"Feels more like barely standing."

Something inside me that is not rational wants to answer that. Something older. Hungrier.

For years I've lived by one rule: control is everything.

Control over my tone.

My thoughts.

My body.

Because control is power.

Because losing control costs more than I'm willing to pay.

But watching her fight for composure?

Watching her hold the line by sheer force of will?

It makes me want to snap it, in the best of ways. Not to break her. Oh, no, never to break, but to let her set aside the weight, even if only for a time.

"I don't need you to hold the line with me," I say, stepping closer. The air between us changes. It's heavier now. Thicker.

She turns slowly, leaning against the glass. Her eyes are clear, but her pulse flutters visibly at her throat.

"That's funny," she says. "You are the line."

I should laugh. I don't.

Instead, I step once more into her space and feel her.

Warm skin. Sweat. Adrenaline. And underneath it, something sweeter. Something sharp and unspoken.

She smells like tension. Like need. Like no one has ever dared get this close.

My body locks. I don't touch her yet. I can't. Not without unraveling everything. It's taking all I have to hold back. I shove my hands into my pockets as an added layer of caution.

"I see you," I say, quiet but certain. "The way you keep breathing through panic, through pride. It's the bravest thing I've ever seen."

Her throat works as she swallows. Her voice is thinner now. "You read everyone like this?"

"No." My tone roughens with the truth. "Only the ones I want."

There it is.

The part I bury. The part that doesn't just want her; it wants to bend her.

To pull the tension from her body one breath at a time, until surrender feels like freedom.

Like being seen.

Like being known.

She doesn't move.

Doesn't flinch.

Her gaze drags down my chest, slow and assessing. She's trembling, but it's not fear.

It's recognition.

Ah, fuck.

I lift a hand, slow and deliberate. I let my knuckles skim the barest line down her arm, stopping above the wrist.

Her breath catches like a snapped wire.

Her pulse hammers against my thumb, fast and needy.

"You always this composed?" I ask.

Her reply is a whisper, and it sounds like a confession.

"Only when I'm not."

The laugh that escapes me is low, dangerous, half-feral.

"Careful, Dr. Nicole. You're going to make me forget why we're here."

She tilts her chin up. Bold. Reckless.

"Maybe that's the point."

And just like that, something breaks free inside me.

Not all the way. Not yet. Just enough to flash its teeth and whisper: touch her again and you won't stop. I do it anyway.

"Green?" A simple check in, because I have to be sure before I take the next step.

PRIVATE ROOM—EMERY

He's so close the air between us vibrates. Not with fear, but with need, raw and reckless. Every nerve in my body seems to have its own heartbeat.

Connor Rives, the man who never breaks, is looking at me like I'm the one thing strong enough to undo him.

"Green." I nod, just in case I only imagined saying the word. He takes my hand and pushes through a door, into a room lit only by the city lights spilling through the tall windows. When he closes the door behind us, his expression is all primal hunger.

His touch isn't hurried or rough. Just intentional. Every slow stroke across my skin sends a fresh jolt through me, stealing my breath.

Connor reaches inside of me and flips a switch I always suspected was there, but never dared get close to.

This is dangerous. Uncharted territory.

And I want it.

Want him.

Not just a kiss. Not just a touch. I want the version of him he keeps locked down.

But he's still too composed. Still restrained.

And I want him to forget.

I want to see what happens when that careful control finally shatters.

The backs of his knuckles graze my collarbone. Skimming, a tease that's too soft.

His thumb traces the line of my throat, then pauses under my chin, lifting.

Forcing me to look at him.

His gaze hits sharp like teeth and hot as sin, and my whole body tightens in response.

"Green." I whisper the word again. Part invitation, part demand, and all prayer. My palms press to his chest before I know I've moved. Solid heat. Barely contained power.

His heartbeat pounds beneath my hands, fast and heavy and barely leashed.

I pull him closer.

Desperate. Reckless. Ready to burn.

His mouth crashes into mine.

The kiss isn't polite.

There's no warning. No easing in.

Just the impact of flesh and fire and hunger.

A collision that starts with shock and spirals into need.

It's a claim.

And I let him take. But the taking is careful, and the care is devastating.

My back hits the wall as his body crowds mine, angled and tense, every muscle straining to hold something back. There's something barely leashed, like he's stopping himself from devouring. My hand slides up into his hair and I clench my fingers into a fist. His low growl of approval curls through me, sending warmth straight between my legs as my world shrinks to us in this space.

Control unravels—mine, his, I can't tell whose first. The kiss turns feral. Tongues tangling. Teeth grazing. Every inch of me aching for right here, right now. His hands trace my sides, gathering fabric, anchoring me between his hard body and the wall. I lift one leg instinctively, bracing against him, every breath a shiver as his hands cup my ass, gripping hard enough to bruise. It's raw and frighteningly honest; not a game, not a performance, just want. And it's still not enough.

The hard bulge of his dick presses against me and I swear I can feel the pulse of it. I want. I want. I want.

His mouth tears from mine, lips dragging down my throat, teeth grazing my shoulder. "Fuck. You make me forget who I am." His voice breaks like gravel. "You make me want things I promised I never would, and I'd burn the whole damn world for a taste."

I don't think. I can't. Logic's long gone, drowned in heat and hunger and the weight of his body pinning mine to the wall.

My head falls back. My lips part.

"Then take it." My voice is wrecked silk.

Not a request or a plea. A command. A surrender. A fucking dare. Take this moment. Take my body. Take the breath I haven't caught since you touched me.

His growl answers before his mouth does.

He grabs my thigh tighter, grinding into me like he could fuck me through our clothes, and I'm so close to letting him. I want him to tear the dress and take me right here, standing, wall to my back, his body caging mine, filthy and frantic and real.

His growl rips from his chest as his hands shift on my ass and I'm lifted higher. My back hits the wall harder this time, held up by brute strength and whatever control he has left, which isn't much.

I wrap both legs around him without hesitation. My legs, my arms, my everything.

His mouth is everywhere; lips searing against my throat, my jaw, my collarbone. His hands drag the straps of my dress down in rough, greedy tugs, exposing skin to the open air, to his breath, to his bite.

"Fuck, Emery—" His voice is fractured. Desperate.

One hand cups my ass, the other slips deeper, fingers curling against my drenched panties. I moan, broken and guttural, when he strokes, grazing over silk and the sensitive skin beneath. Not inside. Just claiming.

My hips buck against him like my body's making decisions without input from my brain and all the air leaves my body in anticipation of his touch. I want him thrusting into me, filling me. Instead, he slides his finger over my panties, stroking from entrance to clit in a soft tease.

"Please!" The word tears from me, desperate and begging.

He hisses through his teeth. "You're soaked."

Like it's a prayer. Like it's a confession.

"I need..."

He silences me with a kiss as his finger teases, sliding back down, circling over my panties. I try to grind down; I need him inside me. His lips curl into a smile and he chuckles.

"Patience. I know what you want, Emery." He taps his finger on my clit, but I want more, so much more.

Without warning, Connor shifts, his other hand comes up in a flash and covers my mouth and my breath stills.

Voices echo in the hall. Laughter. The slam of a door. Then footsteps. More laughter.

Connor freezes, every muscle locked so tight I feel the strain in his arms. But he doesn't step back. Doesn't even pretend. He holds both of us steady, one hand on my mouth, the other still stroking my pussy through my panties. It should feel like danger. Instead, it's hotter than anything I've experienced before.

His head drops to my shoulder like it's the only way to keep from losing his mind.

"Don't move," The words scrape against my skin, wrecked and raw.

I don't. I can't. I'm too wrung out. Too wet. My head is spinning and my body is strung tight. He slides his finger up, circles my clit again, stroking harder until my body begins to shake. The hand on my mouth presses harder.

"Nod if you're okay." His breath is hot on my ear and I nod. Several times.

I'm in bliss, and all I care about is his touch. His body grinds against mine, creating delicious friction, but oh I wish he would tear my panties off and finger fuck me. Or fuck me.

More laughter in the hallway and it sounds like it's right outside the door. Connor's strokes speed up, focusing on my clit.

"I want to make you come like this. No penetration. No skin on skin. Not yet. I want you coming from my touch. Pinned against a wall with people right outside the door, while you're begging me to fuck you."

His touch turns rougher and I pull air in through my nose. He is every fantasy of mine come to life. He presses his lips against my ear and slides his hand from my mouth.

"Beg me, Emery. Beg for what you want. You won't get it. Not right now. Probably not tonight. But I will make you come."

I don't care where we are, I will do whatever it takes to keep him from stopping.

"Fuck me, please, Connor!" I don't recognize my own voice. It's a raspy plea, breaking as if I'm about to cry. "Please, I need..."

His hand clamps over my mouth again as the noises from the hall get louder. But Connor keeps his word. His touch is expert, perfectly riding the balance of tender and rough. In seconds, I'm shaking again.

"That's it, Emery. Such a good girl."

The praise rocks through me like fire. Connor's hips grind in time to the strokes of his fingers. It's like being fucked, but only on the surface. Except there's nothing strictly surface about this. My body responds to every stroke, every kiss, every grind like we're naked and in bed.

"There it is. Right there." He croons against my neck and his hip thrusts speed up. He's pounding my body into the wall with his while his fingers do delicious magical things to my clit.

The door rattles like someone fell against it. Someone yells something.

"Pay attention to me." Connor's teeth graze my neck, then bite down hard. "The door is locked. You're safe. Come for me, Emery."

Maybe it's hearing I was safe, or the knowledge the door is locked. Or maybe it's his command, but the dam breaks and an orgasm tears through me fast and hard. The world blurs and my vision goes fuzzy. Connor doesn't stop. He keeps grinding against me, letting me ride wave after wave of aftershocks.

A door slams down the hall. There's a rush of loud voices and fading footsteps.

Connor doesn't move. It feels like forever. Me still pinned between him and the wall. His fingers still resting against my now throbbing pussy. His hand slowly peels away from my mouth, then his other hand withdraws, glides over my ass, and he lowers me slowly, reverently, until my feet touch the floor.

I'm barely standing. My dress is bunched at my hips. My breath's a goddamn ragged mess.

His forehead finds mine, his hands cupping my face like I'm something he wants to both worship and ruin.

"Color?" It's almost inaudible. He looks wrecked. Like he's seen the edge and is still hanging over it.

"Green." Maybe tomorrow I'll second-guess myself, but not tonight.

He nods and his lips curl into a seductive grin. "That was..."

"I know." The words scratch out of my throat. "We almost—"

"Almost?" He closes his eyes like it physically hurts to stop. "That was far more than almost. I think we're past pretending now."

Silence. Thick and trembling. My hand flattens on his chest again, not pushing him away, but grounding us both.

The space between our bodies is minimal, but it feels like a chasm.

And still, neither of us moves.

My panties are damp against my skin, and my thighs are trembling. I want more. More of whatever this was. More feeling so free, so lost in the moment that I didn't care who walked in. My brain kicks back into gear.

"That was reckless," I whisper. It's the only word I can form that doesn't come with a moan attached.

He leans back enough to see me, and the look in his eyes is wreckage. Not regret or guilt. Just the ghost of everything he didn't let happen.

"That was real," he says, voice low and rough and stripped of all polish.

And there it is. The line. Not between us, but around us. The moment wraps its claws around my ribs and refuses to let go. Boundaries, I remind myself. We draw them. We cross them on purpose.

We start to pull ourselves back together. He smooths his sleeves like armor. I tug my dress down, fingers trembling. I don't even bother with my hair. It's too late. I look like I've been kissed breathless, fucked up against a wall, even if I haven't.

Not yet.

He looks at me like he knows exactly what I'm thinking. What I'm still feeling between my legs.

And I hate how much I love that.

"Next time," he says, voice like gravel and promise, "we won't stop."

I should shut it down. Should remind him, and myself, that this is already a fucking mess. That next time can't happen.

But I meet his eyes and my pulse stutters.

There's nothing clever left in me. Nothing defensive. Just the echo of his hands on my skin and the orgasm he pulled from me like it was easy.

"Then you'd better plan it."

His answering smile is a slow, dangerous thing. Predator. Gentleman. Maniac.

"Already am." He presses his forehead to mine again, slower this time. "Ready?" When I nod, he ghosts a kiss over my cheek. "I'll go out first. Wait two minutes and follow."

He steps back, leaving the scent of his cologne and the memory of his restraint all over me like fingerprints.

When I finally push off the wall, my knees are still shaking. My body still aching. My brain a chaos of noise.

Whatever that was, it wasn't a lapse.

It was a promise.

And I don't know if I'm more terrified he'll keep it, or that he won't.

SATURDAY, MARCH 28

THE MORNING AFTER—CONNOR

On the surface, everything is normal. My condo is its usual oasis of calm. I keep business confined to my home office, or outside these walls. In the office, organization reigns supreme. Four monitors scrolling updates. Everything digitized so there's not even the clutter of files. Just a single notepad for jotting things down. Half-empty coffee mug sitting on a coaster.

Yeah. Situation normal.

Inside, I'm chaos.

I've read every update from my analyst twice. Things are looking good. While Emery is still trending, the tide is turning from public outcry to a more reasoned debate, with some positive voices beginning to rise. Every measurable metric says the storm is passing.

But I still feel like I'm standing in the middle of a maelstrom. Because last night, I lost control. And I wanted to.

I should be thinking in risk matrices and containment trees, and leveraging the positive turn to our advantage, not in the taste of Emery Nicole's mouth or the sound she made when I stopped pretending I didn't want her. She isn't just a complication. She's a client. I've got a contract with both our signatures. There's a clean boundary line that wasn't just crossed, it was obliterated.

The rule is simple: don't blur with clients. Don't touch what you're meant to fix.

I scroll through a cluster of social posts, harmless memes, think-piece snark about 'sex-positive education,' a few performative pearl-clutchers, and force my breathing even: in four, out six. Optics are stable. Containment holds. I'll have good news for my meeting with the Prescotts. I should feel relief.

Instead, I tap out a message to Emery before I can think better of it.

Status check. You holding steady?

Blinking cursor. Nothing. Unread.

Fine. I set the phone face-down like that makes the urge disappear. It doesn't. I've added Steph Rawlings and Joe Macon to my social media watch list, and so far, they're both pretty basic. She posts about knitting, and he's all about gaming and 'gardening.' Still, haven't written either of them off when it comes to letting Drake into the building. I haven't written Erin off, either, despite Emery's trust in her.

The canary hasn't sung. There's no traceable lift of the fake Q&A. No matter how often I tell myself the knot in my chest is professional, it doesn't stick. Then I grab my keys.

The Prescotts' condo smells like citrus and quiet money. Davis is pacing near the floor-to-ceiling window, the skyline reflecting off his glasses. Melanie sits on the sectional, legs crossed, posture perfect, but her fingers are pressed so hard against her teacup it's a wonder the delicate thing isn't cracking. The news is muted on the TV, the chyron looping familiar words—public backlash, political fallout, therapist at center of controversy. They make it sound like analysis, but it's just another way to watch a woman burn and call it news.

"Tell me something good, Connor," Davis says before I've even shut the door.

"The numbers are better than good. Drake's audience engagement is down forty percent, his reposts are drying up, and the only thing trending under your name right now is a local volunteer event. We're in the cooling phase."

Melanie exhales and her fingers loosen their death grip on the poor teacup. "Thank God. I can't tell you how many people called to check on us this week. I've been reassuring everyone that we're fine, but they're still sniffing."

"Politics attracts bloodhounds," I tell her. "The goal isn't to stop them from sniffing. It's to make sure what they do find is unremarkable."

She nods, but I can see the worry still working underneath. "And Emery? Is she okay?"

Interesting. There's not a trace of anger in her tone. It's all genuine concern. Too many people are happy to have a scapegoat and don't give a passing thought to anyone but themselves. More than that, seeing that concern is another testament to the kind of person Emery is.

"She's... holding the line," I say. "Which isn't the same as okay."

Melanie's brow furrows. "I hate that she's shouldering all of this. She's been incredible for us from day one. I don't think we'd have made it this far without her. You know she helped me navigate that entire mess with my sister's addiction. She didn't have to, but she did."

"I didn't." The news doesn't surprise me, the fact that I

missed it does. "She's good at keeping people standing." Even when she's barely standing herself.

Davis stops pacing, scrubs a hand over his jaw. "She's been a godsend for us, no question. But the association." He grimaces, as if uncomfortable with the word. "If it looks like we're defending her, we inherit the hit."

"She knows that," I assure him. "She's not asking for defense. Her focus is on protecting you."

He looks at me for a long beat. "And who's protecting her?"

I don't answer right away. My client list is confidential, even to other clients. I had to tell Emery about the Prescotts. I don't have to tell them I'm the line between her name and the torches, the strategist who keeps her standing when the spotlight turns cruel.

That's what I'm supposed to be. Instead, I'm the man who can still taste her lipstick and remembers the sound she made when I told her to stay still. The one who touched her like he was starving and still wanted more.

"I am." It comes out like a growl, a statement of possession, or maybe that's how I feel. Which is dangerous. Davis studies me for a second longer than comfort allows, then nods.

"Then we trust you," he says. "And her."

Melanie offers a faint smile. "Tell her... tell her we're grateful. If there's anything she needs, she just has to ask."

"I'll pass it along," I promise, even though I know she won't ask for anything. Emery would rather bleed out alone than risk anyone else getting dirty. I know because I watched her do it. I felt it under my hands.

They both look steadier by the time I stand to leave, the weight redistributed where it belongs—on me.

The elevator ride down is quiet. My reflection stares back

from the mirrored walls: shirt crisp, expression calm. I look like control carved into a human shape. It's a good disguise. It always has been. Except now, I'm not sure who I'm trying to fool. Them. Her. Or me.

Outside, the air is damp and gray, the kind that smells like static before a storm. I check my phone again. Still no reply from Emery.

For half a second, I consider texting Alex with some sanitized excuse to check in. Professional oversight or team morale.

Despite what happened last night, I'm not her anything. Yet. It went further than I intended, and whether we reel it back or jump all the way over the line requires a conversation. Right now, I'm her fixer, and I let things get out of hand.

The echo of last night hums under my skin. The heat of her breath, the word green, and the way she trembled against me but never once looked afraid. That's what undoes me most. The trust. The awareness. The way she looked at me like she knew exactly what I was holding back. Like she wasn't afraid of the part of me I know no one could ever want.

"Distance is discipline," I tell myself. It's the practice that's kept me steady all my adult life.

But today, it sounds less like a mantra and more like a warning.

Fuck it. I pull out my phone.

BARELY HOLDING ON—EMERY

I've been working since sunrise. Curled on the couch in my pajamas, muttering random voice notes for future podcasts. The radiator ticks in the background like a countdown. My coffee's gone cold. I reach for my laptop and scroll social media. It's still a mess, but at least the avalanche of emails canceling appointments has slowed down.

All evidence Connor's doing his job.

I was trying not to think about him today, but my body remembers the weight of him. The way he said good girl like it meant something. The way I let go, completely, and never once felt afraid.

Instead, I felt freed.

I bury the thought, pull my laptop closer and open my email. I can't afford that kind of want. Not now. There's a cancellation, and a potential new client. That's not so bad. I reach for my coffee and my phone tumbles to the floor; the screen shows a missed text.

Connor's name.

Status check. You holding steady?

The timestamp hits harder than the words. Two hours ago. How'd I miss that?

I don't answer. I want to, but I don't trust what answering means.

If I let him in, I'll remember the rasp of his voice against my skin. The weight of his body pinning me safely against the wall. The contradiction of safety and sin in the same breath.

I press the phone into the cushion, like I can smother the memory, then stand in a rush. I need fresh coffee. I need to eat something. Today is supposed to be about getting back to normal. There are podcast episodes to outline and I've got a column due next week.

The refrigerator is a sad space populated by a couple takeout containers and a tub of cottage cheese. Guess I'm ordering in. Again. Or going grocery shopping, and I'm not sure I'm ready for that.

My phone lights up with Connor's name and I snatch it off the counter and tap the answer button without thinking.

"Please tell me something didn't explode." I brace for the bad news, but his chuckle starts low then gets louder.

"Nothing exploded. I was calling to say let's grab lunch. Meet me at Noodle House?"

The relief crashes over me in a wave and a laugh threatens to bubble up. I stuff it down, hard. It's my first real clue that I'm keyed up tighter than I thought.

"Perfect spot. Sounds good. Give me thirty minutes?"

"Great."

The line goes silent and I stare at the phone like it can answer the million questions rolling in my head. Like why is Connor suggesting lunch at Noodle House—a labyrinth with private booths and a strict no phones policy. Getting ready takes longer than expected and I'm ten minutes late to the restaurant. The hostess leads me down a corridor to a booth with a beaded curtain where Connor sits with a pot of green tea and two cups.

His usual precision is a little off. The surface looks right. Even on a Saturday, he's in a crisp shirt with the sleeves cuffed up. But he looks like a man who hasn't slept, or who's thinking too hard about something.

His smile is warm and welcoming as I slide into the booth. He pours tea and pushes a cup toward me, forearm muscles flexing with every move. I swear if men knew what rolled up cuffs do to women, they'd never wear their sleeves down. Or they would, just so they could roll them up in front of us.

"I wanted to deliver updates in person, and I took a gamble that you hadn't eaten yet."

"So you call last minute?" I don't know why I'm being so sharp. Or why he has me so on edge.

"I texted. You didn't answer. I called as soon as I was able."

His tone is level. Of course it is. Connor Rives never loses control. Except last night, when he almost did. "I took the liberty of ordering."

He slides closer, but not too close. Like he's keeping a safety buffer between us, and I can't blame him. He smells like cool air, rain damp cotton, and the faint hint of soap.

"You've been at this all morning," he says.

"Trying to get back to normal." My voice sounds raw. "Or something like that."

"Containment's solid," he says, lowering his voice. "Prescotts are in the clear. They send their regards, by the way. Drake's engagement's down and falling. You're winning, even if it doesn't feel like it."

It doesn't feel like winning at all. I'm not surprised the Prescotts know Connor and I are in contact. They are mutual clients, after all, and as bad as this mess is for me, it could be far more devastating to them.

"Good." The word comes out small. "I had a cancellation this morning, but things are slowing down."

He nods. "Short-term losses. People panic fast, forget faster."

"Easy for you to say." I try for humor. "You deal in erasure. I deal in visibility."

His mouth tilts. "You deal in truth. That's harder."

It's a small thing, one line, quiet and precise, but it lands somewhere beneath my ribs and stays. My eyes drop to my hands, shaking more than I'd like to admit. "You say that like it's noble, but it doesn't feel that way. I'm at risk of losing everything I built."

He moves closer again, slow and deliberate, until his shoulder almost brushes mine. Until I feel the gravity of him pulling at me.

"You're not losing it," he says quietly. "You're reinforcing it. Integrity costs extra."

I laugh, soft and uneven. "Do you rehearse this stuff?"

He smiles, faint. "Only the parts that matter."

Food arrives and the silence between us stretches as we eat. Not uncomfortable, but charged with something warm. Outside of this quiet space, the city hustles on and my reputation and career hang on a thread. Inside, it's just the two of us breathing in sync. The quiet feels like shelter.

His hand lands on mine as I push my plate away. Those magnificent forearms hold my attention.

"You don't have to carry all of it alone."

"If I stop, it falls."

"Then let someone else hold it for a while."

"I wouldn't know how."

"You do, in small ways." His gaze is steady. "You delegate to your team all the time. You trust Alex and Dee."

I glare, but it doesn't hold. "That's different."

"It's not." He tilts his head, studying me. That look, part assessment, part confession, strips me bare.

"Start small," he says softly. "Breathe. I'll stay."

Something inside me unclenches. I don't look at him, not yet. Just breathe. Slow and deep. Minutes pass as we sip tea, quiet and calm. No performance or spin. The heat between us a soft glow instead of a raging fire. He's an oasis of strength I didn't know I needed and the kind of safety I didn't think I could have. I thought we'd talk about last night. Or about plans and strategy. Instead, he's helping me do what I couldn't do for myself, reset and recenter.

The plates are cleared and the check comes, Connor pays, and still we sit in silence. There's a peace I've never known with anyone else. I pour the last of the tea and sit back.

"Is this in the contract?"

Connor laughs, soft and low. "No."

A single word. A single syllable. But it carried so much weight.

"Are we going to talk about..."

"Yes, but not today."

That should sound ominous, but it doesn't. Instead it sounds like Connor, steady and sure. Whatever his reason for asking me to lunch, I appreciate it. Nothing has changed, I still have so many questions and so many conflicting feelings, but I don't feel like I'm being tossed around in a windstorm.

I take the risk and lay my hand on his arm. The electric pulse of contact surges, but this time, it's quieter somehow. "Thanks."

"Any time." His hand covers mine and he squeezes. Once. He leans in and the heat flares, bright and hot. It's a tug I can't resist, or don't want to. His eyes close, his jaw clenches and he pulls back.

"Emery." My name is a prayer from his lips. There is nothing routine about his response. It's a promise, and it echoes with something deep and real.

He leaves first. When he stands, he hesitates like he wants to touch me, but knows better. Then he's gone. I wait a few minutes, then go back to my condo. The radiator still hisses, steady and judgmental. I wash my coffee cup and put it away, then grab my laptop, ready to get some work done.

MONDAY, MARCH 30

GETTING BACK ON TRACK—EMERY

The worst of the storm seems to have passed, but the silence it left behind is almost worse. It feels like the eye of a hurricane—still air, waiting for the next hit.

My laptop hums on the desk, the cursor blinking on the outline title for a new episode. Rebuilding Trust: When the Truth Hurts. Too on the nose. I delete the title and try again. Every try collapses into static.

I lean back and press my fingers to my temples. My mind won't unclench. Every time I exhale, Connor's voice slips in—low, steady, impossible to forget. You're safe. Let someone else hold it for a while.

I hate that my body remembers.

I hate that I don't really hate it.

I flip open my planner, forcing my brain into structure. Monday. Afternoon client session. I haven't canceled yet, though I considered it. I've only seen her a few times. High-functioning anxiety and corporate burnout getting in the way of dating and finding pleasure in life. Safe territory. Manageable. Something I can help with.

My therapist brain clicks in automatically, reaching for what it knows: containment, control, rhythm.

If I can help someone else feel grounded, maybe I'll start believing I am too. Though Connor did a fine job of getting me to that point Saturday.

No. I don't need him intruding.

Erin breezes in, tablet in hand, hair perfectly imperfect in a way that makes me feel a hundred years old.

"Morning! You've been all over my feed again," she chirps. "It's not all bad—people are arguing about free speech. You're trending for empowerment. Should I boost those?"

I inhale through my nose. I'm not feeling very patient or charitable today. "Empowerment's not a trend, it's a practice. And let's not feed the algorithm."

She blinks, smile faltering but still bright. "Right. Totally. I thought you'd want to know people are, you know, defending you. You really should jump in. This is what it's all about."

She's got the right idea, but I've seen the things that excite her and I am not about to agree with a group of posters who think doxing people is acceptable.

"We're sticking to the outlined plan," I say gently but firmly. "Ignore it. Let it burn out."

"Sure." Her phone buzzes. She flips it over fast, face unreadable. "Glenda emailed about next month's workshop schedule. Should I confirm the dates?"

The Honey Pot. The thought of stepping back into that room makes my stomach tighten. Dee swears no one on Glenda's staff leaked anything. The jury is still out on possibly creepy Joe Macon. Connor's less certain, but supports still working with them. His exact words: Keep the schedule. Push forward. Normal is a weapon.

Normal. Right.

"Yes," I say finally. "Confirm the dates. I sent over calendar notes—make sure everything's updated. If any slots open, pull from the waitlist and use the standard email form."

"You got it, Dr. Nicole." She gives a quick, too-bright smile and dives back into her screen.

I watch her type, trying to ignore the tiny itch of unease under my ribs. She's efficient and enthusiastic, if a little careless at times. Connor warned me to be careful what I share. Now, even routine feels like walking a tightrope.

The office quiets again. Dee and Alex are both working offsite today, which means it's me and Erin, and my thoughts.

I try to focus on the outline for my client session: breathing exercises, emotional reframing, self-compassion tools. Words I've said to others a thousand times.

But the echo of Connor's hands still lingers. The weight of his body holding me in place. That dangerous calm he wears like armor. It's infuriating how safe I felt pinned to that wall.

And even worse how much I miss it. Our lunch Saturday left me even more confused. The only people who've ever shown up for me like that are Dee and Alex. I never expected it from Connor. I really never expected myself to relax and give in to it as easily as I did. It felt...good.

I shut the laptop before I can spiral, grab my notebook, and write three clean words across the top of a page:

Focus. Boundaries. Balance.

Professional first. Always.

I take a steadying breath and look toward the end of the table where Erin's humming softly to herself, oblivious.

Time to practice what I preach. If her pattern holds, Celeste will be here ten minutes before her appointment.

The intercom buzzes. "Dr. Nicole? Your one-thirty has arrived."

"Thanks, Bridget, send her up." I turn my attention to Erin. "I've got a session starting. Remember, stay here in the workroom. If you need to go out, go through the kitchen."

"Of course." She smiles, polite but distracted, thumbs flying over her phone as she nods.

I stand and smooth my slacks, the shift into therapist mode sliding over me like muscle memory, then move into the front office, locking the door behind me. The quiet settles and I breathe it in, letting my pulse slow and the cares of the outside world fade.

A soft knock follows a minute later. My client, Celeste, steps in, hair frizzy from the wind, blazer a little too formal, smile stretched thin.

"Hi," she says. "Sorry I'm a few minutes early."

"Early is fine," I say, gesturing toward the couch. "You're on time for you. How've you been?"

She laughs once, brittle and self-conscious. "Overwhelmed. Between work and trying to have some kind of dating life, I feel like I'm failing at everything."

"Failing or overextended?" I ask gently. "There's a difference."

Her laugh softens, embarrassed. "I guess... both? I canceled another date last night because I was too tired to pretend I'm fun."

"That's not failure, Celeste. That's burnout, especially the sexual kind." I keep my voice steady, clinical but kind. "When your body and brain are in survival mode, desire doesn't take a back seat, it pulls the emergency brake."

Her shoulders relax a fraction, her relief palpable. "God, thank you. Everyone keeps telling me I just need to try harder. Like that's magic or something."

"Trying harder doesn't work when you're exhausted," I say, leaning forward slightly. "You can't build intimacy on fumes. Let's look at what's draining you first, before we start rebuilding your connection with pleasure or motivation."

She nods, tears welling but not falling. "That actually makes sense."

"It's supposed to." I offer a soft smile. "You're wired for pleasure, Celeste. You don't need to try harder; you need to find ways to make space for yourself so you have the capacity for real pleasure."

Her breath shakes out, slow and deliberate. We move through grounding techniques, anchoring her in breath and body, teaching her to recognize arousal as an invitation, not a demand. By the end, her voice is steady.

"That felt... real," she says. "Like I wasn't faking calm."

"Because you weren't. You gave yourself permission to rest."

When she leaves, her smile looks genuine. Mine almost feels that way.

The quiet after she leaves isn't as hollow as before. It feels earned. I jot quick notes in her file, body awareness improved, breathing technique successful, then glance at my phone.

A new text blinks on the screen.

How are you holding up?

I type back before I can overthink it.

Coping. Thanks for checking.

A few seconds later:

Good. Keep breathing. One day at a time.

It shouldn't make me smile.

But it does.

I set the phone down beside my notes and underline the word I wrote earlier. Balance.

If control is a practice, then this counts as progress.

Tomorrow, I'll try again.

CLIENT ON FIRE, EYES ON HER—CONNOR

The apartment smells like coffee and steel polish—my version of calm. I try to focus on the data scrolling across my monitors. All clean. All manageable.

None of it helps.

My mind keeps slipping back to her.

The way she went soft in my hands. The sound she made when control snapped—mine and hers. The way she walked into lunch, shoulders tense and her smile too tight. I'd wanted to talk about Friday, but while she may have wanted to discuss it, she needed something else. She needed someone to provide her space to breathe, and I was happy to meet that need.

It didn't help ease my own tension.

I'm supposed to compartmentalize. It's a skill I learned early and honed to perfection. Emotions in one box, clients in another. But she's under my skin like a splinter I can't stop touching.

I've broken every boundary I have with her. Well, almost every one, and odds are good the few left standing won't be for long.

A sharp ping cuts through the quiet. Encrypted inbox. Unknown sender.

One line, no traceable address.

Your girl's trending again soon. Keep her close.

No signature. No metadata. Just a timestamp.

I frown and lean forward, running a trace. Nothing. Whoever sent it knows what they're doing. I flag it and send to my analyst with a short note—investigate source, possible social-engineering attempt—then lock the screen.

Could be Drake's people. Could be someone chasing clout. Could be something else entirely.

I shove open a window, needing the air. Late-March wind cuts through the city, sharp and damp with recent rain. Nearby, Dupont Circle hums—traffic, laughter, the illusion of normal life.

I tell myself I'm worried because that's my job. Because a warning like that, no matter how vague, deserves attention.

But that's not the whole truth.

I want to see her.

Make sure she's okay.

Maybe hear her laugh again.

I slide my hands into my pockets, staring at the phone one more time. The screen stays black.

"You're already in too deep," I mutter. The city answers with the wail of sirens, a reminder that there's always another crisis waiting to start.

Inside, the monitors still glow, steady, ordered, controlled. Everything I built my life around.

And all I can think about is the woman who makes me want to lose control again.

The air in the condo feels wrong. Too still. Too tight. I pace once. Twice. It doesn't help. The energy in my body is a live wire with nowhere to ground.

I change, grab my keys and gym bag then head downstairs.

The gym's mostly empty this time of day—one guy on a treadmill, earbuds in, oblivious. I hit the weights first, fast and punishing, every rep an act of defiance against the restlessness clawing under my skin. Shoulders, arms, chest. Again. Harder.

By the time I switch to the heavy bag, my muscles are on fire. The first hit lands with a satisfying thud. Then another. Then another. The rhythm takes over. Hit. Breathe. Pivot. Hit.

It's not about anger. It's containment.

I can still see her. The smooth fabric of her dress. The sound of her voice. The way her pulse kicked under my thumb when I told her not to move. Then at lunch. Her eyes questioning. Her body vibrating with tension.

The bag swings. I hit harder.

Control, I remind myself. Control is what keeps things safe.

But all I want is to lose it.

I stop when my breathing turns ragged, sweat dripping down my back, pulse pounding in my ears. The gym smells like rubber and adrenaline. I press my forehead to the bag, closing my eyes.

This is what being caged feels like. A body that knows what it wants, and a mind that refuses to give in.

She's the reason. I know it. Every time I touch her, every time I don't, it drags something feral closer to the surface.

I tell myself I can handle it. That this is chemistry, proximity, part of the job.

But I know better.

I keep working until my muscles shake with exhaustion, and it still isn't enough. When I go upstairs, the place looks exactly the same as when I left—perfect, contained, silent.

I'm toweling off after a shower when my phone buzzes. Analyst.

"Talk to me," I answer.

"Preliminary trace is dead," she says without preamble.

"The message bounced through a relay in Iceland, then Singapore, then through a burner VPN. But—"

"But?"

She hesitates. "The timestamp matches a known pattern from the same accounts that pushed some of Drake's recent leaks. Either someone's playing games, or this is another coordinated drop."

My pulse steadies, not from calm but from clarity. "Timeline?"

"Hard to say. Could be tonight. Could be nothing."

"Nothing is never really nothing," I mutter.

She exhales. "You want me to escalate?"

"Quietly. Eyes only. Keep it off the formal channels."

"Understood."

I end the call and set the phone down. For a second, I consider calling Emery, warning her, preparing her, but she's had enough impending doom, and what could I say? Hey, there's a vague something that maybe could hit?

No. Not yet.

I'll let my analyst dig deeper first. I'll keep an eye on the chatter myself and prepare to push back.

I grab a clean glass, pour water, and drink it in one pull, cold and sharp. The silence creeps back in, broken only by my own pulse.

Discipline. Distance. Control.

The holy trinity of survival.

And she's burning holes through all three.

TUESDAY, MARCH 31

THE SMEAR CAMPAIGN—EMERY

The air outside the office tastes of outrage. A handful of protesters cluster across the street waving homemade signs in bright posterboard, some wrapped in clear plastic against the drizzle. The rhythm of their chants rises above the steady noise of traffic. Protect Our Kids. Stop the Smut. At least they spelled my name right this time. Progress.

From the second-floor window, the colors blur and the bobbing umbrellas become restless punctuation marks in the gray morning.

The office has that eerie kind of stillness that feels like the world is holding its breath, waiting to decide if it'll clap or combust.

I drop my bag by the table, flick on my computer and wait. My inbox explodes across the screen.

Subject: You're evil.
Subject: Disgusting!

Subject: Thank you for saying what no one else will.

For every hateful message there's one full of gratitude, but somehow the hate always screams louder. At least I had a warning about this one. Connor texted that some conservative morning show ran a segment where a pastor spoke out against me and called my classes and podcast abominations. Nothing new there.

Then he called to walk me through handling it. And this time, he wasn't talking spin, or containment. He suggested pushing back. Being myself.

I should make a coffee. Instead, I settle in and scroll through the noise until it all blurs into fonts and fury. I've been through this kind of hate more than once, and Erin can sort through looking for emails that need a real response.

A horn blares outside; the chants rise and fade. I stare out the window at the handful of people pacing the wet sidewalk.

"Congratulations," I mutter. "You found your villain. Why not grab pitchforks next time?"

The kitchen door opens before I can gather my composure. Alex breezes through, umbrella dripping, Dee on their heels, both holding caffeine like armor. The familiar pattern of them, Alex's efficient calm and Dee's grounded warmth, snaps me back into place.

"Morning, boss." Alex drops a latte onto my desk. "Before you look, yes, the internet's on fire. Again."

"I saw." I force a thin smile. "At least it's all focused on me and what I teach. If I'd known it was a roast, I'd have brought marshmallows."

Dee exhales, setting his laptop on the conference table that doubles as our team desk. "We can put out a pause statement. Call it a 'scheduled hiatus.' Buy some time."

"No." I'm already standing, marker in hand, the scent sharp and clean. "We are not disappearing because the yelling got louder and more targeted. We're going to double down."

Alex arches an eyebrow, looking halfway between impressed and terrified. "You want to change the new episodes?"

"Yes. I want to remind people why we exist." I start writing across the whiteboard, the words bold and slanted: Consent. Power. Shame.

"If they're going to talk about sin, let's give them vocabulary. Three new episodes. This week."

Dee whistles low. "That's not playing defense."

"It's offense. The best kind. They want a culture war? Fine. I'll fight it with facts."

Dee grins, a mix of awe and worry. "You realize this is how revolutions start, right?"

"I'm counting on it."

The kitchen door creaks open again. Erin pokes her head in, her phone clutched tight, screen lighting her face, water still beading on her raincoat. She looks young. Too young.

"There's a livestream out front," she says breathlessly. "You should see—people are quoting you."

My stomach tightens, but I keep my face neutral. "Then I hope they quote accurately."

"I could—um—jump in the comments? Clarify things?" Her tone's hopeful, too eager.

"Don't engage," I say softly but firm. "Let them yell and posture. When we respond, it will be on our terms." I'm beginning to sound like Connor. I'm not sure how I feel about that, but it's necessary.

Erin hesitates, thumb hovering over her phone, notifications flashing so fast they reflect in her glasses.

"Right," she says. She stands half in the doorway, looking like she doesn't know what to do.

"We can hear and see them perfectly fine from here, but if you are so inclined, you can go watch."

Part of me hopes she'll do just that. I doubt she'll get any work done if she's distracted by the spectacle out front. The way her face lights up tells me I'm right.

"Remember. Do not engage." I yell the words at her retreating back and shake my head. The door clicks shut behind her, and the quiet seeps back in.

Alex murmurs, "She's trying to help. I think."

"I know." I cap the marker, feeling the sting of recognition under the irritation. "She's enthusiastic. I was like that once. All heart and idealism."

Dee hums in agreement. "And you turned out pretty okay."

I give him a look. "Define 'okay.'"

He smirks, and it almost makes me laugh. Almost.

Alex leans in, their eyes lingering on me, sharp and assessing. "You sure you're good?"

"Relative term." I step closer to the window. The chant outside hits a rhythm, words blending into a single wave of noise. "But I'm done hiding."

I rest my fingertips on the cool glass, watching the signs flap and sway in the wind. For a second, the reflection shifts, and I catch my own face—tired, yes, but still standing.

And underneath it, faint but clear, I hear Connor's voice: You don't have to hold it all up alone.

For the first time since this started, I almost believe him.

CONTROLLED BURN—CONNOR

Sitting in my office, staring at media feeds and trying to manage the chaos from a distance feels cowardly. I should be in the office with Emery. Offering support. Another hand to tackle the work. But there is no way I could be in the same room with her and not want to wrap her in my arms and tell her it will all work out. We'll get through this.

So much for just a client.

The data feeds scroll across my monitors in neat, color-coded columns. We had the calm, and now is the pivot. Outrage hits a saturation point, then mutates. A new voice emerges. A different spin. Then a headline becomes a hashtag, a hashtag becomes a movement, and the movement starts looking for a villain.

And it's Emery.

A low buzz from my phone cuts through the hum of the monitors. My analyst's update pings on-screen a second later.

> Prescott quiet. Nicole trending again. Hashtag #CancelLetsTalkAboutSex increasing 12% hour over hour. Her response is brilliant.

It damn well better be. She and I spent a tense half hour on the phone working it out. I click the link. Emery fills the screen. She's in her front office, framed by the windows, camera angled to show the protestors outside.

"We talk about sex because silence hurts more than honesty. You don't have to like my words to know they matter." Her voice is steady and sure and she's the picture of professionalism. She's skipped the pinup queen look I'm used to seeing in much of her content. This is the softer side and she's stunning. I lean back in my chair, drag a hand down my face, and swear softly.

"Christ, she's fearless."

It's part professional admiration and a whole lot of things that have nothing to do with the job and everything to do with the woman filling my screen.

Every line of her face burns behind my eyes. The tilt of her chin and the sharp set of her jaw that scream defiance, and that's the part that draws me in.

I roll my shoulders back, force myself to breathe. Distance is discipline. I've said it a hundred times. But the cage of discipline is starting to feel very small.

My email pings again.

Unknown sender.

You can't protect her from everything.

Same phantom encryption signature as before. I trace what I can—headers, metadata, handshake points. Nothing.

Whoever's behind this knows how to stay invisible.

I forward it to my analyst with a brief note: Trace origin. Compare to previous. Possible persistent actor.

Then I sit back, reading the line again. It doesn't feel like a threat. More like a warning.

Was the first one a threat about this morning's episode? Or a warning.

I pull up the livestream of the protest outside her office.

Maybe twenty people. Homemade signs, predictable chants. No visible coordination, no corporate funding. But that could change in a heartbeat.

Online chatter is one thing, but a group of people riled up enough to protest in a constant drizzle, and fueled by righteous indignation can turn dangerous. At least she has Dee, and the big guy would never let any harm come to Emery.

In any protest, there'll be the true believers, a few clout chasers who want to be seen as part of the movement, and inevitably those who take things too far.

The camera pans the crowd then turns to the building and I see her. Whoever is doing the live feed has some serious equipment going. Maybe I need to reassess the no corporate funding. Or maybe this is what they do. Social media is full of folks with great camera set ups.

She's in the office window, wearing the same coral blouse she wore in her post. Her hands move as if she's talking to someone. Animated. Alive. There's a glow that wraps around her like stage lighting and it hits me.

This is intentional. She filmed her statement, and must've left the lights up. She's close to the window, knowing people will take pictures. The image? Unflappable.

The tension in my chest loosens a fraction.

"That's what survival looks like," I murmur. "That's what winning looks like."

I should stay behind the screen. Keep my distance.

Instead, I grab my keys.

Twenty minutes later, I'm parked across from her office, windshield wipers squeaking against a misting rain. The air smells like exhaust and wet asphalt. It's a chill that seeps under your collar.

Through the windshield, I can see her office window glowing against the gray afternoon. Movement inside—shadows crossing, her hand gesturing mid-sentence. I can almost hear her voice even from here.

I shouldn't be this close.

But I can't bring myself to leave.

I lean back in the driver's seat, close my eyes for a beat, and try to imagine being anywhere else. Gym. Roof. Hell, even a bar. Somewhere with noise and distance.

It doesn't work.

The truth is simpler: I want to make sure she's okay.

That's what I tell myself, anyway.

My phone buzzes again—analyst callback. I swipe to answer.

"Rives."

"Nothing substantial yet," my analyst says, voice flat through the line. "Whoever sent those masked the route through four relays—two domestic, two offshore. Could be a crank, could be targeted social probing. Pattern looks human, not automated."

"Meaning?"

"Could mean anything," she says. "Either someone's flying by the seat of their pants and can't plan enough ahead to schedule or automate things, or they have a plan and are getting off on pulling the trigger each time."

My grip tightens on the phone. "Great."

"The timing with the morning show and protest could be coincidence. I'll keep digging. Still, I'd keep my distance for now."

"Got it."

The line clicks dead.

I stare at the dark screen until my reflection looks like a stranger's—jaw tight, eyes tired, shirt collar half undone. A man who pretends he's made of control.

The rain picks up, soft and steady. I rest my head back against the seat, forcing my breathing to slow. I could leave. Go to the gym, lose the tension under iron and sweat. I could run until my lungs burn and the world narrows to rhythm.

But instead, I stay.

I pull up her social media again, sound off this time, and watch her mouth move, watch her hands paint conviction into the air.

Eventually, I give up pretending it's about strategy. I open a new text.

> You're winning today. Let me buy you dinner tonight before the next round starts.

I hit send. So much for distance.

For a while, nothing.

Then her shadow shifts near the window. A second later, my own screen lights up with a single thumbs up. A low laugh escapes me, rough and quiet. Not yes. Not no.

But I know the answer.

I pocket the phone, eyes still on her window, and whisper, "Game on, Doctor."

THIS IS A DATE—EMERY

The city hums outside my condo windows. Horns, wet tires on asphalt, the pulse of nightlife gearing up. I stand barefoot in front of my dresser, a half-zipped garment bag slumped at my feet, trying to decide between dresses. The truth: every choice feels like a declaration.

The green wrap dress wins because it makes me feel reckless. It skims my hips when I move, ties at the waist like a secret I get to choose whether to release. I add knee-high boots, gold hoops, and the lipstick I only wear when I'm daring myself.

My reflection stares back—hair loose, eyes sharp, mouth painted with confidence I almost believe. The woman in the mirror doesn't look afraid. Not tonight.

Images from Friday creep in uninvited. His body caging mine. The sound of his breath when control snapped. That rough-voiced promise that next time, we wouldn't stop. Heat flares low in my belly, sharp enough to sting. I shake it off.

"It's dinner," I murmur to my reflection. "Strategy. Optics. Not foreplay." I'm kidding myself if I believe a word of that. Enough of the pep talk. I call an Uber, then grab my bag and a coat and head for the elevator.

The mirrored walls show a woman far more pulled together than I feel, and I use the ride down to do a few breathing exercises. By the time the car reaches the first floor, I'm doing a much better job of pretending to be calm. Then the doors open and my pretending grinds to an abrupt halt.

Connor Rives exits the car across from me. Black shirt open at the throat, sleeves rolled, and looking like a fantasy come to life. A grin ghosts across his mouth when our eyes meet across the elevator lobby. What the...

"You live here?" The words escape before I can stop them.

His brows lift, that half-amused, half-predatory expression doing dangerous things to my pulse. "Ah, so you're the one who moved into the place on three."

"You've been casing me?" I ask, part accusation. Mostly something else entirely.

He shakes his head, slow and deliberate. "I'd have noticed sooner. Your address isn't listed anywhere. I checked."

"You checked?"

"It's what I do. And maybe I was curious."

The honesty hits harder than a lie ever could. "For a man who preaches discretion, you have terrible boundaries."

He smiles like he's fully aware of it. "Boundaries are situational. Cancel the Uber." He points at the phone, screen still glowing in my hand.

The ETA is still ten minutes out. I cancel the ride, then step aside as a group of women, talking and laughing, one wearing a 'bride to be' sash, exit the elevators and navigate around us. We're sort of in the way, but I'm not ready to move on yet. I cross my arms, mostly to keep from reaching for him.

"We live in the same building and it takes a scandal of career-ending proportions for us to meet? The universe has a sick sense of humor. "

"I've lived here for several years," he says. "Who's casing who here? And this isn't career ending. You've got me on your side to ensure that."

I arch an eyebrow. "Huh. You know this makes this dinner highly suspect?"

"Does it? Was it ever innocent?"

The words land between us, quiet and certain. My breath catches before I can stop it. He doesn't move closer, but somehow the space feels negotiated, intentional, like an unspoken dare we're both pretending not to accept.

"I'm in the garage." He nods toward the elevators again. Sharing a car with him is an exercise in restraint. The faint hint of his cologne makes me want to draw closer. Catching his reflection in the floor to ceiling mirrors isn't helping. His shirt has to be custom tailored. There's no other way it could fit so perfectly, hugging his broad shoulders and stretching across his biceps, then tucking tightly in along his ribs.

In the garage, he leads me to a sleek silver sedan then opens the passenger door.

"Your ride, Doctor."

The way he says it—Doctor—turns my title into a pulse point.

I exhale, pretending it's steady. "So, is this just dinner?"

"Maybe."

My laugh slips out before I can catch it. Quiet. Unsteady. The air is thick with rain and the scent of wet concrete mixes with whatever heady combination is Connor. My dress whispers against my legs as I slide in, and his gaze tracks every inch of movement.

He rounds the hood, gets in on the driver's side, and starts the car. The low purr of the engine fills the silence, soft jazz spilling from the speakers. The city lights streak across the windshield as we pull out of the underground parking—two people who should know better, heading straight into trouble.

A CAMPAIGN TO MANAGE—CONNOR

The garage gate lifts, and the sound of rain against metal fades into the hum of the city. Emery's quiet beside me, her hand resting loosely on her thigh, the green of her dress flashing in the light every time we pass a streetlamp. I keep my eyes on the road. It's easier than looking at her and remembering the way she felt under my hands.

The city's alive tonight. Wet pavement gleaming, headlights reflecting off slick blacktop. The kind of night that promises trouble and makes you want to chase it anyway. Every part of me is tuned to her. The shift of her breath. The faint scent of her perfume—warm, clean, a little citrus. Fresh and light, but a hint of sultry underneath.

She stares out the window like she's trying not to think, which means she's thinking too much. I could tell her I know that look. I've seen it in clients trying to hold their world together one decision at a time. But she isn't a client anymore, not really, and what she needs from me tonight isn't strategy. It's space. Stillness. Relief.

"Nice car," she says finally, voice casual but soft around the edges.

"Makes a good impression," I answer. "Stylish but reliable. A little flash that's backed up by substance. Nice enough to convey success but not extravagant."

Her mouth curves faintly. "You say that like it's a metaphor."

"Maybe it is." I glance at her, then back to the road. "Fits my brand."

Her laugh is low. "That's one way to look at it."

Traffic slows at the next intersection, a snarl of headlights and pedestrians darting between cars. I ease off the gas, one hand on the wheel, the other resting against my thigh to keep from reaching across the center console. Every second she sits next to me feels like an argument between instinct and discipline, and the leash I keep on both is starting to fray.

"You've been quiet," she says.

"I'm thinking."

"About work?"

"Always." I let the word hang before adding, "And about what happens if we stop pretending we're working."

Her eyes flick toward me. "What am I tonight?"

I glance over, take in the slow rise of her breathing. "The one I want to feed, not fix."

The light turns green. I press the accelerator a little harder than necessary.

She tucks a strand of hair behind her ear and looks out at the rain again. My hand tightens on the wheel. It's the only thing keeping me from reaching out and guiding her chin back toward me. She's the first person in years who makes me want to stop managing outcomes and start taking control.

We reach the restaurant, all glass and low light spilling onto wet pavement. I pull to the front and nod to the valet, shifting the car into park.

Emery unclips her seat belt but doesn't move. The tension between us hums like a live wire—unspoken, undeniable.

I step out, hand the valet my keys, and circle to her side. She opens the door before I touch the handle, her eyes catching mine as she steps into the halo of the awning lights.

"Still pretending this is just dinner?" she asks quietly.

I almost tell her yes. Instead, I smile. "Absolutely not."

Her lips twitch like she's fighting a grin. "Good. I hate false advertising."

I gesture for her to go ahead of me, then catch her hand to hold her in place. "Next time, let me get your door."

Emery cocks her head to the side and smiles slow, then turns toward the restaurant without a word. The green dress catches the light with every step. I keep pace behind her—not following, guiding, and admiring the view. This isn't about work, or headlines, or damage control. She's been carrying too much for too long, and I can see it in every inch of her posture. Tonight, I can take some of that weight. Then we'll talk about what comes next—because whatever this is, we're past pretending it's nothing.

DINNER AND HEAT—EMERY

The host leads us to a booth tucked into the far back corner, so quiet I can hear the low hum of the air vent over the muted clink of silverware.

Private. Removed. No chance of being overheard.

I slide into the leather seat, pretending not to notice Connor's eyes tracking the length of my legs as I cross them. The heat in that look is concentrated, unblinking, and so direct it's like he's testing how long I can hold it without squirming. Spoiler: not long.

"You pick this place on purpose?" I ask as he takes the seat opposite me.

He smiles, slow and knowing, like I've walked into something without realizing it. "I like to be able to hear the person I'm with."

It sounds innocuous. It isn't. Not when he says it like that. Like everything else in the room is irrelevant. Like I'm the only one worth focusing on.

The server appears, takes our orders, leaves. And suddenly we're alone again, save for a couple in the distant corner.

His gaze skims my mouth before locking on my eyes again. "So. What's your tell?"

"My what?"

"Your tell. Everybody's got one. Something they do when they're turned on, even if they don't mean to show it."

"That's bold for a dinner opener."

"It's not like I haven't already picked up on a few." His tone is maddeningly calm. "Half the fun's in the observation, but I do want to hear you admit it."

The man makes foreplay out of eye contact.

I snag a piece of bread from the basket between us, tear it apart to have something to do with my hands. "Maybe I'll be harder to read than you think."

He leans back, arm draped along the top of the booth, watching me like he's already clocked something. "Maybe you're hoping I'll try hard enough to prove you wrong."

My pulse jumps, traitorously. He notices. Of course he notices.

Somehow, we make it through drinks and dinner. Through it all there's this low-grade hum, a current underneath the small talk. A brush of his leg against mine under the table. His hand settling on my knee when he makes a point, thumb rubbing slow circles that have nothing to do with emphasis.

When we're waiting for the check, he says, almost casually, "One thing before we leave."

"Mhm?"

"My last STI test was a month ago, I can show you if you want, but all negative. I don't do anything unprotected without knowing for sure."

I could bristle and call him presumptuous, but we'd both know better, and I find his bluntness is refreshing. Hot, even. "I'm good, too. Last test was in January. And I'm on the pill, but condoms are a must anyway."

He gives me a look that makes the air feel heavier. "Good. I've got that covered." There's a pause, then his mouth curves. "Fit matters."

The implication of that is enough to pull a shiver up my spine, then send heat cascading through me like liquid.

By the time we walk out, I'm hyper-aware of the space between us. It lasts exactly until we reach the curb where the valet has his car ready.

At the passenger door, he cages me without touching. The scent of soap and cedar clings to him; the glint of the streetlights catches at his jaw.

"Emery," he says softly, not a whisper, just quiet and intimate. "Before we go, is there anything I shouldn't do tonight? Lines you don't want crossed?"

Every muscle I've kept braced for years wants to exhale. Consent isn't a speed bump; it's the key turning in a lock.

"No lines," I say, meeting his eyes so he can see it land. "I want this."

He holds my gaze a beat like he's testing for cracks, then steps aside. "Good."

The door clicks. The seatbelt whispers. The city slides by

in slow strips of shadow and sodium light. His hand is on my thigh before we hit the first turn—broad, hot, unapologetic. The weight of it hardly shifts when he speaks.

"You've been crossing and uncrossing these legs all night," he murmurs, and his palm slides higher. "Trying to get comfortable?"

"Adjusting." It's supposed to be flippant. It comes out husky.

The corner of his mouth cuts like something wicked. His fingers skate under the hem of my skirt. Skin on skin is a shock and an answer.

"That's not what it looks like from here."

I keep my eyes up, on him, on the windshield, anything but the hand on my thigh, because looking at his long fingers splayed over my leg makes me want to whimper. Streetlights carve his profile into gold and shadow; his eyes stay on the road, the tendon in his forearm shifting when he turns the wheel. His thumb draws slow circles that notch closer and closer to heat.

He presses against my thigh, gently urging my legs apart. I don't know whether to wish for traffic to clear up so we can get to his place sooner, or for it to slow to a crawl so I can enjoy the delicious torture of his touch.

When he finally grazes the damp edge of my panties, my breath catches hard enough to sting.

"Good girl," he says—quiet, iron sure—and the praise strikes through me like pulling a cord.

He toys with me the entire drive, mimicking Friday night. Approach then retreat. The barest touch, then nothing. I turn liquid and restless, thighs trying to chase his touch, hips arching in a silent plea for more. At a red light, he slides under the lace, drags through wetness, and sets his finger to my clit in light, unhurried circles. My gasp fogs the window as my head rolls against the seat. His eyes flick once to my face—cataloging, claiming—then he drags his fingers from me and puts them in his mouth, tongue slow over his fingertips.

"Better than dessert."

By the time the gate shuts behind us in the garage, I am a taut wire. Every nerve is tuned to the possibility of touch.

At the elevator, Connor pulls me close to him and presses a gentle kiss against my cheek. Another couple enters and Connor's breath tickles my neck.

"Too bad we have company. I was hoping to do unspeakable things to you on the ride up."

Inside his apartment, dim lights and the faint scent of cedar greet me as the door snicks shut behind us. In half a breath, Connor has me pinned against the wall and his mouth claims mine. Deliberate and deep. His tongue taking and coaxing at once. My bag thumps to the floor. His hand cups the back of my neck and presses down. My knees find the rug without hesitation.

The shift is so clean I feel it physically—the second my knees hit, something inside me loosens and settles. Not fear. Rightness. Like a puzzle snapping into place.

His belt slides. Leather whispers through loops and his zipper rasps down. Then I see him.

Holy fuck.

Thick, heavy, flushed dark, the vein along the underside a line my tongue is already desperate to trace. My fingers don't meet around him. I swallow on instinct.

"Open," he says, and I do, heat rising up my neck, the thrill of obedience shocking and sweet.

The first push fills my mouth, stretches my lips until a soft ache flares. I wrap my hand at the base to manage the heft, stroke what I can't yet take, and draw him deeper, the weight of him settling on my tongue like gravity.

"Look at you." His fingers thread through my hair, holding gently—not forcing, guiding. "On your knees, mouth so pretty around me."

I glance up. His eyes are dark, focused, a single crease at the corner like he's trying not to grin at how undone I already am.

I breathe through my nose, relax, let him slide further. The head nudges my throat and my eyes water; spit slips over my bottom lip onto my fist. He strokes my cheek with his thumb. My gag reflex flutters and I swallow against it.

"Fuck, yes. Tears on your face, my cock in your throat... you were made for this." The filth is praise and my whole body answers to it. I pull back with a wet pop, strings of saliva catching the low light, and dive back down, hollowing my cheeks, letting the thick weight rub along my tongue on the way out, then pressing down to take him as deep as I can.

He groans. His hips twitch. I feel the control in him like a wire drawn tight between his teeth.

I want to give him more.

I grasp his wrist, a little signal. He understands instantly. His hand tightens in my hair and he holds me in place, deep, until my lungs burn and my eyes flood and the needy ache between my legs spikes into something feral. When he lets me go, I suck in air, drool slicking my chin, and I like the mess. I like his eyes on me while I make it.

I go again. Deeper. Slower. Worship as a verb.

THE DROP—CONNOR

The moment her knees hit, I saw it—the drop. The invisible armor she keeps stitched under her skin loosens by degrees, and she looks up at me like she's offering me the key to her undoing. Not compliance. Surrender.

It's gasoline on everything I am. Every flicker of desire I've held back roars to life like a firestorm fed oxygen.

Her eagerness, her tears and spit, destroy my plans to savor and take my time. Instead, I get a firmer grip in her hair and guide her back down my cock. She gags a little but doesn't push against my hand.

"That's it. Take it like a good girl."

She learns me like she was made for the task. Opening. Relaxing. Going deeper until I feel her throat closing around me and the tightness that says she's fighting not to gag. I hold her there and count slowly, keeping my eyes on her. The moment her chest starts to heave, I pull back, letting her suck in air and swallow before I plunge back into her waiting mouth.

"You love this," I tell her, because it's obvious she does. "Love choking on me."

Her hum vibrates down the length of me, a muffled, aching affirmation that hits like a lightning strike to the base of my spine.

I hold her down again, a heartbeat past comfort. The squeeze of her throat and the struggle as she fights her body's reflexes all signal her trust. I ease her back before she taps out. Saliva strings from her swollen mouth to my cock. I could finish at that sight. I don't. I didn't spend the last two hours winding her up to cut it short without making damn sure she's taken care of first.

"Bedroom. Down the hall. On the right."

She obeys instantly. If I wasn't already raging hard, the way she hops up and scurries down the hall would do it. As much as I want to get her naked and see how much she can handle, there are things we need to discuss.

"What's your safe word?" I trust that she understands the concept. If not, it's time to dial things back. A lot.

"Red." She's standing loose and comfortable at the foot of my bed. Her eyes fixed on mine, lips still puffy and red. God, she's gorgeous.

"You know the stoplight system. If I check in, I want to hear a color. Or you can give me a thumbs up or thumbs down. A nod is acceptable. That work?"

Her head bobs in a fast nod. A second later, she gives me a quiet 'yes.'

"Any questions? Concerns? Anything I need to know?" I wait for the shake of her head. "Okay. Strip. Everything off. You can put your things on that chair. Then I want you sitting on the foot of the bed."

I lean against the wall, cross my arms and watch as Emery does as told. No questions. No hesitation. But there's a slight tremble in her hands and her legs shake as she takes off her boots. Still, when she sits and looks at me, her expression reads confidence, even though she has her knees pressed tightly together.

"Ready?"

She gives another nod and I cross to her, slide my hands between her thighs and press them apart. I keep pressing until I feel her muscles resist. Her eyes fix on mine and I see her hunger.

"I want you to watch." I prop pillows behind her, then lay her back so she's half reclined. "Don't look away. Don't close your eyes. Watch."

I sink to my knees between her legs and lower my head. She's a taste of heaven. Sweet and salty with the scent of musk. This isn't about making her come fast. This is about building her up to something explosive, something so intense it shuts off her brain. I work my tongue over her pussy until I reach her clit. A soft lick and she jumps. Another and she sighs, legs parting wider. I seal my mouth over her clit and flick my tongue until her hips try to climb my face.

"Stay." I pin her hips with my forearms. Her entire body quivers and I work her like a problem I enjoy solving. Mapping the pressure and speed that make her gasp, the things that make her moan, and the ones that make her curse. She's vocal, sweet and filthy, and it makes me greedy for more.

She's right on the edge when I pull back the first time. Her whine hits the same place in me as the sight of her tears did. I give her two fingers, slow, sink them to the knuckles, curl up. Her mouth opens on a perfect, hurt-sweet oh.

"You come when I let you and not until then," I tell her, thumb dragging a tight circle over her clit. She grabs at air like she needs something to hold. I make her hold still. I take my hand away at the edge again. And again. She trembles and cusses and begs prettier with every denial.

"Please." She sounds wrecked after half a dozen rounds of build up with no release. "Please, Connor—"

"Beg me to claim you."

Her eyes glass. "Please take me. Make me yours. I want—" Her voice breaks into a needy sound that shoots straight to my cock.

That's enough.

I flip her. Get her knees on the edge of the bed, perfect ass in the air. I roll on a condom, press the head to that drenched heat, and make myself go slow. Tight. Hot. Home. I breathe through the slam my body wants.

I keep her there at the first stretch, then sink in, making sure she feels every inch until I'm buried in her, hand splayed low on her belly. She makes a desperate, grateful sound into the sheets and pushes back like she's trying to crawl onto me.

She shifts just right and rubs the cleft of her ass along my pelvis like an accident that isn't. My thumb slides between her cheeks almost without me deciding to, circling the other tight heat. I press—gentle, testing. Her moan goes lower, filthier, like I've tuned a hidden string inside her.

I've played this instrument before, but never with someone who opens like this. Who offers her hunger like a prayer.

"Not tonight," I growl into her shoulder. My thumb presses against her ass again, the barest intrusion, enough to mark the trail. "Soon."

I pull almost all the way out of her pussy and hold. She clenches like she can drag me back.

"Stop teasing," she pants, head turning so I can catch the wet heat in her eyes. "I want it all. Please."

There it is. Surrender wrapped in demand. The ask with her whole self.

I slam home.

She screams my name into the mattress, and the way her body grabs me borders on violent. I set a pace meant to undo —deep, hard, relentless, hips snapping, my hand fisted in her hair to arch her throat so I can watch her mouth when she comes. She goes in ripples, first one sharp, then another stacked on the first because I don't give her time to recover. I drive her through it and she breaks beautifully, voice ragged, submission pouring out of her like heat.

The control I've leashed all night—weeks, really—loosens and surges. I want to own every breath, every tremor, every filthy word she doesn't know she'll say until I take it from her.

I flip her onto her back because I want her eyes. Pin her wrists in one hand over her head. Line up and sink in again, slower this time, so deep my hips pin her to the mattress. She whimpers when I roll my pelvis and grind right over the place inside that makes her pupils blow.

"Mine tonight," I tell her, mouth at her ear. "Say it."

"I'm yours," she breathes, then louder, rawer: "I'm yours."

Her legs lock around my hips like she's afraid I'll leave. I won't. Not when she's looking at me like that, not when every line of her body is saying more. I give her more. I pull her legs up and put her heels on my shoulders then fold her in half so I can watch my cock disappear inside her. I keep her open with my hand under her knee and my other hand pressed against her chest.

When she tips her head back, baring her throat and keeping her eyes locked on mine, I slide that hand up, resting it at the base of her neck. She smiles and clenches around my cock. My grip tightens, firm but not choking, and I angle my hand to keep her head back.

"You want to come?" I ask. She nods, wild. Her breath punches out in a sob. I slide out and down and eat her again—mouth greedy, tongue ruthless, licking my own taste from her as I work her clit with precision. She writhes, trapped between my forearm and the mattress, begging with words that come apart.

When she's right there, about to detonate, I stop. She yells and I smile into her thigh. I give her two fingers, curved mean, drag them slow against that spot inside that makes her clutch, then three, my palm up so I can keep rubbing her clit with my thumb. She took my cock, so I know she can handle more.

"You take me so well." I slide a fourth finger in, past the knuckles until my palm is flat against her pussy.

Her whole body screams yes, even when her mouth can't form the words. She opens for it, not just physically but emotionally, trusting me to push her this far.

She fights the flinch, breathes, opens to it, and the pride that surges through me is pure and hot and possessive.

I fuck her with my hand, slow at first, then building harder until my palm slaps against her pussy with every thrust.

Emery's body shakes and her moans could make me come in my pants. I curl all four fingers into her and stroke slow.

"What do you want, Emery?"

Her hands scrabble; I catch both and pin them with my free hand, and she breaks.

"Connor—stop teasing—please, I need it—give me all of it—"

"Ask pretty."

"Please. Please fuck me. Take me. Make me come."

Leash off.

I drive into her in one ruthless thrust and feel the scream leave her chest against mine. My hips pound a rhythm that's closer to fighting than dancing. The bed answers with a punishing creak; the slap of skin is filthy percussion. She's sobbing and smiling at once, gone loose and tight in all the right places, her body opening more each time I push. I feel when she crosses from control to flood—the moment the last stray piece of pride dissolves and it's pure need. I catch her face in my palm and make her hold my eyes while I take her apart.

The first orgasm hits fast and the second climbs quickly behind. Emery throws her head back and arches against it. By the third, she's got her teeth in my shoulder, I don't mind. I pull out and turn her again, pushing into her from behind, holding her back against my chest. One hand tangled in her hair and the other fingering her clit while my cock slams into her. She comes apart again with a ragged cry that scrapes my name raw.

I don't stop. I flatten her on her stomach, spread her legs wide apart, palm her shoulder blades into the mattress, and fuck her in a long, grinding line that keeps me buried and her sobbing, every inch of me slick with her. When I slip my hand back between her cheeks and press the tip of my thumb into her asshole, she moans like a secret and pushes back until my thumb slides in all the way. It takes everything in me not to take what I want. Not yet.

"Soon," I promise, voice broken gravel. "You'll take me in your ass. But not tonight."

Somehow, that promise sends her over the edge again. I feel it roll through her, clutching and fluttering around me. This time, I break with her. The intensity tears a groan from my chest and makes my vision go gray around the edges. My whole body locks and shudders as I empty into the condom.

The come down feels like a fall I don't want to stop and the silence after is loud: our breathing, the tick of a vent, the distant city hiss through glass. I ease out slow, knot the condom, toss it in the trash without leaving the bed. She mews when I move like her body is convinced I'm part of it now.

I gather her in. She's wrecked—flushed, damp, hair a wild halo, mouth kiss-bruised, eyes heavy—but there's a softness under the wreckage that I haven't seen on her face before. Satisfaction like warmth from the inside.

"You okay?" I ask, palm smoothing down her spine, checking, really checking.

Her smile is lazy and sure. "More than okay." A beat. "I liked the ass play." She flicks a glance south, a wicked glimmer through the haze. "Soon?"

"We'll get there," I say, kissing her temple, the crest of her cheekbone, the spot under her ear that made her gasp earlier. "We'll talk. You did perfect."

I get up long enough to bring water, press the glass to her hand, hold it while she drinks because her fingers are doing that lovely post-orgasm tremble. I wipe her gently with a warm cloth, kiss the inside of her knee when she giggles at being fussed over, then pull the sheet over us and drag her into my chest. She tucks there like she was built for the space.

Her breathing evens fast. I watch the secondhand sweep of

the clock for a while with her hair tickling my chin, the room still thick with sex and her.

She gave me more than I planned to take. She went further than I thought she could. And I didn't open the final door.

There haven't been many women who could handle anal with me. I think Emery can, and if I play it right, she'll be happy to beg me to take her ass. I can feel it in the way she melted when my thumb pressed in and the way her yes turned from words to body.

"Good girl," I whisper into her hair, a benediction for sleeping ears.

WEDNESDAY, APRIL 1

FRIENDS, RIGHT?—EMERY

I wake up to heat.

Not just the kind clinging to my skin, but the slow-burn kind that hums between bodies. That stretches like satisfaction and smells like Connor and safety.

His breath brushes the back of my neck in a steady rhythm. One arm is wrapped around my waist like a seatbelt he forgot to unbuckle. His palm rests flat and wide over my stomach, his touch doesn't ask for anything but claims everything.

I don't move. Not yet. My body's too sore, too warm, too content in that way you only get after being thoroughly and completely fucked, and fucked well.

And God, I was. That man's dick should come with a warning. He's bigger than anything in my drawer, and those toys don't mess around. Better still, he knows how to use what he's got. And his fingers, his mouth, his everything.

He shifts behind me and the sheet slips lower on both of us. His nose nuzzles into my hair and he murmurs something unintelligible before he lifts his head and kisses my cheek.

"Mmm. You always wake up this pretty?"

I smile. I can't help it. "You say that like you've seen me wake up before."

"Maybe I'm hoping it's not the last time."

My stomach flutters, and I pretend it doesn't.

Instead, I stretch—a slow, catlike arch that rolls my ass back into the cradle of his hips. His answering groan is low and full of promise. I feel him start to harden against me, and my pulse jumps like it didn't spend the whole night wrung out.

I want more. I don't know how, after everything last night, but I do. Still, it's morning and I need caffeine. "Does this ride come with coffee? Or is that extra for one-night stands?"

He stills.

Then he leans in, presses a kiss to the shell of my ear, and says, voice rough, "Not a one-night stand. You oughta know that."

Oh.

"Coffee's doable," he adds, already starting to move. "Stay."

It's not a question. It's not even a request. Just quiet certainty. Like he knows I won't leave.

And he's right.

I prop myself up, watching as he stands and stretches. The morning light does sinfully wonderful things to him. He's built like a swimmer, muscular but not too ripped, and the deep V down his lower abs makes me want to lick him, all while pulling my eyes lower. I don't even pretend not to look.

Dear God, he's hot. That dick? Still thick and lethal, even soft. My body remembers every inch and wants more. That, I can handle. It's the rest of me I'm trying not to think about.

He kisses my forehead then leaves the room as I pull the covers higher, trying to get my brain to settle. But there's no distance between us anymore. Not in memory. Not in want. And definitely not in the way I already know the shape of his body by heart.

He returns with two mugs, hands one to me, and leans against the dresser like it's a negotiation table.

"Thanks," I say, wrapping my hands around the heat.

He watches me for a moment. "You're quiet."

I sip and try not to stare at his body. "Thinking."

"Oh?"

"Hmm." I meet his gaze. "About what happens next."

His brow lifts, unreadable.

I clear my throat. "We're obviously compatible."

"That's one word for it."

"And I think we both know last night wasn't a fluke."

"No arguments here."

"So," I continue, careful and deliberate, "maybe we don't make it a thing. But we don't pretend it can't happen again."

Everything in me wants more, but I know how risky that is with a man like Connor. His expression sharpens. He doesn't answer right away, instead he keeps that sinful gaze leveled on my eyes.

"So, you're suggesting what? Friends with benefits?" His tone says he likes it even less than I do.

I tell myself it's for the best and nod. "With boundaries."

"That's what you want."

It's a little too quiet. A little too fast. I nod and keep my expression neutral.

"No expectations."

"None." But there's something under the word. Something that tightens between us.

I keep going. "No weirdness if one of us, say, starts seeing someone else."

He cocks his head and the look he gives me is smoldering. "You planning on that?"

"No."

"Me either."

The air thickens, the quiet more honest than anything we've said.

I lick my lips. His eyes drop to my mouth.

"Then we're good?" I ask softly.

He takes a step forward, mug abandoned on the dresser. "We're perfect."

And then he kisses me.

DANGEROUS KISSES—CONNOR

Kissing her is dangerous. I know what that will stir in me, and I've never known a woman who could take me again so soon after a night of vigorous sex.

But the second her mouth softens under mine, it stops being a choice.

She tastes like sleep and coffee and something sweeter underneath—something warm and open and dangerously addictive. I pull back enough to see her face. Her eyes are soft, half-lidded. Her cheeks flushed. Her lips swollen from my mouth and last night's heat.

There's a mark at the base of her throat—mine. My teeth.

A streak of guilt slices through the heat. Not because I hurt her. But because I liked it.

Because I wanted to leave marks, and some part of me wants to leave more.

There's a version of me I don't let out. Haven't in years.

Even with lovers, I've kept control, kept tight boundaries so I didn't overwhelm.

Because I learned what happens when I let go.

But with her? It's too easy to forget I'm supposed to be holding it back.

For years, sex has been another type of performance. I take pleasure in touching, in driving someone to the brink. It's good for me, but leaves me wanting more. And the hunger that's caged up, fed on scraps, snarls for attention.

But with Emery? There's no performance. She sees too much.

And I want her anyway.

God, I want her.

I try to breathe through it. Rebuild the walls. Go slow.

She kisses me again, her tongue tracing my lips and her arms winding around my neck, fingers curling in my hair. She moans into my mouth—barely a sound, but it's enough to undo me.

I break the kiss, just enough to speak. "Tell me if this is too much."

Her breath hitches. "I don't want you to stop."

"You sure?"

She nods, already pulling me down. "Connor..."

It's the way she says my name. Like it's permission. Like it's hers.

I duck my head and kiss the hollow of her throat, right above the bruise. I should stop. I know how this goes. She'll flinch when I slide in, and that's not the kind of pain I get off on.

Emery pushes the blankets down, baring her body for me. Revealing a thumbprint along her thigh. Another stab of guilt twists in me, then she's pulling at me, arms and legs wrapping around me and I reach for a condom before covering her body with mine and keep a close eye on her expression.

She welcomes me with a smile and a sigh then arches against me. Not a flinch to be seen. I should have known. Emery doesn't flinch. I capture her hands in mine and hold them over her head, partly to hide how bad my hands are shaking from how much I want her.

"You feel so fucking good," I murmur, my voice wrecked and too honest as I press deeper into her, forcing myself to go slow.

Emery wraps her legs around me and lifts her hips, grinding in small, eager circles that damn near wreck me.

I laugh, but it comes out low and feral. "You're dangerous."

"Nah, I'm here for the coffee," she whispers, her breath already hitching as she keeps grinding on my cock.

I hear the lie in her words and know. She's as conflicted as I am. I groan against her neck.

"I want—" I start, then stop. Everything. That's what I want. But I bite it back. The last time I let someone get close was college, and that didn't end well.

Instead, I press my mouth to hers and let it take over—every ounce of hunger poured into her lips, her body, her breath.

I kiss her like I'm starved and take her in a slow grind. Forehead to forehead. Chest to chest. Breath mingling. I rock against her until she's coming apart under me. When she comes, I don't stop. I take my time and show her just how far from casual this really feels.

THURSDAY, APRIL 2

SOMETHING WE'RE NOT SAYING—EMERY

By Thursday, everything hurts.

Not in the aftermath-of-sex kind of way—though Tuesday night and Wednesday morning left their share of marks. Not even in the god-is-this-my-life kind of way. This is the bone-deep ache of a woman who has been trying to outrun her own stress for two straight weeks and is finally running out of road.

The worst part? I slept like a baby Tuesday night with Connor wrapped around me like he meant it. Safe. Warm. Held.

Last night? Alone?

My brain wouldn't shut up. Every second was some combination of: What the hell are you doing? This isn't smart. You're going to get attached. You're already attached.

Undeniable. Despite the whole 'let's just do casual' that I gave Connor. And now, with three hours of fitful sleep and a schedule full of fires, I feel like a peeled nerve in lipstick.

The office is a war zone. Alex is juggling four color-coded fires. Dee is slamming keys with righteous fury.

"Charlotte affiliate is dropping the podcast," Alex says, not even looking up from their screen. "Scheduling conflict. And they said you're 'too much.'"

I sigh. "I'd be insulted if that weren't true."

Dee looks up. "The Richmond event venue's waffling. Something about 'community standards.' I'm going to need to go full litigation threat in five."

"Let me know if you need backup," I murmur. "I'll bring snacks."

Alex rolls their chair back and stares at me. "You okay?"

I nod. I have to be okay. Alex and Dee are great and they've been through the fire with me, but this time is different. This time, someone slipped through our carefully built defenses and now it's not just my reputation on the line, but my clients and seminar attendees are at risk as well. Alex gives me another deep look and I force a smile.

"Yeah, it's a lot, but we'll get through it. I'm fine."

I turn back to my client session notes, pretending to focus. Epic failure. Instead, my fingers hover over the message icon. It would be so easy to text Connor and find some time for some much-needed stress relief. Which is exactly why I don't.

A knock cuts through the tension and chaos in the room.

Not frantic. Not tentative.

Just solid.

The door swings open.

Connor.

His calm enters the room and takes up space, spreading over everything like a balm. He's in tailored slacks and a long-sleeved knit shirt, sleeves pushed up like his forearms are a weapon. His eyes scan the room once. Absorbing everything. Saying nothing.

I sit up straighter, though I couldn't explain why. My body understands perfectly as still tender parts clench in anticipation.

"Not trying to interrupt," he says, already walking in. "Was nearby. Figured I'd stop in."

Alex blinks. "If 'nearby' includes downtown and two levels of security, sure."

Connor shrugs. "I make things happen. Emery. Got a minute?"

I narrow my eyes. "Are you here in a professional capacity?" Bitchy, I know, but him popping in right when I'd been thinking about him is not doing good things for my self-control.

"Define professional."

"That's a no."

He shrugs. "Actually, it's a sort of. Purely professional? This could be an email, but I like delivering good news in person."

He walks over to the desk and sets down a folder. I stare at it like it's a trap.

"What is this?"

"The Baltimore Journal piece is taken care of. I intercepted it. Redirected the reporter to a PR contact I trust and pushed a statement under your name to get ahead of it. Stuff pulled from your podcast."

I blink. "You intercepted a journalist?"

"It's a thing I do."

I open the folder. There's a clean, prepped statement. Not spin. Not fluff. My words. My mission. Clear and precise.

He's been listening.

"You didn't tell me you were doing this," I murmur.

"Comes with the territory."

"I..." Part of me wants to be angry. This is the whole

spin thing I hate, but it's not. All he did was use my own words to reframe the narrative. "I didn't know I needed help."

He doesn't flinch. "You did."

Dee pipes up from the other corner. "I got an email. Richmond's back on. Apparently their regional manager called the whole thing a 'misunderstanding.'"

Connor doesn't even look smug.

I look up at him, heart doing something inconvenient.

"You fixed that, too."

"I smoothed it," he corrects. "You're the one building the damn thing."

I don't know what to say to that.

He picks up a to-go cup of coffee—where the hell did that come from?—leans in close, lips brushing my ear.

"I've got an event tonight. But tomorrow night?" His voice is low, certain. "You're mine."

Then he turns and heads for the door, leaving me with my thighs clenching and my brain short-circuiting.

"I'll send the rest of the update by five," he says.

And then he's gone.

Just like that.

Like it didn't matter. Like it wasn't huge. Like he didn't show up in a way no one ever has.

The silence after he leaves is loud.

"I made him the coffee." Alex settles back at the table and hands me a cup. "Don't think I didn't see the question on your face. Honestly, I was skeptical at first, but you two balance each other."

I sputter on my first sip of coffee and try to protest, but Alex shakes their head.

"You call it 'radical honesty,' but it's still a performance. You choose which truths to tell. He chooses which ones to hide. You're playing the same game with different language and rules."

As much as I hate to admit it, they're not wrong, and that's going to take some processing.

"Anyway..." Alex leans forward and braces their elbows on the table. Even Dee looks up. "Are we all pretending that wasn't insanely hot?"

"Shut up." I refuse to look up.

"Don't even deny it," Dee chimes in. "It was."

"See?" Alex fans themselves. "That wasn't just him looking good, either. And you know he looks good."

"So does he," I mutter.

But I'm already replaying the scene. The way he walked in like he belonged. The way he didn't wait to be invited. The way he acted like protecting my work was just obvious.

I exhale, long and low.

He's not staying, I remind myself.

He's not part of this.

Except, he already is.

FRIDAY, APRIL 3

SAFE AND WRECKED—EMERY

I don't try to pretend tonight. I can't even muster the pretense of being fine. Every time we take a step forward, it's like there's another blow waiting to land. It's been a day full of manufactured outrage that paints me as some moral corruption that needs to be stamped out of this country. I have no brain left. No witty one-liner when I open the door to Connor's place. Just me—tired, wired, and aching for something I can't name.

He takes one look at me and knows.

Of course he does.

He doesn't ask what happened. Doesn't try to fix it. He hands me a glass of water and holds out one arm like a lifeline. I step into it without hesitation. Into him.

His body is solid and warm. His chin rests on top of my head. I melt there for a minute, letting my chest rise and fall against his, trying to remember how to breathe.

He kisses my forehead. "Bedroom."

That one word takes my stress down another notch. I

don't ask why. Or what he has in mind. I trust and turn for the hall.

His room is dim and quiet when I walk in. Clean sheets, faint cedar scent, the low thrum of possibility.

I sit on the edge of the bed, fingers tangled in my lap, trying not to vibrate out of my own skin.

Connor walks in behind me, silent and sure. He sets a pair of cuffs on the nightstand, and my breath catches.

"Color?" he asks, voice like warm smoke.

"Green," I answer. No hesitation.

He steps closer. "You trust me?"

"Yes."

"You want to let go tonight?"

I nod. "Please. I need to."

His mouth curves a little. Not smug. Just settled. Like he's relieved I asked.

He moves with slow precision, stripping me down to my panties, then guiding me back to the bed. Cuffs first—soft and padded, no sharp edges. He buckles them around my wrists, then clips them together above my head, letting the tension in my arms stretch me open. It doesn't feel restrictive.

It feels like being held in place by someone who knows exactly what I need.

Connor settles beside me, trailing the backs of his knuckles along my collarbone, over the swell of one breast, down the line of my ribs.

"I'm going to take my time with you tonight," he says, voice quiet but certain. "Every inch."

My breath stutters. "Okay."

He leans in, brushing his lips over mine. It's not rushed. Not even close. It's worship.

Then his mouth moves lower. Kisses down my neck, over my chest, his tongue circling one nipple until I arch into him.

His hand slides between my legs, cupping me through my panties like he's confirming something he already knows.

"You're soaked," he murmurs. "Didn't even touch you yet."

I whimper, hips rolling. "Connor..."

"I've got you," he says, like a promise. Like a fact.

He slides my panties down slowly, kissing the inside of each thigh as he goes. Then he spreads me open and devours. There's no other word for it. Slow at first. Thorough. His tongue drags through my folds, lips sealing around my clit just long enough to make me cry out before pulling back again.

He teases me to the edge. Once. Twice. The third time I gasp his name, he lifts his head and says, "You're doing so good for me."

I can barely breathe.

He slides two fingers inside my pussy and I clench around them instantly, the pleasure dizzying.

"So fucking tight," he murmurs. "And you haven't even taken all of me yet."

I let out a laugh that's mostly a moan. "That's what they all say."

He stills. Cocks an eyebrow. "Are you okay with anal play tonight?"

Of course he'd bring that up.

"Yeah," I breathe. "I like it."

That gets a slow, dark smile from him. "Yeah?"

"But I've never done it like this."

His brow furrows. "Like what?"

"Like this." I angle my head, nodding toward my cuffed wrists and swallow hard. "It's different. You're different. I don't know..."

I'm a therapist, I should be able to find the words I want, but this is the thing I've left unnamed for so long. The only word I can think to describe what I crave is the scariest word there is. Connor's eyebrows raise, as if he's waiting for me to finish. I screw up my courage and say it.

"Never from a place of surrender."

Something flashes in his eyes. Not softness. Something deeper. Like I've handed him a piece of truth he wasn't ready for, but wanted anyway.

His hand stills inside me, and his other hand coasts lower, pressing my thighs apart. I've done anal, but never while cuffed and trembling, and never with anyone like Connor.

"One day I'll bury myself in that gorgeous ass. Tonight, you get fingers, but that's all. Do you want that?" he asks, voice low and careful.

"Yes," I say, steady now. "I trust you."

His breath shudders. His fingers flex before he slides them out.

"Color?"

"Still green."

He slicks a finger with lube, presses a kiss above my clit, and murmurs, "That's my girl."

And something in me, something hidden and locked away, unravels.

RUINED AND REVERED—CONNOR

She's still trembling.

Her hands are cuffed above her head, her body flushed and open and so fucking ready for me.

But what floors me isn't how beautiful she looks.

It's what she said.

'This is different...never from a place of surrender...I trust you.'

Not just permission. Not just curiosity.

She wants me. My pace. My control. My hands.

I take a breath, slow and deliberate, because what's inside me wants to devour her. But that's not what tonight is. Tonight isn't about pushing to the limit. It's about building something for us.

I press one finger to the tight ring of muscle, circling. She's already relaxed, body trusting mine, hips tilting in silent invitation.

I go slow. Breach her with care. Just the tip, then more. Watching her face the whole time.

She gasps. Her thighs quake.

"You okay?" I ask, stilling.

"Yes," she pants. "More, please."

God, she's incredible.

As requested, more fingers, more pressure. I keep one hand on her clit, circling slow and easy while I finger fuck her ass in smooth strokes. She's soaked. Wrecked. Her body's giving me everything I want without hesitation.

"You take it so well. Like you were made to be filled. Open. Owned."

She whines. Tries to move. The cuffs hold her in place. Her body shakes, every muscle drawing tight.

"Connor—please—I'm so close—"

"Come for me," I growl, fingers relentless. "Right here. Just like this."

And she does.

She shatters beneath me, crying out my name, body clenching around my fingers, breathless and honest and so fucking mine in that moment I can barely see straight.

I ease her through it. Unclip the cuffs. Pull her into my arms until her body is cradled in mine.

"You okay?" I murmur against her temple.

She nods, barely able to speak. "I didn't know it could feel like that."

I stroke her back, slow and steady. "That's the point."

She's quiet for a long time. Then she lifts her head and whispers, "Still just friends with benefits, right?"

It's a knife in my ribs, but I nod.

"Best damn benefits ever."

She huffs a tired laugh and drops her head back onto my chest and folds into me like a prayer.

But I don't close my eyes. She's unlocked something in me and there is nothing casual about what she let me do tonight. Or about the way I never want to let her go.

SATURDAY, APRIL 4

IF IT BLOWS AGAIN—EMERY

The conference room is too bright. Too cold. Too quiet.

I sit in a chair molded for function, not comfort, across from the eight board members of the East Coast Women's Crisis Centers—an organization I've worked with for years. We've built therapy access programs together. Created trauma-informed workshops from New York to the Carolinas. Held hands with survivors while the world looked away.

Today, they won't look me in the eye.

This is their regular monthly meeting. Always on a Saturday, rotating through the dozen centers. Normally I'd come to present outcomes and collaborate on the next quarter's goals. Instead, I'm handed a paper agenda with my name listed under 'Discussion: External Partnerships.'

Those three words tell me all I need to know.

They talk around it at first. They make it about donor unease and concerns from faith-based partners, or a spike in calls from concerned constituents. Someone uses the phrase 'moral clarity.'

Another says, "your podcast has become too polarizing for us to remain publicly affiliated."

"We're not terminating our partnership. Think of it more as a pause, at least until things die down." The chair of the board doesn't look at me as she speaks and her words hang in the air, polished and bloodless.

I sit a little straighter. "Pause? After ten years of collaboration? After everything we've built?"

She issues a sigh. Measured and sympathetic and very rehearsed. "You know how it is, Emery. We need a little distance while the situation settles. All of this... notoriety is not a good look for us."

"Notoriety," I repeat, tasting the word like metal. "I'm the same person who redesigned your trauma outreach last fall. The same person your donors praised for 'changing lives.' You mean that notoriety?"

Her pause is long enough to make its own statement.

"We appreciate your passion," the chair says finally, which is how people with power tell you the decision's already made.

As if this is temporary.

As if they don't want to admit I've been branded with a scarlet S.

S for slut.

Because I speak openly about sex.

Because I believe everyone deserves pleasure without shame.

Because I talk about kink and boundaries and healing and autonomy like they're not filthy things.

I'm dangerous because I'm too loud.

The board thanks me for my time and says it isn't personal.

They tell me "this doesn't reflect the value of your work."

But I can see the judgment in their eyes. The fear is tangible, and the relief at cutting ties before the fire spreads even more so. I won't lie to myself and believe it's a pause.

I thank them. I stand. I smile. And I leave with my spine straight and my insides unraveling.

Outside, the wind slices through my jacket. I make it to my car before my hands start to shake. The rearview mirror shows a woman too red in the cheeks, too bright in the eyes, too practiced in holding it all together.

The drive home is a blur. Through the garage. Into the elevator. To my condo. There's a small package hanging from my doorknob. I snatch it off and turn for the trash, ready to toss whatever it is, then I stop. This is a secure building. My address isn't public. Even Connor couldn't find it.

Connor. The box is matte black and wrapped in a red satin ribbon. No note or label. But I know.

Inside my condo, I set the box on the kitchen counter and drop my bag like it's burning. Kick off my shoes. Shrug out of my coat and return to the small box.

Inside, a pair of silver earrings shaped like miniature vintage microphones. A whisper of power tucked inside elegance.

Beneath them, a folded notecard in familiar handwriting.

You were made for this.

My knees nearly give. I catch myself on the counter, earrings clenched in one hand, the note shaking in the other.

Who knows when he bought these. It doesn't matter. They're a reminder of who I am. Who I've always been. And they're a gift from a man who sees me, sometimes better than I see myself.

When the knock comes, I know it's him before I open the door.

Connor steps into the doorway, eyes locked on mine. Tall and gorgeous and more casual than I've ever seen him.

"I didn't know if today was one of the days you needed quiet."

I nod, throat too tight to speak. "It was."

He starts to step back, to give me space.

"Stay," I say, barely above a whisper. I'm not sure what I want, but I know I don't want to be alone.

He makes coffee. Finds my favorite mug and puts on music. Something soft and warm that soothes. When he puts the mug next to me, there's a small plate with two macaron from my favorite shop around the corner. I don't need to ask the flavors—mocha and dark chocolate. Then he sits beside me, not touching, not speaking, just there, cradling his own mug and a plate with two salted caramel cookies.

He's solid and steady.

And mine. At least for now, and that will have to do.

I lean my head against his shoulder.

I don't cry. But something inside me loosens.

"Thank you for the earrings. They're beautiful."

He doesn't respond, just kisses the top of my head, then tucks me closer to his side.

And for the first time since I saw the agenda item with those three words next to my name, I take a deep breath.

SUNDAY, APRIL 5

TRUTH DRAFTED—EMERY

I stare at the blinking cursor like it's part of the problem.

The outline for my next Let's Talk About Sex episode is open, perfectly color-coded, courtesy Alex. Of course. Yellow for core themes, green for listener questions, blue for research links. I've even written a suggested title: The Illusion of Safety.

But the space beneath it, the part where I'm supposed to actually say something, remains blank. Never mind the carefully transcribed voice notes Erin typed up on Friday.

My fingers rest on the keyboard. Then curl back. Then reach again.

It's not that I don't have thoughts. I have too many and they're not aligning with the intended topic. I could give an impromptu TED Talk on how safety is a myth we sell to survivors. Or how vulnerability does more to expose you than protect you.

Right now, I'm thinking more about how shame isn't born from consensual sex, but from the systems that police it.

On a good day, I could work that in, but today, none of it comes out clean. It's all jagged edges and salty attitude.

I try to type the first line. Delete it. Try again. Delete that too.

All I can think about is yesterday.

The paper agenda with my name under 'External Partnerships.'

The chair's voice as she thanked me for my service and cut me loose.

The expressions of disdain, or worse, embarrassment as they all looked away from me.

And when I got home—him.

From the earrings on my door to him showing up and not asking for an explanation, but stepping in and doing what I needed. He made caring an action.

Coffee. Cookies. The soft weight of his silence beside me.

He didn't try to fix anything. Or tell me what I should have done. None of the typical male responses to a woman's stress.

I close the laptop.

In the kitchen, I move by muscle memory, pulling out things I bought on my last grocery trip. Onion. Garlic. Carrots. Celery. I dice by feel, not thought. Let the rhythm of the blade settle my breath. Leftover rotisserie chicken, pulled apart with my hands. Broth poured from a box, not homemade, but it'll do.

The scent of simmering soup slowly fills the condo. It's something earthy and warm that reminds me I'm still here.

I tell myself I'm cooking because it helps me think. Because it's functional. But really, I'm trying to build something no one can take from me.

When it's done, I ladle a spoonful into a small tasting bowl and take a sip. Rich. Familiar. Could use a little salt, like maybe I was afraid of going overboard.

I glance at the pot. There's enough for eight people. Easy.

Too much for one person. Way too much for someone who isn't really hungry.

My phone's in my hand before I know what I'm doing. I hit Connor's contact and type.

> Got too ambitious. Made enough soup for a small army. Want some?

I stare at the message.

Then hit send. Friends do this sort of thing. It doesn't have to mean anything big.

UNSENT UNTIL NOW—CONNOR

The message lights up my phone as I'm pouring whiskey. The bottle tips a little too far, splashing liquid onto the counter.

"Fuck."

I set the glass down, grab a paper towel and wipe up the spill. Read the text again. Then I stare at it.

> Got too ambitious. Made enough soup for an army. Want some?

It's simple and casual. There's no reason for it to punch the air out of my lungs. I don't overthink it. Don't give myself time to. Just grab my keys and turn to the door, taping in a response while I walk.

> On my way.

Halfway to the door I glance back. The bottle of whiskey

sits on the counter, cap still off. I hesitate for half a beat, then grab it.

She'll have glasses.

A short elevator ride later, I get out on Emery's floor and the hallway smells like lemon cleaner and someone's takeout. Her door opens before I even knock.

She's barefoot. Leggings, oversized sweater, sleeves pushed up to her elbows. Hair in a loose knot, a few strands curling at her temples. No makeup. No armor.

I have to look away for a second, afraid of showing too much.

"It smells like actual comfort in here," I say, holding up the bottle by way of greeting.

She smiles. It's small, tired, but real. "The soup might be edible. No promises."

I follow her in. The warmth hits immediately. Broth and butter and garlic, rich and earthy and exactly what the night needed. She's already ladling soup into two bowls and cutting a grilled cheese into quarters like it's a sacrament. She nods at a cabinet, like I haven't already figured out where she keeps things. I fish out two glasses and splash in whiskey.

"Not sure this is a normal combination, but here we are." I hold up the glasses. Emery loads up a tray with food and silverware.

We eat on the couch. Legs curled. Bowls balanced. The heat of it seeps into my chest like something I forgot I needed.

Halfway through, she passes me a grilled cheese triangle without asking. I take it without a word.

The TV's tuned to some nature documentary in soft British narration, all low rumbles and whispered awe. We're not really watching.

Our shoulders brush. Barely.

But then they stay touching.

Her skin is warm through the sweater. Her presence so close I can taste it. I sip the whiskey slowly, willing my body to behave.

She leans her head on my arm and I hold still like it might break the spell.

I want to say something. Anything.

That I thought about her all day.

That I've never wanted someone more in silence.

That the gift I left yesterday wasn't just care—it was need.

That this, right here, might be the most dangerous thing I've ever done.

But I don't say any of it.

Instead, I shift my hand enough so our fingers brush. Let them rest there. Let it feel like an accident.

She doesn't pull away.

Her pinky curls slightly toward mine. The lightest contact. The smallest surrender.

For one long, aching moment, we sit like that. Not lovers. Not friends. Just something fragile and unnamed. Something holding its breath in the space between.

MONDAY, APRIL 6

UP AGAINST A WALL—EMERY

By a quarter after three, I've had it.

Not with my team. They're saints. Alex pulled two podcast guests out of thin air, Dee fixed an entire livestream with caffeine and code, and Erin hasn't flinched once, even after catching a protestor on TikTok chanting "Cancel the sex witch!" outside our building. Though something tells me she delighted in that in some way. She stood around long enough to get a five-minute video.

I've had it with myself. I'm the problem.

Too many thoughts. Too many fires. Too many feelings I don't have time to name.

I haven't been able to focus since I woke up. Not because of the inbox. Not because of the noise.

Because I didn't wake up next to him.

Friday still lingers on my skin. The stretch. The surrender. The way he whispered 'that's my girl' like it was truth carved into bone. And Saturday morning—curled into him, cuff marks fading on my wrists, both of us pretending it was just really good stress relief.

Then that horrible meeting Saturday. It threw off my whole weekend. Connor came by both days and he was amazing. Sweet and supportive. A genuine friend.

But he didn't stay over. Didn't initiate sex. Not that I blame him for that. I wasn't giving off seduce-me vibes, and I sure as hell know I can ask for what I want.

I didn't sleep much Saturday night, or last night, because I missed him. Not just the sex, but the feel of his body next to me, and I don't have the spoons to process that right now.

So I stop pretending.

I grab my phone and text him one sentence.

I need to turn my brain off.

His reply comes before I can lock the screen.

Tonight or now?

I consider the question for less than a minute.

Now. Later. Both.

On my way.

Meet me in the basement. Storage room.
End of the hall.

I don't wait for his response. I'm already on my feet, ignoring the questioning looks from Alex and Dee.

"Back in twenty," I mutter.

"Uh-huh," Alex calls after me, not buying it.

Downstairs is quiet. First floor, empty hallway, then the stairwell that leads to the basement. Down the old concrete steps and into the cool air, and a rush of adrenaline I don't try to name.

The storage room at the end of the hall is barely marked. Just a steel handle and a key lock. I unlock it, step inside, and slap the light switches. Too bright. I click them off one by one until the only light is pooled near the door, leaving the rest of the space in shadows that shift as people walk by the window high in the far wall.

If someone walked past on the sidewalk above, they might see shadows moving in the room. Might hear something.

The risk shouldn't thrill me, but it does.

I shut the door behind me and breathe in the quiet.

Half-empty shelves line the walls. A few standing lockers on one side and a sturdy worktable near the far wall. Remnants of when this was a single-practice building. Now the shelves contain holiday decorations and building maintenance supplies.

I'm pacing near the door when it opens.

Connor steps inside, shuts it, locks it.

Then looks at me.

Eyes scanning. Breathing shallow. Entire body coiled like he already knows what this is.

Neither of us speaks.

I walk backward, deeper into the shadows.

He follows. Like a big cat on the prowl.

When my back hits the wall near the table, I exhale like I've been holding my breath all day.

"How much time do you have?"

Leave it to him to think logistics. I could tell him I'm the boss; it doesn't matter.

"Fifteen minutes. Ish."

His laugh is low and seductive. "I've never been the quickie type, but I'm sure we can make it work. Bad day?"

I nod. "Please."

That's all I say.

Please.

His mouth is on mine before I can think again. His hands already under my skirt. No slow tease, no warm-up—just need, fast and consuming.

His fingers slide between my legs and he groans into my mouth. "Jesus, you're soaked."

I gasp when he finds my clit, strokes me hard and fast like he can tell that's what I need.

"I knew you'd be like this," he murmurs against my throat. "Knew you'd be dripping for it before I even touched you."

"Connor—" My voice breaks.

"You want to forget?" he growls. "Let me fuck the thoughts out of your head."

I nod wildly. "Yes. Please, yes."

He spins me toward the wall, his chest against my back. I feel his dick, already hard, pressing through his jeans.

I lift my skirt.

He yanks my panties down, then slides his fingers through me again, slow this time, savoring.

"Fuck," he whispers. "So ready. You want me to fuck you right here? Use your words."

I moan. "God, yes. I need this. I need you."

He pulls a condom from his back pocket. Planned, prepared, and that shouldn't make me ache the way it does.

I hear the tear. The slick slide. Then his voice right against my ear:

"I know you like it rough." His hand slides between my thighs again. "You ready to play with that?"

I choke on a breath. "Yes."

"Good. We're about to see how hard you can go."

He leans in, pinning me against the wall, and slams into me in one deep, devastating thrust.

HOLD NOTHING BACK—CONNOR

She's molten heat, clenching tight around me, her hands scrambling for something to hold as I bury myself to the hilt. No hesitation or pretense.

Emery gasps, eyes wide.

"You okay?"

Her lips part. "You feel... so fucking big."

I groan against her shoulder. "And you love taking every inch."

She does. Like her body was built for me. And maybe it was.

Because the second I got her text, every part of me snapped into place. Like she'd pulled a trigger only I could feel.

'I need to turn my brain off.'

No flirting. No coy pretending.

Just need.

And fuck me, I live for that.

I thrust harder. Her breath stutters.

"This what you needed?" I growl. "My cock, hard and fast, buried so deep you can't think."

She nods, whimpers. "Don't stop."

Her head falls back against my shoulder. My hand slides to her throat, not tight, just there. Her pulse pounds beneath my fingers. She's mine in this moment. Open. Gutted and desperate.

"You're dripping down my cock," I mutter. "You like being used like this, huh?"

"Yes," she gasps. "God, yes! Harder."

The sound of our bodies coming together echoes in the

small room. Emery's thighs tremble and she tightens around my cock. In minutes, she's ready to explode.

Not yet. I pull out, ignore her cry of protest and drag her away from the wall then bend her over the big wooden table that's bolted to the floor.

"Spread your legs." I don't wait for her to comply, instead, I use my feet to push her legs further apart. I slide two fingers through the wetness of her pussy then press them against her asshole. A little spit and I'm able to slide both fingers in. I wrap my other arm around her hips and trap her clit between the fingers of my other hand.

"What do you want?"

Emery grinds her hips, gliding between the fingers in her ass and the fingers on her pussy. Her hands clutch the far side of the table so hard the muscles in her arms stand out.

"Fuck me, please!"

The moment the words are out of her mouth, I slam my cock back into her, burying myself all the way. Her breath rushes out in a gasp as her body is pressed into the table. I don't give her a moment to recover before pulling back and doing it again and again. She's going to have bruises on her hips and thighs in the morning.

Seeing her like this makes me want more. I want her hands and ankles tied to the table and my cock buried in her ass after a slow round of spankings. I nudge the hood of her clit back and stroke harder, faster, keeping time with the thrusts into her pussy and ass.

That tips her over. The shaking starts in her legs and spreads. I lean down, pressing into her. "Come for me. Come while you're bent over this table, getting fucked senseless, and knowing someone might hear you."

She does. Body spasming. Clenching around me. Her mouth open in a silent cry as she rides it out.

I don't last.

The second her body squeezes me like that—tight, wet, perfect—I slam into her once, twice more, and let go.

We stay there. Breathing hard. Her head drops to the table as I slowly slide my hands from her. I pull out and ease the condom off; thankful I thought to grab a handful of paper napkins and a hand towel. I clean her up as best I can, then turn her over and lift her to sit on the table and cradle her in my arms.

Her cheek lands on my shoulder and I almost say something I shouldn't. Instead, I kiss the spot behind her ear and whisper, "Anytime you need to forget, you call me."

She lifts her head and locks her eyes on mine and for a second, a heartbeat, I see it. This isn't just sex anymore. I'm not sure it ever was.

Then she nods once and the moment disappears. "Deal."

Like it's nothing.

Like we're still in control.

BAREFOOT IN HIS KITCHEN—EMERY

There's something sacred about the smell of garlic in a pan.

That and the clink of silverware, the low hum of jazz from Connor's speakers, and the blissful, impossible fact that, after a high demand day, between our afternoon quickie, and more when I finally left the office, my brain has relaxed a little.

I lean against the counter in his kitchen, sipping wine and watching him stir something with far too much focus for someone who claims not to cook.

"This feels suspiciously domestic," I say, lifting a brow.

He glances over his shoulder. "You're in my shirt. Drinking my wine. Watching me cook. It's domestic because you started it. No way in hell were we making it out to dinner tonight."

"Is that how this works?"

"You texted me mid-afternoon to meet you in a basement then let me fuck you in a most disrespectful way. Later, when you got off work, you knocked on my door and dropped to your knees the second it closed behind you. What part of that says, 'let's go out for dinner?'"

My face goes hot, but it's not embarrassment. It's memory.

"I was highly motivated."

He turns back to the pan like he's not smirking. "Understatement of the year."

He's right, though. I haven't stopped thinking about the basement. About the way he locked the door behind him like he was stepping into a ritual. The way he saw my need and filled me so fast I forgot my own name.

The way he whispered 'let me fuck the thoughts out of your head' then did exactly that before he told me to come for him.

My thighs clench under the hem of his shirt.

Connor stirs the sauce, oblivious or pretending to be.

"So what are we having?" I ask, trying to steer myself back to neutral ground.

He lifts the lid and releases a cloud of steam that smells like oregano and victory. "Pasta. Chicken. Something that might pass for cream sauce."

I narrow my eyes. "After everything else, I'm surprised you didn't order delivery."

"Needed to burn off energy."

"Oh my god."

"You're welcome."

We eat and it's good. Like, annoyingly good. Especially for

a man who railed me over a worktable five hours ago, then throat fucked me the moment I walked in the door.

"This is really good. Thank you," I murmur between bites.

He doesn't look up. "You shouldn't sound so surprised."

We clean up, move to the couch, and fall into stories—his worst Tinder date, my most absurd DMs—and the laughter comes easy. Dangerous, easy. Like the weight of the day is melting into the walls of this apartment.

"You're making that up," I say, nearly choking on wine.

"I'm not. I have the screenshots."

"You always have screenshots."

"I like evidence."

"So I've noticed."

His eyes flick to mine across the table. "I liked how you looked today."

I blink. "Which part?"

"Bent over. Panting. Nails scraping wood."

My mouth drops open.

"You said that so casually."

He shrugs. "You looked perfect."

It's a simple statement that sounds like filthy praise coming from him, and I like it. It makes me believe he's still thinking about it, because I know I am.

I try to keep it light. "You're obsessed."

"Absolutely."

The air shifts. Not heavy. Just honest.

STILL THINK THIS IS CASUAL?—CONNOR

She shifts on the couch, legs across my lap, glass loose in one hand. The flush in her cheeks hasn't faded, and it's not from the wine. It's from this. From us.

The laughter's quieted, but something else hums between

us now. Warmer. Slower. Built on all the things we're not saying.

My fingers trace lazy circles on her thigh. She doesn't stop me. Doesn't shift away. Her breath changes enough to tell me everything I need to know.

I glance up, voice low. "Still think this is casual?"

She hesitates.

Just for a second.

Not enough for most people to notice.

But I'm not most people.

She shrugs, that slow, practiced kind of move that's meant to look effortless.

"Sure."

Liar. I don't call her on it. Not directly. Instead, I nod slowly.

"I think we're lying to ourselves really well."

Her eyes flick to mine. "I don't lie. It's kind of my whole brand."

"Emery."

She knows what I'm asking. Still think this is just sex? I sure as hell don't, and I don't believe she does either.

She sets her glass down. Doesn't answer. Not in so many words.

Then she exhales and says, "Okay. Fine. We're totally liars. Both of us."

There it is.

I reach for her without thinking—pull her into my lap like it's the only place she belongs. Her body folds into mine, soft and sure. Like she's meant to be here.

She looks up at me, eyes wide, lips parted. Her voice barely a whisper.

"What are we doing?"

I don't have a clean answer. But my hands slide under the

hem of my shirt—still draped on her, still the only thing she's wearing.

She sighs when I touch her.

"Well, I don't know about you," I murmur, "I'm trying to make it harder to pretend."

Her fingers curl into the fabric at my shoulders. Her legs shift, hips arching toward me. And I feel the heat, slow but undeniable, already pulsing beneath the surface.

I lean in to kiss her, keeping it soft. Reverent. I want her to know this isn't about the basement. Not this time.

She opens under me, lips parting, thighs loosening. My hands roam freely, memorizing the shape of her again.

But then she tilts her hips again. Just enough.

She breaks the kiss to whisper, "You're holding back."

My breath hitches and a groan tears from me. "Emery, dammit."

She smiles. Small. Dangerous.

"I don't want you to," she adds. "Not tonight. Not ever. Not with me."

The part of me I usually leash tight, the one that devoured her against a wall and growled in her ear and made her come while her panties were still on, that part stirs.

And I don't fight it this time.

She cups the back of my neck, pulling me down. Her voice is low and electric.

"Show me."

Fuck.

She doesn't have to say more. My hand fists in her hair, my mouth crashes into hers, and she moans, already gone for it.

She likes what I become for her.

And for the first time, I'm not afraid of it.

TUESDAY, APRIL 7

FIVE WORDS, NO REPLY—CONNOR

I finish the last set of pull-ups with a grunt that tastes like blood and shame. I've pushed myself hard enough that my hands are raw and my shirt clings to me with sweat. Still not enough.

The gym is quiet. Empty. It's why I go early mornings or late nights. So I can avoid eye contact. I drop to the floor, chest heaving, and stay there.

Yesterday.

The way she called me. The way she sounded. 'I need release.'

I answered without thinking, without hesitation, because something in her voice unspooled me. And what we did—fast, rough, feral in that basement storage room—wasn't something you walk away from untouched.

I haven't. The sex at my place later only cemented her in my brain.

There are scratches on my back, faint bruises on my shoulders from her fingers digging in. My sheets smell like her and I almost left them on the bed as a reminder. I didn't. But the temptation said too much.

It wasn't just sex. I don't know that it ever was.

And it scares the hell out of me. Because I don't know how to love someone without destroying it.

Back in my condo, I move through my space like it offends me. The rooms are too clean. Too still. The silence, once soothing, now presses in.

I sit at the kitchen island with my laptop, not working. Just clicking.

When I open the video, it's not an accident.

It's old, pre-DC. Pre-New York explosion even. She looks fresh out of college. Emery, on a cramped stage with bad lighting and a shitty mic. Her hair is shorter, her heels higher. Her voice, though—clear, commanding, alive.

She's talking about desire and power and the way women are taught to fear both. She laughs at her own joke, and the audience laugh with her. Her body language is open, her fire impossible to look away from. Even then, she had presence and the ability to captivate a room.

I watch it twice. Then a third time. Each viewing cuts a little deeper.

Because that woman—that confident, radiant force—is still inside Emery.

But now I only see her in moments. When she's working. When she's performing. When she's building armor out of posture and tone.

In private, she's quieter. Frayed at the edges. Still strong. Still sharp. But carrying so much weight.

This past weekend, she let me in, a little, and yesterday, she chose me.

Not just to fuck her. That was the surface. Her asking for that showed trust. But what came later, holding her, feeling her yield control and allowing me to strip her of the tension until she could finally breathe.

I could've ruined it.

I still might.

I open a message to her.

You okay?

Delete.

Yesterday was more than you let on. I see it. I'm here.

Delete.

Then I open a thread with Alex.

> Keep an eye on her today. Quietly. Let me know if anything shifts.

No emoji. No explanation. But Alex will get it.

I set my phone down like it burns.

My mind flashes to the press of Emery's back against the wall. Her fingers clutching my shirt. The whimper she made when I commanded her to take it. All of it.

I told myself it was what she needed. But that was a lie.

I needed it too. Not the orgasm. Not even the dominance.

The trust.

She saw me. All the parts I hide. The hunger. The control. The leashed beast inside my soul.

And instead of flinching, she opened herself to it.

Let me in.

She trusted me with her body yesterday. I want to earn her trust with everything else.

I replay the video again. Watch her smile. Watch the fire behind her eyes.

"You made me want to be seen," I whisper. "And now I don't know how to stop."

On the screen is a woman who, even then, owned the room. She still burns as bright, but with all the stresses pressing on her, I'm not sure she can keep it up much longer.

I close the laptop. And sit in the quiet, finally letting myself feel everything I've been avoiding.

WEDNESDAY, APRIL 8

WHEN SHE BREAKS—CONNOR

The text comes at 4:12.

Do you have five minutes?

I'm in the middle of reviewing access logs for a new client—four monitors lit up, one earpiece in, half-listening to my analyst talk about probabilities.

I mute everything and call Emery immediately.

She answers on the second ring. "Hey."

Her voice is off. Too quiet. Too careful.

"What's wrong?"

"I—" She stops. Breathes. "A client canceled. One of my long terms. Said the press made her feel unsafe. That her husband saw the clip and didn't want her associated with..."

In the pause, I hear it. The sniffles. The sigh and hitch in her voice.

"He doesn't want her associated with a woman like me." Her tone is heart-breakingly bitter.

I say nothing. Let the silence hold while her breath hitching does the talking.

She's trying to hold it in and she's losing.

"Where are you?"

"Garage. Just finished an interview. Got the email in the car."

I hear the wetness in her voice now. A breath through her nose. The slight, sharp inhale of someone trying not to cry. Or who's trying to stop crying.

"Can you drive?"

A pause. Then: "Yeah. I think so."

"Okay. Go to the lowest level of the garage. Find the darkest corner you can. Somewhere with no cameras. Text me your location. I'm leaving now and I'll let you know my ETA."

She doesn't argue.

Just says, soft and wrecked, "Okay."

And hangs up.

She called me. Not Alex. Not Dee. Me. And if sex helps ease the ache, I'll give her that. Every goddamn time. Casual my ass. The reality is, I don't need to be a therapist to recognize that she's turning to sex to deal with her stress. It's healthier than many of the alternatives. She's under a lot of pressure and I know how to trip her release valve. Whether it's emotional support or making her come so hard she forgets her name.

The map says she's ten minutes away. I make it in seven.

I don't remember the drive.

I remember white knuckles on the steering wheel. I remember the ache in my chest when I pictured her alone, crying in the dark. I remember the sound of her voice—how small it got.

What I don't remember is trying to calm down.

Because I didn't.

I pull in fast and find her immediately. Back corner. Low light. No foot traffic. Her car tucked neatly into the shadows.

She's already out when I kill the engine.

Face blotchy. Eyes red.

She looks like she's about to apologize.

I don't let her.

I close the space and pull her into my arms, tight and immediate. Her cheek presses to my chest. Her fists bunch in my shirt.

"I didn't know who else to call," she whispers.

My throat closes.

Always me. That's what I want to say.

Instead, I bury my face in her hair and say, "I've got you."

We stay like that for a long breath. Maybe more.

But then she shifts.

Her hands slide down. Her body presses closer. Her breath turns warm against my throat.

It's want and need. Sharp and demanding.

I pull back. Just enough to see her face.

"Are you sure?"

She nods. "Yes."

"Tell me."

"I want it. I need you."

That's all it takes.

Whatever control I walked in with evaporates.

I fist her hair and kiss her like I've been starving. Like the only way to soothe the ache in my chest is to fuck it out of both of us.

She moans, hands clutching my back.

I spin her. Press her back against the hood. The metal

groans under her weight as I lift her effortlessly, set her there, and drop to my knees on the garage floor.

She gasps.

"Connor—"

My hands slide under her skirt. Find soaked lace. I growl when I feel how wet she already is.

"You need this," I say, voice rough. "Don't you?"

"Yes—fuck—yes."

I pull her panties aside and press my mouth to her like it's mine.

Because it is.

She tastes like heat and desperation. My hands grip her thighs tight, spreading her open, and I devour.

No teasing.

Just tongue, pressure, claiming.

Her body jolts. Her moans echo off the concrete.

She tries to stay quiet. Fails.

"You're so fucking responsive," I groan into her. "Come for me. Right now."

Her hands slam against the hood. Her hips buck. She shatters fast and loud, like her whole body forgot how to hold tension.

I don't let her rest.

I stand. Fumble the button on my jeans. Roll on a condom with hands that shake more than I want to admit.

I grip her chin and tilt her face up to mine.

"Turn around."

She does.

Over the hood. Back arched. One yank and her panties pool around her ankles.

I line up and slide in with one brutal thrust.

We both groan.

"Fuck—Connor—"

"So tight. So fucking good."

I grab her hips and start to move. Hard. Deep. Unforgiving.

She takes all of it.

Her fingers grasp at the metal. Her back bows. She throws it back into every stroke.

"God I love seeing you like this," I snarl. "Taking me like you want to be wrecked."

"More," she pants. "Please, more—"

My hand slides into her hair. Fists.

"Mine."

"Yes—yours—"

I lose it.

Thrust after thrust, I slam into her. My hips slap hers. Her moans go sharp. High.

"You gonna come again?"

"Yes—yes—Connor—"

"Do it. Let them fucking hear you."

She breaks. Again.

Clenching, trembling, sobbing my name.

I follow her into it. Body locked. Mind gone. Every part of me buried in her, shaking with what I can't say.

When I pull out, she collapses against the hood, breath ragged.

I curl an arm around her. Press my forehead to her spine. Try to remember how to breathe.

BENT AND BLAZING—EMERY

My cheek is still pressed to metal.

My legs are jelly. My heart's pounding. My body is still echoing with every thrust, every filthy word, every shudder that ripped through me.

Connor is draped over my back, his breathing just as ragged. His hands—those big, callused hands—are braced beside mine.

He doesn't move and neither do I.

Because this? This wasn't escape.

It was possession, and not the scary kind.

The kind that made me feel wanted. Like I was his release. His tether. His sanctuary.

"I shouldn't want you like this," he whispers into my skin.

"Says who," I whisper back.

His breath catches—sharp and broken.

But it's not over.

His hand slides down my back. Gentle at first. Tracing the line of my spine, the curve of my ass.

His hand lands on my ass with a crack that echoes off the concrete.

Not hard enough to hurt. But enough to shock me. Claim me. Center me.

He growls low in his throat, and the sound reverberates straight between my legs.

He smacks my ass again and I start to tremble.

Connor drags his fingers through the slick mess between my thighs, and then—without hesitation—slides two inside me.

My hips jerk.

"Still so fucking tight," he murmurs, voice dark and reverent.

"Connor—"

"You think I'm done with you?" His fingers curl. "You haven't even seen what I can do when I let go."

My moan breaks open.

One hand on my hip, the other inside me, he fucks me with slow, ruthless precision. Curl, drag, pressure—again and again. His other hand smooths up my back like he's calming a wild thing he owns.

And the whole time?

He's whispering to me. Not soft words. Not sweet.

But steady. Raw.

"You take everything I give you. Every inch. Every word."

"You're mine like this."

"I'll wreck you if you let me."

"I'll rebuild you slow."

I'm shaking. Helpless against it. My body pulses around his fingers, tighter and tighter until the orgasm takes me again —sharp and fast and too much.

I sob out his name.

He groans behind me, pulling his fingers free only when I collapse fully onto the hood, chest heaving, legs useless.

Then he touches my face. Drawing a fingertip along my jaw. Tender, as if he's scared of himself.

He helps me stand. Gathers me up against his chest.

Straightens my clothes with the same fingers that just made me fall apart.

He presses his lips to my temple.

And for a second, I swear I feel him shake. I search his face for clues and see it. He's still holding back, and losing the battle.

I don't say anything, because if I say a single word, I'll cry, and I'm not sure I'll stop. But I know this much: Whatever's happening between us?

It's not pretend anymore.

It's not just sex anymore.

It's him.

And I want all of him.

Even the parts he's afraid to give me.

Especially those parts.

UNZIPPED AND SILENT—EMERY

There are cuffs still clipped to my headboard, hanging open like they're ready to be used again.

One of my toys sits on the bathroom sink waiting to be washed.

My thighs are still sticky. My hair's a mess. My heart hasn't quite found its rhythm again.

Connor is beside me, warm and steady, one arm slung low across my waist. His fingers trace the shape of my hip like he's memorizing me in pieces.

We've had each other twice more since the garage.

And now, the fire's settled to embers—but the connection hasn't.

It's in the quiet that the truth slips out.

"I used to think secrets were currency."

His hand stills. Just for a second.

"I didn't always hate them," I say softly, eyes on the ceiling. "When I was little, secrets made me feel powerful. Like I knew something other people didn't. Like if I held them close, I could protect the people I loved."

My voice drifts.

"But they never protected me back."

I feel him breathe. Feel the way his chest rises behind me.

"My family was full of things we didn't talk about. We thought if we buried them deep enough, they couldn't hurt us. But secrets rot. They don't stay quiet forever."

My pulse kicks up. I should stop.

But I don't.

"I didn't learn to hate secrets until they tore everything apart."

A pause.

"First when I was a kid. And later... when I thought I was in love."

His touch is still gentle. His presence steady.

And that—God, that's why I keep going.

"He said I was the one. That I made him feel safe, seen, like he could finally be honest."

I laugh. Quiet. Bitter.

"I didn't know he was married."

The silence thickens. Not judgmental. Just heavier.

"I found out the same day everyone else did. The day everything went up in flames."

My throat tightens, but I keep talking.

"You know the video. The red dress."

I exhale.

"Someone commented on it. Tagged his wife. She saw it and put it all together."

I don't describe the messages. The emails. The way it spread like wildfire.

But I don't have to.

I swallow hard. "She didn't come at him. She came at me. Painted me as the villain. The homewrecker. The fraud."

My voice drops. "And the worst part was, I couldn't fight back. Because I didn't know. And because no one cared. My employers wanted me silenced."

Another breath. Fragile.

"I lost everything. Clients. Reputation. Everything. All because of something I didn't choose."

I go quiet.

And then, without looking at him, I murmur, "You probably already know all of this."

Because of course he does. He's Connor.

There's a beat.

Then his voice, low and sure. "I do."

I brace for more. Judgment. Discomfort.

But it never comes.

"I also know what you built after," he says quietly. "I know the people who trust you now. The community you created. The reach you have."

His fingers tighten on my hip. "I know Alex and Dee would walk through fire for you."

I blink, and something hot stings behind my eyes.

"You rose from ashes most people never crawl out of. You didn't just rebuild—you lit the fucking match and said, watch me."

My throat goes tight. Still, he doesn't ask for more. Doesn't offer anything about himself. And that should sting. But it doesn't.

Because he's here. He's holding me like I'm something worthy. He's not looking away from the messy parts.

It's enough.

So when I shift under the covers and press a kiss to the warm skin of his hip, it's not a deflection. It's a thank you wrapped in devotion and need.

My fingers slide down. His breath catches.

And when I whisper, "Let me take care of you."

His groan encourages me. When I wrap my lips around the head of his dick, the hissing intake of air fuels me. And then his words wash over me.

"That's my good girl."

THURSDAY, APRIL 9

TOO LATE TO FOLLOW—EMERY

The front office door closes with a soft click that sounds too final. I stay seated in the chair across from it, staring at the empty cushion where my client had been sitting not thirty seconds ago.

"I can't risk being seen here anymore. I hope you understand."

No blame. No anger. Just that polite, practiced tone of professional detachment. The same one I use when I'm trying not to shatter.

I do understand. I understand too fucking well.

A knock comes at the door to the inner office, then Alex pokes their head in, brows creased. They hesitate.

"There's an email you should see. From the syndicate. Contract status change."

I nod. It's too much. "Thanks. Gimme five?"

Alex disappears without a word.

I make it to the hall bathroom before the tears come. Not a sobbing breakdown. Just quiet, gasping exhales as I brace my hands against the sink and stare down the drain. I don't cry often, not like this. Not at work. But this week has been a slow unspooling of every rope I've tied around myself to hold it together.

The client walking out? Not the first. The contract suspension? Neither the first nor the last.

My reflection looks older today. Eyes ringed in exhaustion, mouth too tight, posture slumped. The glossy version of myself—the confident, composed expert—has been stripped down to bare vulnerability. And beneath it, there's just me. The woman holding too many secrets and not nearly enough silence.

The door creaks open behind me. I don't flinch. The footsteps are soft, deliberate.

Dee.

He doesn't say anything. Dee steps up beside me, his reflection joining mine in the mirror.

After a beat, he reaches into his pocket and offers me a hair tie. The simplest, most practical thing and it's an anchor in the storm.

I take it with shaking fingers. Loop my hair up into a knot. Pull it tight until it hurts.

Dee meets my gaze in the mirror. Nods once. Leaves.

I don't thank him. Don't need to.

Back at my desk, I look at the email Alex flagged. When we landed in DC, I busted my ass to get a syndicate deal for the re-launched podcast. A six-month contract that they're not renewing.

It's a financial hit. Maybe the biggest one yet. Book sales have actually gone up, which doesn't hurt, but that won't pay the rent. Speaking engagements, seminars, classes. There's not one thing that's my bread and butter. Individual clients and the podcast are the two biggest pieces of the pie.

Maybe I should talk to my publisher about another book. Controversy sells, after all. It wouldn't take much to put together a collection based on my podcasts.

I close out the email and scan the schedule. I have a presentation tonight in Baltimore and tomorrow is a workday, no clients.

"Erin, there's an email from my sexual assault survivors group asking if we can meet offsite. I sent you some notes, if you'd draft a response and get it ready before you leave today. Then take tomorrow off. With pay." Her eyebrows go up, but she doesn't say anything. "In fact, you two do the same. We all need a mental-health day. I'm booking a damn massage."

Dee lays a big hand on my shoulder and squeezes. Alex, for once, has no smart remarks. They both know what losing the syndicate can mean.

When I finally meet their eyes, Alex's voice comes out rough. "You think I'd ever walk away now? You're the reason I made it this far."

The words hit harder than they should. I swallow, throat tight. "And you two are the reasons I'm still standing."

For a second, the three of us just breathe—together, bruised but unbroken. I shoo them away before I start crying again, then open my phone and click on Connor's name.

Is your offer to make the noise stop still open?

Always.

Are you free Friday night?

I close my eyes. Breathe in. Breathe out.

Letting go has never felt more necessary.

Or more dangerous.

ALREADY ON MY WAY–CONNOR

Shit. I'm committed to an event tomorrow night. I could cancel, but it would look bad. I make a snap decision.

Sort of. Fundraiser I need to attend. Be my plus one? A night of dancing. Dinner. Then I'll make you forget your name and make sure you never forget mine.

I set my phone down and wait. She asked about tomorrow, so she's not at a breaking point like she was before. I snatch my phone at the first hint of a buzz.

I can do that. Dress code?

I can read between her silences and see beneath her self-control. She's stressed and trying to prevent a meltdown, and she's clued me in. This time, I'm not going to wait until she breaks to catch her.

Let me handle everything. Meet you at your place at five. Trust me.

I make the call standing in front of my open laundry closet, earbud jammed in and digging through the hamper. The call picks up on the third ring.

"Connor Rives!" Darla's voice is lilting and full of warmth. "To what do I owe the honor?"

She's the wife of a former client and runs a boutique dress shop. It'll be expensive, but worth it.

"I need a favor. Quiet and fast."

I can hear the wheels turning in her head as she puts two and two together.

"Is this about the recovery gala? I assumed you were going solo."

Yeah. So had I. Showing up at a formal event with your client on your arm is maybe a questionable choice, but I need to be there, and Emery needs me, and what the hell, we can have some fun.

"I'm not."

A pause. Then a hum of satisfaction. "Give me her size and your budget."

She deserves to feel untouchable. If it costs four digits, so be it. Some things aren't meant to be budgeted.

"No budget. Just right." My fingers land on what I was searching for. The dress Emery was wearing Monday. She slept over and wound up going home wearing one of my hoodies and not much else. Hot as fuck, really.

"Hang on, I'm trying to figure this out."

Darla laughs, clear and bright. "Switch to FaceTime and show me."

I tap the phone and turn the camera toward the dress. Darla tells me to zip it. Then splay my hand over the bust, then the waist, and finally the hip.

"I have exactly the thing. Royal blue silk. Backless. Slit high. Sexy, but it says elegance, not bait. She'll look like power on a pedestal."

I close my eyes. "Can you get it to me tonight?"

"I'm wrapping it now. You'll have it by dinner."

"Let me know how much."

"Darling, you said you needed a favor. It's taken care of."

I thank her, profusely, then hang up. She carries only independent designers and I was prepared to cough it up.

I check on Emery via text. Just a small touchpoint. I know she's in Baltimore tonight. I get a smiley emoji back. The rest of the evening drags as I try to focus on work. Try to stay detached.

The courier buzzes at seven and when I open the package from Darla, any attempt at detachment goes right out the window.

The dress is breathtaking. Silk so fine it floats in my hands, cool to the touch. Understated, luxurious, and bold in its simplicity. A piece meant to drape over a woman who knows exactly who she is.

Except Emery is on the edge of forgetting, because the world is trying to make her small.

I lay the dress back in the box and stare at it, haunted for a moment by the image burned into my memory—the video of Emery in that red dress. Lips painted to match, eyes bright with purpose. The fire in her body language, the fury behind her message. The judgment she never saw coming.

She'd been devoured for daring to be honest. She wore that same dress for the flirting class. The night I first kissed her.

I trace a finger along the silk. This time, no one will get to tear her down.

She'll walk into that room a goddess. And I'll be there beside her, making sure the world knows exactly who she belongs to.

Not because I need to own her.

But because I want her to feel worshiped.

Seen. Safe. Desired on her terms.

No blood-red sacrifice. No spotlight as punishment.

Just shimmering silk, a private car, and my unwavering presence.

It's not vulnerability.

It's devotion. Disguised as control.

FRIDAY, APRIL 10

COME FOR ME—EMERY

I've never felt this naked in public.

Which is ridiculous, considering the dress Connor chose for me covers all the important parts. Technically.

But nothing about it feels modest.

It drapes over me like a second skin, not tight, but not loose either. Deep blue silk cut shockingly low at the back, and a slit high enough to whisper danger. No bra. No jewelry. Just a barely there thong, shimmery body lotion, a pair of gold heeled sandals, my body, and his attention.

And God, his attention.

He hasn't taken his eyes off me since I stepped out of the bathroom wearing one of the most beautiful pieces of clothing I've ever seen. His eyes didn't waver when we entered the marble atrium. Not when people turned to look. Not even when someone stopped to greet him with a practiced smile and a drink in hand.

He's in full social mode—calm, confident, immaculate in

a perfectly tailored tuxedo. But beneath the surface, I can feel it.

The pull.

The leash.

His hand rests at the small of my back, warm and steady on my bare skin, guiding me through the crowd like he owns the floor. Every time his fingers press, I feel it between my legs.

And I can't stop reacting.

Every glassy laugh I manage for a donor, every polite nod, every pass by the silent auction table—underneath it all is the fact that Connor dressed me tonight. That he showed up at my door with this dress. That I wore it without hesitation.

Because it was never a request.

And because I wanted to.

We're halfway through our second round of mingling when he leans down, lips grazing my ear.

"After your next drink," he says softly, "you'll go to the bathroom and take off your panties."

My breath stops.

His mouth brushes the shell of my ear.

"You'll bring them to me. In the hall. No questions."

A beat.

"They're already wet, aren't they?"

My cheeks flush. My legs threaten to buckle.

I take a sip of champagne to hide the way my hand trembles.

This man. This fucking man.

He pulls back like nothing's happened, greeting someone with a small nod and a handshake. The conversation shifts. We move on. But I don't hear a single word after that.

I'm too busy spiraling.

Five minutes later, I slip into the marble bathroom.

It's empty, thank God.

I lock the stall, brace one hand against the wall, and hook my thumbs into the waistband of my panties.

They're soaked. Of course they are.

Because I've been wet for him since the moment we walked in.

I slide them down, fold them neatly, and tuck them into my hand. My hands are shaking. My heart is racing. And I've never been more turned on in my life.

When I step back into the hallway, Connor is already there. Waiting in a quiet alcove just past the coat check, half-shadowed under a sconce.

He holds out his hand.

I place the panties in his palm, face flushed, thighs slick.

He doesn't even glance around before lifting them to his lips.

He inhales.

My knees go weak.

"Wet," he murmurs. "Good girl."

I exhale through parted lips; dizzy from how little it takes for him to ruin me.

He folds them and slips them into his jacket pocket.

"You obey so easily," he says. "Do you even realize how much I could do to you right now?"

"Connor—"

His fingers graze my inner wrist. Just a brush. But it feels like ownership.

"Later," he whispers. "On the floor. You'll come for me."

He takes my hand and leads me back to the ballroom.

Back to the performance.

And I follow, like I'd follow him anywhere.

We separate and mingle more, each of us talking to different people, making connections, before meeting back up by the bar. The music slows. Something lush and orchestral.

Connor holds out his hand.

I place mine in his without question.

He takes me to the center of the floor, where couples sway in practiced rhythm. The lighting is low, golden and warm, casting long shadows and soft glows across satin gowns and pressed suits. Champagne glasses sparkle on the tables.

Connor steps close.

One hand settles at my waist. The other laces with mine. The contact is smooth. Confident. Like he's done this a thousand times, but we've never danced together.

And then we move.

I expect stiffness. Some kind of formal, rigid choreography.

But no. He's fluid.

He glides. Leads.

Owns.

He doesn't just dance. He commands. Without hesitation. Without apology.

Every step draws me closer.

Every turn tightens the invisible tether between us.

And then his palm drifts lower, resting at the small of my back, above the swell of my ass. His hand is warm, wide, certain. Anchoring me.

He leans in, his lips grazing my temple.

"You feel it already, don't you?" he murmurs.

I blink. "Feel what?"

He moves us into a spin, pulling me back against him. His thigh slots between mine.

"That pressure in your belly. That heat between your legs. The way your nipples have been hard all night."

My breath catches. I try to press my thighs together, but he's there, forcing them to stay parted.

"Yeah," he says darkly. "Right there. I can feel it. Every time your leg brushes mine."

I gasp softly, but he keeps us gliding across the floor like we're in a dream.

"I haven't even touched you where you need it," he says. "But I don't have to, do I? Your panties were soaked when you gave them to me. How wet are you now?"

God.

My pulse kicks up. I try to look away.

He doesn't let me.

His hand tightens on my hip, pulling me flush against the hard line of him.

"No panties. Because you followed orders like a good girl."

His breath is hot against my skin. His tone never rises. Never falters.

"Tell me something," he says. "Does it feel different dancing like this without them?"

I swallow. I can't speak.

"Every step," he whispers, "your thighs rub together. Slick and bare. Every movement presses the silk between your legs. And the only thing holding you up is me."

I whimper.

The sound is swallowed by the music.

No one hears it but him.

He pulls me close and guides us into a series of quick steps, making a tight circle, then presses his lips against my ear. "You get so wet for me Emery. I'm trying to decide what you like most. Maybe it's my cock."

A slow sliding move has me tight against him and the feel of his dick, already half hard, throbbing against me.

"You definitely like that. And you seem to love my tongue. You come so sweet for me when I eat your beautiful pussy. Maybe that's it."

Another turn. His hand dips low again, grazing past bare skin and burning hot through the tissue thin dress.

"But no, I think it's more. You like it when I take control. When I own your body and your pleasure."

I don't know how I'm not falling over my own feet. My brain is lost in Connor's words and my body awareness has narrowed to the point where the only things I care about are where he's touching me, and where I wish he were touching me.

"I think that's getting closer. When I make you beg to be fucked. Do you want to beg for it tonight, Emery?"

I clamp my mouth shut, afraid to answer out loud, but I nod.

"Good girl. Here's the deal. Later, at the hotel, you're going to beg me to fuck you. Beg me to make you come. I have surprises in store for you, and I know you'll like them."

His eyes catch mine and hold. My breaths are coming fast and shallow, and I can't look away.

"I know you will like them because what you crave is surrender and control."

If any other man said those words to me, I'd laugh at them. But this is Connor. And he's right.

"I will make you beg later, Emery, and if you want the reward, if you want me to fuck you until you're totally spent, you have to earn it."

I want to drag him off the dance floor, find a quiet corner and wrap myself around him. Or leave the event and go straight to the hotel to find out what he has in mind. My pussy throbs with an ache that only Connor can soothe.

"If you want all of that tonight, you're going to come for me now."

I stop breathing.

"Right here," he says. "While we dance, and I won't even have to touch your pussy to make it happen."

He guides my hips. Subtle pressure. Nothing indecent. But I can feel the suggestion in the way he moves against me. In how he pulls me through the rhythm, pressing and dragging and guiding until my body is humming with it.

"Feel that?" he whispers. "Let it build. Imagine my fingers stroking inside your pussy. My mouth on your clit. Your thighs are trembling, like they do when you're about to come. Is your clit pulsing? Your pussy aching and throbbing?"

I nod.

"Good girl. Let it happen. Don't speak," he warns. "Don't make a sound."

My nails dig into his shoulder. My pulse is everywhere.

His voice lowers, thick with praise and filth.

"You're so easy for me. So fucking ready. So good. Let it go, baby."

The world blurs. My hands shake. Connor keeps talking but it's turned into a haze of sounds. The tone of his voice stokes the fires higher and higher until it feels like I'm about to burn up.

"There it is. Give it to me. That's mine, just like you."

His arm tightens around me as my body clenches. The orgasm hits low and sharp, a burst of heat that spreads fast, twisting through me in tight waves. I shudder once, hard. A woman dancing nearby shoots us a curious glance, but Connor pulls me into a deeper embrace, shielding me with his own body and keeps us dancing. Keeps me upright. Keeps me moving.

Like it never happened.

Like it's our little secret.

My head spins. My body aches for more

He smiles like everything is normal.

And maybe it is, because he's right—I'm his.

CAUGHT IN THE FLASH—CONNOR

Flash.

I feel it the moment it happens.

Not just the photographer's strobe, though that's unmistakable. The hollow click of a professional shutter penetrates even through the music. A tight smile from a man in a crisp blazer, camera hand low at his side, pretending like he hadn't been aiming at us.

No. What I feel is her.

Tense. Just for a second.

The way she registers it in her bones, but doesn't flinch.

Good girl.

I keep us moving. One hand steady on her lower back, the other holding hers like we're just another elegant couple in a well-rehearsed spin.

But inside?

I'm not calm.

I'm coiled. Tight. One more breath away from snapping the thread I've been holding all night.

Because this dance? It's not business.

It's not press or optics or the PR guy waltzing his client around a high-profile event.

That moment is mine.

Emery is still blushing, glassy-eyed, and trembling from a whispered orgasm in my arms. Her nails still grip my shoulder while her body follows my rhythm.

There's no walking it back now.

No denying it.

And I don't want to.

My mouth lowers to her ear again, and this time, I don't filter the hunger.

"You feel what that did to me?"

She nods, barely perceptible, but her breath hitches when my hand shifts lower.

Still polite. Still acceptable.

But possessive as hell.

"You came in front of everyone," I murmur, dragging my nose along her jaw. "Letting me control you without lifting a finger."

She shivers and I take the risk of escalating.

"You're such a good girl, such a dirty girl, I could do it again right now. Make you fall apart in front of a senator and a CEO without touching your pussy."

Her step falters, and fuck if that doesn't make me harder.

I want her open for me. I want her wrecked. I want her mine.

She turns her face slightly. "Connor—"

I smile against her cheek.

"I promised to make you beg for it if you obeyed, and you did. And I keep my promises. You'll beg, Emery. You'll beg to be taken. Owned. You think this is just sex?" I whisper. "You still pretending?"

She doesn't answer. Doesn't need to. Her body tells me everything. So I lean in one final time, voice low and full of grit.

"We're leaving."

Her breath catches again.

She wants it too. All of it.

I slide my hand down to her hip and press a soft kiss to her temple—one that looks sweet enough to pass, but lands like a brand.

Then I straighten. Adjust my jacket.

Keep my palm against the small of her back as I guide her off the floor, through the glittering room, past the murmurs and champagne and the lingering heat of too many eyes.

None of it matters.

Because tonight?

She's offering me everything.

And I'm going to take.

The valet barely looks at us when he opens the car door. I hand him a tip without breaking stride and pull her in beside me.

The door closes, cutting off the noise of the party. For a moment it's just the two of us and the steady thrum of the city outside.

She shifts beside me, legs crossing, the slit of that damned dress riding higher. My jaw tightens.

"Connor—"

"Don't." My voice comes out rougher than I intend. "You speak when we're upstairs."

Her breath stutters. She nods once.

The driver merges into traffic. I rest my hand on her bare thigh, just below the place that's been mine all night, and watch the lights slide over her skin.

BREAK ME ANYWAY—EMERY

The hotel room door clicks shut, and Connor stops and strips the dress off of me, leaving me standing in nothing but my heels.

I'm still shaking from the ride over—Connor's hand on my thigh, his order to stay silent, the way he looked at me like he already had me spread open in his mind.

He doesn't say a word.

Just walks toward the bed and begins unpacking his overnight bag like a man laying out weapons.

I stand frozen. Breath shallow. Skin flushed.

Dildo. Lube. Condoms. A black velvet pouch I've never seen.

He glances up. Nods once toward the bed.

"Up."

I climb on all fours, heart thundering. My ass in the air. My body already soaked.

He steps behind me, the bed dipping slightly as his weight joins mine. His hands stroke down my back, soothing—until they don't.

Until they grip.

"Warm-up first," he murmurs. "You will be begging before I give you anything."

His fingers slide between my folds. Stroking, not penetrating.

"You're soaked already. Good girl."

He strokes my clit and I moan, pressing back, hungry. It's not enough. It's never enough with him. He withdraws and I whine in protest.

Then I feel it. The rounded tip of the dildo, slippery with lube, pressing at my asshole.

Not him—but not small. Thick. Firm. Unforgiving.

"This is all you get," he says. "Until you earn more."

He circles the head around, never pressing deeper. My back arches.

"Fuck—Connor—" I push back against the toy and it's removed quickly.

"Ah, ah." His palm lands hard across my ass. I yelp.

"You know how to ask."

My breath hitches. I'm already on fire.

"Please. Please give it to me."

"How much?"

"All of it."

"You sure?" His voice is pure sin. "This is one of yours, and it's pretty good size. It's not as big as my cock, but it's enough to stretch that sweet ass and make you feel it tomorrow."

I gasp. He adds more lube, eases the head in and pauses.

"Beg for it," he growls.

"Connor, please. I want it—I want to feel full. I want you to fuck me with it. Make me come."

"Good girl."

He drives it deeper, and my cry turns to a moan that echoes.

He fucks me with it slow at first. Controlled. Deep. Twisting it enough to make me clench. Then faster. Rougher. With his hand on my lower back and praise falling from his lips like worship.

"Look at you. Taking it so well. Look how your body opens for me. Like it was made for this."

He reaches around to play with my clit, bringing me right to the edge of orgasm before stopping. I barely have time to catch my breath before he pulls out.

"I want your ass filled when I fuck your pussy."

Wait. What? My whole body tenses.

I glance back. He's opening the velvet pouch. He pulls out a plug. And it's big.

Nearly as thick as he is and longer than a typical butt plug. It's silver, looks heavy and it's intimidating as fuck.

"I picked this up for you. You'll beg for this too," he says. "And I won't come in your pussy. I want to fuck your throat while you've got this big plug in your ass. I want your ass clenching around something that almost matches me."

Oh god.

He lubes it slowly. Watches me squirm.

"Ready?"

I nod.

He spanks me. Once. Sharp. "Words."

"Yes, Connor. I'm ready. Please..."

"Not good enough."

I pant. "Please fill my ass. I want it. I want to feel it stretch. I want you inside me—any way I can have you."

"Better."

He braces one hand on my low back then presses the plug to my rim, and works the tip in.

"What are you supposed to be doing, Emery?"

Shit, he meant it when he said he'd make me beg for it all. I squirm and he holds me down.

"Do you want me to stop?"

"No!" The word tears from my throat without thought. "Please don't stop."

"There you go," he growls, sliding the plug in deeper.

Another push and it's in. I feel stuffed full. It's almost too much. His hand lands on my ass with a resounding crack.

"You should be thanking me."

I nearly sob. "Thank you. Oh my God, Connor, thank you."

My reward is him fucking me with the plug. Sliding it in and out, then grinding it just right. His other hand slips under me, teasing my clit.

"Do not come," he demands.

I hold it back somehow. Moaning, shuddering, and gasping into the sheets. My whole body shaking with need.

But Connor owns my pleasure. The bed shifts and he kneels behind me and I realize what he's doing. My body clenches in anticipation as the head of his dick brushes my pussy.

"Color."

"Yellow? Maybe green?"

Connor's hand glides down my spine. "We can take it slow. Stop if you need. I won't move. If you want my cock in you, back yourself up. Show me how much you want it."

WORSHIP HER RUIN—CONNOR

She's fucking beautiful like this. Ruined.

Red cheeks. Shaky thighs. Her ass stuffed with a plug that's nearly the size of me and her mouth parted, waiting.

She takes a deep shuddering breath then inches her ass back. The head of my cock slides between her pussy lips. The fit is tight with her ass stuffed full of the big plug, and Emery pauses twice to breathe, but she doesn't stop until she's taken all of me. Then she bends forward more, until her chest is on the mattress with her ass high in the air.

"Please Connor. Fuck me."

She's going to be the death of me. I grip her hips and rock forward slowly at first, giving her time to adjust to being double stuffed. Soon she's begging for harder, faster, deeper. I push her legs wider apart and lower her to the mattress, then pound into her hard, and still Emery moans in pleasure.

Her muscles clench and I stop before I lose control. She pouts when I pull out, but I flip her over and slide four fingers into her pussy with no warm up, then hold still. Emery's eyes pop wide open, but she doesn't complain. She arches her hips and spreads her legs wide.

"Do you want to come?"

"Yes, please!"

"You can come when I taste you. But, you're going to have all of my fingers in you and it's going to be hard and rough and fast."

She nods and rocks her hips against my hand. So beautiful. I lower my head and pull her clit into my mouth. True to my word, I don't take my time. There's no slow build up. I push my fingers in deeper and piston them like I'm fucking her. Hard and deep. Then I suck her clit between my teeth and use my tongue to get under the hood, lashing directly on the sensitive nub.

A scream rips from Emery's throat and her back bows. She clenches, trembles, and finally goes into full-body shakes as a gush of wetness covers my arm and face. I don't stop until she's begging me for a break, then I wipe my face on a towel and pull her from the bed.

"On your knees. I want your lips around my cock."

She scrambles to kneel, breasts heaving. Still flushed and open and wrecked, eyes glassy, tears clinging to her lashes.

And she's beautiful.

Not because she's polished. Not because she's perfect.

Because she's mine.

I grip the back of her head, and she opens for me like she's been waiting for it her whole life. That mouth—wet, ready, reverent—closes around my cock like worship.

"Fuck, Emery."

She moans around me, and it shoots straight through my spine.

I start slow. Letting her feel every inch.

But it doesn't last.

"You're so fucking good," I groan. "My dirty girl. Be a good girl and finger that beautiful pussy. Make yourself come again while you swallow my cock."

I grip her jaw, holding her open and fuck her mouth like I own it—because I do.

Then she does something amazing. Emery, my beautiful fucking Emery, tips her head and my next thrust slides deeper.

She grabs my free hand and brings it to her hair. I fist my fingers and push deeper.

She's gagging and drooling. Crying beautifully as the last inch of my cock disappears between her lips.

Her fingers work her clit as I hold her there.

"Look at me," I growl.

Her lashes flutter up. And fuck, that's a sight.

"My perfect girl." I pull back a little and come hard. With a sound I've never made before.

She holds me there.

Swallows.

"Good fucking girl," I breathe. "Open."

She does and I slide out as she shows me her tongue.

Clean. Empty.

My control shatters.

I push her back onto the bed. Never mind that I've had her all night. Or that I've made her come repeatedly. I need more.

"Don't move."

I slide between her legs and yank her thighs open wide. The plug is still deep in her ass, her cunt glistening and twitching.

"Spread yourself."

She reaches down with shaking hands, holds herself open for me, and I devour.

There is nothing soft or sweet about it. If earlier was hard and rough, this is brutal. I'm ravenous.

My fingers slide back inside her—two, then three.

She arches.

I growl.

Then four.

Her whole body locks up.

The stretch. The plug. My tongue.

It's perfect.

I feel her tighten, clench, break—and then she lets go.

She soaks my face again with a cry so raw it punches straight through my chest.

I don't stop.

Not until she's twitching, whispering my name like it's the only word she remembers.

Not until I've had every drop.

And even then?

I stay there.

Mouth on her. Hands gripping her thighs like she might disappear if I let go.

Because I don't want her cleaned up. I don't want her put back together.

I want her like this—wrecked, gasping, mine.

And I want to believe that maybe... just maybe...

She wants the same.

STILL HERE—EMERY

I don't know how long I've been lying here.

The sheets are twisted. My body's boneless. My lungs still hitch every few breaths. My thighs are sticky, sore, trembling.

But I've never felt safer.

Connor hasn't said a word.

He's just here.

First, his hands. Gentle on my hips, coaxing me onto my side. I let him move me, pliant and quiet, my cheek pressed to the pillow as he slips the plug free with slow, reverent care. I hiss softly. His hand smooths down my back in apology.

Then warmth. A soft cloth. Tender touches cleaning the mess we made—the corner of my mouth, across my thighs, between my legs.

Still no words. But none are needed.

He handles me like something breakable, but not broken.

He disappears for a moment. I hear water. The faucet. The opening of the minibar fridge.

When he returns, I feel the dip of the mattress behind me. He helps me sit up, hands me an open bottle of water and waits while I drink. Then he tucks me in. The duvet rustles as he pulls it up over both of us.

His body presses along my back. Solid and grounding. One arm slips around my waist.

Possessive in a good way. Staking a claim.

His palm rests low on my belly. His thumb strokes idle circles against my skin.

I feel held.

I've had sex like this before. Rough. Intense. Dominant. But Connor took it to whole new levels. Never had someone stay like this.

Where they bring warmth and comfort after stealing your breath. Where they touch you like they mean it all.

My fingers find his where they rest on my stomach. I lace ours together.

He squeezes. Still no words. But I hear him. In every touch. Every breath. Every quiet, steady beat of his heart at my back.

I'm here.

You're safe.

You're mine.

And I believe it.

SATURDAY, APRIL 11

TRENDING AND TORN—EMERY

Sunlight bleeds in around the edge of the blackout curtains. There's a delicious ache in my body, reminding me of everything we did last night.

Connor's arm is draped across my waist, his breath warm on my neck, one knee hooked over mine. His body is all heat and weight and steadiness.

Last night still hums through me—the tension, the surrender, the way he touched me like he wanted every broken, beautiful part of me. And I want more of that.

I don't want to move. But habit wins. I reach for my phone.

And freeze, wishing I'd ignored my phone and woken Connor with kisses or my mouth on his body instead.

Dozens of texts. Hundreds of alerts. My inbox is a disaster. Slack. Instagram. Every social media outlet. Even the practice line is blowing up. I pick the one from Alex.

> You seeing this??

I click.

There's a video.

It's us. At the gala.

Dancing. There is nothing obscene or even scandalous about the video. It is, however, unmistakably intimate.

Connor's hand at the small of my back. My body tucked close to his. The way we move—fluid, practiced, like we've done this a thousand times. Like we know each other.

My head tilted back against his shoulder. His lips at my ear. A moment frozen in time, framed in golden light and the suggestion of something deeper than sex.

It's romantic. Devastatingly so.

I don't have to look to know what the comments will be like, but I look anyway.

> *'The Let's Talk About Sex Lady cozying up to a fixer? That feels off.'*
>
> *'Preaches radical honesty. Dates a guy who gets paid to spin lies. Cute.'*
>
> *'So much for transparency.'*

I scroll, take a deep breath trying to slow my pounding heart, then scroll again.

Because I've done this before. And I know the difference between criticism and collapse.

This is criticism. I can handle it.

I wake Connor gently.

He stirs, groggy, blinking against the morning light. "Mornin'."

I hand him his phone.

His body goes still.

And the quiet vanishes.

"What?"

THIS IS GOING TO COST US—CONNOR

The look on Emery's face shocks me fully awake and I tap my phone screen. I don't have to look far. The video takes seconds to load.

We look good.

Too good.

The kind of good that makes people assume things. That sparks narratives. That makes clients nervous that I've crossed a line.

The kind of good that's a problem and can get you dropped.

I already have three emails. Two clients requesting postponement. One citing "ethical considerations regarding recent developments."

I know what that means.

She sits up beside me, the sheet falling to her waist, calm and composed like she knew this was coming. Meanwhile, I feel like I've been sucker punched.

I realize Emery expected it because this has become her normal.

"They think it's hypocrisy," she says. "That I talk about transparency while dating someone who makes a living protecting secrets."

"Yeah, I get it."

She lays a hand on my chest, her eyes soft and understanding. "You look like a man who's lost objectivity. Like you broke your own cardinal rule."

I grit my teeth. Because she's right.

They don't care that I never lied. That there was no NDA breach. No conflict of interest. No actual misconduct.

They care that I look compromised.

And image is everything.

"We need to step back," I say. "Let it cool. No more events. No public anything." It tastes like failure. Like running from something I want too badly.

Her eyes narrow, but she doesn't argue. Not yet.

"Discretion is one thing, Connor. But I won't pretend this isn't happening. I won't lie."

"I'm not asking you to lie."

But I am. And we both know it.

I pick up my phone again, jaw tight. Another email. Another client "reevaluating."

She walks to the window, the curve of her bare back marked by everything we did last night. She doesn't hide it. Doesn't cover the bruises or the bite on her shoulder. It's the one thing in this mess that makes me smile. Emery isn't shying from us, even after I asked her to publicly step back.

She stands there in silence.

And I watch her.

A woman who won't run from the fallout. And a man who just realized he might have to.

SUNDAY, APRIL 12

WHAT WE DIDN'T SAY—EMERY

The silence between us isn't awkward.

It's practiced.

Polished like glass—clean, unbroken, perfectly clear.

We worked all day Saturday and into Sunday night to manage the fallout. The hours blurred together. Talking points, media spins, endless review. Released a statement. Curated the narrative. Public interactions: paused. Private ones? Very much not.

Connor sits across from me at my kitchen table, reviewing final notes for a media session we prepped long before the dance floor detonated the illusion.

He's wearing what I've come to realize is his armor. Crisply tailored shirt. Perfectly fitted slacks. Unapologetically polished. His entire look curated to perfection. The image of control. Of credibility.

But I remember how it felt to peel his clothes off him. The heat of his hands. The way he trembles, just for a second, when I whisper his name like a promise or when I swallow him deep.

I study him while pretending not to.

His focus is sharp. His posture straight. No sign of the man who bent me over a bed Friday night and kissed the bruises he left behind. No evidence of the whispered praise, the low growl of my name, the way he buried his face between my legs like prayer.

He's back in professional mode. Controlled and untouchable. But I'm not.

I feel every beat of distance. I know what we are—what we've become. I'm past pretending it's nothing but sex. That fiction died somewhere between his mouth on my body and the way he held me after.

And now we're here. Being polite and civil and pretending we're safe.

Except I'm splintering under the surface.

I thought, hoped, that what we shared meant something beyond the dark. That we were building something real, even if we didn't call it that. Even I refused to call it that.

A spin of my own. Just friends. Keep it casual. Not anything big. Except all of that was a lie. Is a lie.

Now we pretend a different game. Like it's strategy or crisis containment. Just sex in private, silence in public.

He stands.

"All set for tomorrow," he says. "I'll reroute any morning fallout through Dee."

I nod, mouth dry. There's so much I want to say. Want to ask. But I don't.

He moves toward the door, but stops halfway.

I rise before I can think and meet him there. It's not instinct. It's ache. I kiss him. Slow. Lingering. No heat. Just presence.

His hand finds my waist. Not possessive. Not pulling me in. Just holding.

I rest my forehead to his chest for a beat. He doesn't move.

When I finally look up, I give him a soft smile.

"Night," I whisper.

He nods and leaves.

I return to the kitchen, turn off the lights. My heart doesn't slow.

I tell myself it's enough.

I pretend we're fine.

I lie.

DON'T GET TO WANT—CONNOR

I almost kissed her again.

Almost dropped my bag and pressed her against the door.

Almost said fuck the optics.

But I didn't.

Because control is the only thing I have left.

I walk to the elevator, jaw tight, chest tighter. The silence on the short ride up doesn't bring relief. Neither does the cool familiarity of my condo.

This isn't sustainable.

We keep pretending. Sex without strings. Just friends with benefits. Now this.

But I'm tangled in her.

Friday night she came apart in my arms, fingers twisted in my hair, whispering my name like it meant something.

Today, we talk about rerouting statements and strategic media releases. Like she isn't the only thing I've thought about since Friday. Fuck, since before that.

I should be relieved she agreed to keep things quiet and not go public with our relationship.

But I'm not. I should have realized on Saturday morning that would have been her choice. She values transparency. Honesty. And I asked her to lie. Not just about me, but about herself. So she retreated to her safe zone. Back to claiming this is casual. And the more she pretends this is temporary, the more I realize I've stopped pretending at all.

I need her. Not just the sex. Not just the peace she brings. The steadiness. The spark. The goddamn passion and heart of her. The way she looks at me like I could be more than what I was.

I sit in my living room, lights off, staring out the window as the city lights come alive. And I let my hands shake.

Because I can spin a crisis. Navigate a smear campaign. Control a room full of liars. But I don't know how to want something this real without breaking everything.

I don't know how to keep her without exposing all the parts of me I've spent a lifetime hiding. But I know I don't want to let her go.

And I think the worst part is, she might not want me to stay.

MONDAY, APRIL 13

SHE'LL HATE ME FOR THIS—CONNOR

The espresso machine hisses and I stand with one hand braced on the counter, the other wrapped around a mug, waiting for the liquid gold to finish brewing, like it might burn something clean. My eyes burn from lack of sleep, but I'm not tired. I'm raw.

Memories loop in my head. Emery at the gala, shaking under my touch. Coming apart in my arms on the dance floor, surrounded by hundreds of people. I knew there would be press there. Of course there would be. It's what I would've warned someone else about. But I didn't care.

With all the attention on Emery lately, it was inevitable that there would be pictures taken. Especially when she walked in looking like a goddess come to earth. And I didn't think twice about what that would mean. Didn't think about who'd be watching.

That's not like me. Because I wasn't thinking like a fixer. I was thinking like a man who couldn't stop touching her. I was so lost in her that I forgot to count the potential cost.

I made mistakes, and that wasn't the biggest of them. No, the big mistake was suggesting we go quiet in public. I've gone through the motions. Done the right things. Played the part. But it's killing me inside.

I open my inbox, trying to shift gears. Trying to be the man who handles fallout, who smooths disasters. It takes longer than usual to scan the new messages, my brain fogged by the memory of her eyes that night—wild and wide and completely mine.

Until she wasn't. Until that moment on the dance floor became an internet sensation.

A flagged thread catches my attention.

RE: Potential Client Inquiry - Los Angeles

My assistant had tagged it as previously declined.

Might as well take a look. At least then I can write a more firmly worded no.

The email is smooth. Polished. Full of vague language and cushioned requests. They want to revisit a proposal I'd rejected in March. The sender wants me to consider a discreet advisory role, given my "past experience with the brand."

Acid creeps into the back of my throat.

I scroll down to the original email chain. There it is.

The name.

Brenner. My former boss. The man who ran the strip club franchise behind Obsidian—the flashy, no-apologies male revue that started in California and spread to multiple states.

I'd been one of the stars. For several years, I danced, flexed, smiled on cue. Women screamed my stage name. I signed more shirts, and cleavage, than I care to think about. Made bank.

I learned how to read a room. How to control it. How to deliver exactly what people wanted.

And how to disappear behind it.

I close my eyes. That version of myself rushes back—oiled and pumped, young and cocky, grinning in the sweat-soaked spotlight. It was performance. Survival. And total detachment. The lights were always hot. The music too loud. But I could feel the hunger from the crowd like heat against my skin. That was the point. Make them want you.

I thought I buried that. Filed it under lessons learned. Under survival.

"Past experience with the brand."

Like it was marketing. Like it was a skill.

I hit delete. Just a quick keystroke. Gone.

My fingers hover over my phone. I open a message window.

Emery.

The cursor blinks.

I need to tell you something...

Delete.

Something came up today. About who I used to be. About something I thought I'd buried.

Delete that too.

The message window stays open for another thirty seconds before I close it.

She wouldn't want this version of me. Not the fantasy. Not the spectacle. Not the man who used his body to survive.

I open my email trash. Stare. Undelete the client inquiry and move it and the whole thread to a secure folder. Locked away where it belongs. Where I can pretend it never happened.

I close my laptop with shaking hands. Fuck.

TUESDAY, APRIL 14

WHERE NO ONE WATCHES—EMERY

The living room is softly lit, all warm tones and worn-in textures. There's tea brewing in the kitchen, and someone brought muffins. The space feels intimate. Safe. Intentional.

The perfect atmosphere for a group session.

I shift slightly on the overstuffed chair, legs tucked to the side. Across from me sit three people I've come to care for deeply. A triad. Survivors of sexual trauma. Truth-tellers. They've been with me for months, working through layered grief, loss, and redefinition.

They asked to meet here. Not at my office.

"It's not that we don't trust you," one of them said, careful and kind. "It's just... people talk. And some of us can't afford the visibility. You understand, right?"

I'd nodded. Smiled. Rearranged my schedule.

Now, seated among them, I listen to their updates. Hold space for their fears and laughter. Gently redirect when someone spirals. The work feels real here. Earned.

One of them brushes a hand against my arm when thanking me for making time. Another jokes about finally baking something edible. We talk about how grief ebbs and love mutate and trust rebuilds.

It feels good. It feels right.

Until the quiet turns.

"Are you still involved with that PR guy?"

The question isn't loaded. It's asked softly, with genuine curiosity. But it lands like a gut punch.

The room shifts. Tension like fog.

I force a light laugh. "We're... taking a step back. Reevaluating. Things have been complicated lately."

No one presses. They nod. Sip tea. The moment passes.

But inside me, something collapses. What I said wasn't a lie, but it wasn't the truth either, and that's not me.

I drive home on autopilot. Don't turn on music. Don't look for easier or faster routes. Just move.

At home, I don't go to the bedroom or the kitchen. I sink to the floor, back against the door, and let the silence stretch.

I'm not ashamed of Connor.

I'm ashamed that I said yes.

That when he asked me to stay quiet—to play it safe—I didn't even hesitate.

I told myself it was fine. Just casual. Just temporary. But that lie is louder than silence.

I hear it in every pause. Every question I dodge. Every part of myself I mute to protect something that shouldn't need protecting.

That silence isn't neutral. It's shaping me, and I'm starting to hate the outline it leaves behind.

My phone is in my hand before I even realize it. I open a message window.

Do you regret me?

No. I can't send that.

Can we talk tonight?

No. Not right either. The screen blurs, and I blink hard.

He sees me. In ways that feel terrifying and holy. But he's still asking me to shrink. To stay silent. To tuck him into a box labeled private and keep that box hidden.

And I've done that before. Even if it was unknowing and unintentional. I've swallowed truths and made myself small to protect someone else's comfort.

It cost me everything.

So what if he feels essential, like air, like gravity. I can't go back there.

I won't fracture myself again, even for him.

Even if it means losing what we almost were.

I press the heel of my hand to my chest, trying to breathe past the ache.

Because the truth I won't say—not even to myself—isn't that I'm scared of losing him.

It's that I already know what it would mean if I did.

And that terrifies me more than anything else.

THURSDAY, APRIL 16

SECRETS STRIPPED—EMERY

I don't even hear the knock.

I've been pacing for so long that the rhythm of my own footsteps has swallowed everything else. My phone screen is still open on the video and promo pictures, the same ones I've stared at for the last twenty minutes. They're burned into my retinas now.

The video? Connor shirtless on a stage. Spotlight in his hair. Sweat gleaming down sculpted abs. Hands gripping a chair as he does a pushup then a slow grind.

The promo photo? One hand behind his head. The other pulling the waistband of his jeans lower. A smile that says, 'I will wreck you.' That fucking smile. Caught somewhere between performance and seduction. The name says 'Knox,' but it's Connor. A lot younger and a bit bulkier and more ripped, but undeniably him. Performing at Obsidian, whatever that is, in Chicago.

The video is pure eye candy. He wasn't just performing. He was commanding. Controlling the room with expert ease.

Like Knox was the real version of him, and Connor was the mask.

He was good. Damn good.

The caption is nothing. The comments are wildfire.

The practice inbox is blowing up. Clients confused. Journalists fishing. A few sleazy messages that make me want to throw something.

But none of that is why my chest aches. Why my hands keep curling into fists. Why I can't sit still long enough to even drink water.

It's that he didn't tell me.

Not once. Not when I told him about my past. Not when we talked about risk and image. Not when we built our entire strategy around discretion, trust, and truth.

Of all people, he should have known. Should have trusted me.

The door opens—he must've used the code—and I whip around to face him.

He stops just inside the threshold. Dressed in dark jeans, navy shirt, sleeves pushed up like he didn't bother changing after chasing down the fire. Like he came here straight from battle.

His eyes lock on mine. "You saw it."

I hold up the phone. "What the hell, Connor."

He exhales through his nose, jaw tight. "I didn't think—"

"Exactly. You didn't think. You didn't plan. You didn't trust me." My voice cracks, and I hate how fast it rises, how unsteady I sound. "You of all people. You're the one who's supposed to see this shit coming."

"I didn't know it was still out there."

I laugh, sharp and humorless. "So what? You thought it disappeared? That no one would ever find out that the man who manages reputations spent years taking his clothes off for strangers?"

He flinches. It's small. But I catch it.

And for a second, I almost apologize. Almost tell him I don't care about the photo, or the dancing, or the past. That it's not the exposure that hurts.

It's being shut out. Being treated like I couldn't handle it.

But I don't say it. Because if he didn't trust me before, what difference would the words make now?

He runs a hand through his hair, pacing now too. "I'm working on finding the source. I have a few names—someone's playing dirty. Probably a client we iced after the gala—"

"Connor." I step in front of him. "Stop. Just stop with the damage control."

He freezes.

"This isn't about your reputation. Or my brand. This is about you not telling me the truth." My voice lowers, sharp and sure. "You let me walk into this blind. You let me trust you with everything, while you hid this one piece of yourself like I couldn't be trusted with it."

His eyes flash. "That's not fair."

"No? Then why didn't you tell me?"

He doesn't answer.

I press forward. "You've seen me wrecked. You've seen every bruised, broken, humiliated part of me, and I never held it back. I let you in."

"I didn't ask you to."

That stuns me.

I take a step back, heart thudding. "Wow."

His expression twists, like he's already regretting it, but the damage is done.

"You didn't ask," I say slowly, bitterly. "So you think I overshared? That I was foolish for trusting you?"

"That's not what I said."

"But it's what you meant."

Silence.

It's so quiet, I can hear the radiator kick on in the hall. The city outside still hums, uncaring. I stand there, staring at the man who's seen my soul in bed but won't let me hold a single part of his outside it.

I shake my head. "You didn't even give me the chance to accept it."

"I didn't want your acceptance." His voice is harsh now. Frayed. "You think it was sexy? Marketable? I was eighteen. Broke. Stripping for bachelorettes while pretending I had control. Knox was a phase. He was armor that I was happy to take off and put away."

My throat tightens. "But you didn't take it off. You changed what it looked like, and instead of trusting me to understand, you gave me this carefully curated version of you."

"I gave you everything I could."

"No," I whisper. "You gave me everything you wanted me to see. There's a difference."

TOO MUCH, TOO LATE—CONNOR

I can't breathe.

Not properly. Not the way I need to if I'm going to keep my head. The air in her apartment is too warm, too close, like it's pressing in around my ribs and daring me to crack.

She's right. That's the worst part.

Every word out of her mouth lands like a punch I didn't block in time.

She's not angry about what I did. Not really. She's angry because I didn't tell her. Because I didn't trust her with the worst of me.

Because she gave me her pain in pieces—biting her lip, eyes wet, naked under me—and I took it like a gift. And offered nothing back.

"I didn't think you'd understand," I say, and it sounds hollow even to me.

Her brows lift, incredulous. "Me? Me? The woman whose entire life exploded on the internet? Who was called a homewrecker and a fraud and a slut and had to start over from scratch?"

I wince.

"You didn't give me the chance to prove I could handle it."

I don't say it, but the thought screams in my skull: Because if you knew the whole truth, you'd leave.

Not the stripping. The reasons behind it. The desperation. The choices I made. The control I had to build, piece by piece, after I spent years being consumed by the lack of it. Of fearing every day I was just like my father.

I can't lose her. And I don't know how to keep her.

"I was trying to protect myself," I murmur.

"And in the process, you made me feel like I was the danger." Her voice is quieter now. Devastated, not furious. "You made me feel like I couldn't be trusted."

I look at her.

Hair messy. Eyes fierce. Standing in the middle of her living room like she's barely holding herself together.

And I feel something inside me split.

I want to reach for her. To ground her with my hands. To tell her we'll get through this.

But the need for her that's clawing up my spine isn't tender.

It's feral.

My emotions are too close to the surface. And the leash I've kept around them is fraying fast. One wrong move, and I'll say too much. Touch too hard. Want too openly.

So I stay where I am. Silent. Controlled. And breaking. I try to get my breathing under control. Try not to shatter.

Behind me, I hear her swallow. The silence that follows isn't practiced or polite. It's raw and bleeding.

It's the silence that comes before something detonates.

BREAK ME, I'LL STAY—EMERY

He turns away from me.

Back to the window. Hands braced on the sill like he's holding himself up with nothing but bone and muscle and willpower. Like if he doesn't grip something, he might implode.

I don't move. Can't.

My skin still hums with the fight. My throat is raw, my chest tight, and everything inside me is twisted up in the wreckage of what we said—what we didn't say.

He's unraveling. I can feel it. And I can't take it anymore. If he were a client, I'd take a different approach. Gentler, letting him set the pace. But he's not and this isn't a therapy session. This is us. Our relationship on the line here.

I move.

Cross the room, slow but steady, until I'm behind him. My voice doesn't shake.

"Connor."

Nothing.

"You didn't trust me," I whisper. "But I trust you."

He flinches.

"Even now," I say. "Even like this."

His shoulders rise—sharp, jagged. "Don't."

"I'm not afraid of you." I take the gamble, trusting years of experience to understand the core of what's eating at him.

"You should be."

The words are low. Not a threat. A confession. A confirmation.

I step closer. Press my palm to his back. He shudders under the touch.

And that's when I see it and know for sure.

This isn't him trying to win the argument.

This is him trying to keep the door locked on something he's terrified to let me see.

So I twist the fucking handle.

"Connor." I press my body to his back, my lips near his ear. "Whatever this is... whatever you're afraid of doing to me, with me—I want it."

He growls. Actually growls. Low and feral and so full of warning it should make me run.

Instead, I press against him harder.

"You think I can't handle you? Let me prove you wrong." If softness won't get through to him, maybe a push will.

He turns.

Suddenly I'm the one against the window, my wrists caught in a single punishing grip.

"You don't know what you're asking for."

I lift my chin. "I do. And I want it. All of it."

His eyes go dark. Dangerous.

And the last of his restraint snaps.

He doesn't kiss me.

He claims me.

Mouth on mine, brutal and all-consuming, like he's trying to erase the fight, the space, the shame. He grinds against me, already hard, already beyond reason.

And I moan.

Because I want this. I need this. I need him unleashed.

He spins me. Shoves me forward until my hips hit the back of the couch.

"I should leave," he snarls. "You want comfort. You want connection. You want—"

"I want the truth, and this is it. This need. This hunger." I spit the words over my shoulder at him. Fuck hinting. "I want your dick in my ass. Right fucking now."

The silence that follows is electric.

Then he growls again—deep, guttural, fucking feral.

He doesn't hesitate.

His hands rip at my clothes. Not careful. Not gentle. He yanks my leggings down, tears the thin strap of my tank. My underwear shreds like paper. And then he's pushing me further over the couch, forcing my knees apart with a thigh, one palm braced at the back of my neck.

I'm soaked. Quaking. My cheek pressed to the cushion, breath coming fast.

He grabs the bottle of lotion from the end table. Not the best lube, but better than nothing.

My stomach flips.

He presses two slick fingers to my asshole and shoves them in without warning.

"Yes," I moan. Arch to give him better access. "Like that." I cry out again as he pulls out, adds more lotion and thrusts his fingers in again.

He groans. "You're so fucking tight."

He scissors them, relentless, and it hurts a little but it's laced with heat. I push back against his hand.

"More," I pant.

He chuckles darkly. "My greedy little slut."

He fucks me with his fingers until I'm sobbing with want. Then pulls them out.

"Beg."

I choke on a whimper. "Please."

"Not good enough."

"Please, Connor. I need it. I need you to ruin me."

Silence.

Then I hear the clink of his belt.

And I break.

He doesn't undress. Just unzips.

He grabs the lotion again, slicks up his dick. I hear it. Feel it.

Then the head of him is pressing against my asshole.

No warning.

Just a brutal, stretching push.

This time I scream, not in pain, but at the intensity. My nails dig into the cushion. Tears leak from my eyes as he forces his way in. Too thick, too deep, too much. And I've never felt more fucking alive. I breathe through it.

"Fuck," he groans. "Emery."

I don't need him to back off. I need him to know he's safe with me. I need him to take me. To claim me. I need to feel the surrender. "Harder. Please—please—"

His hands clamp on my hips, and he fucks me.

Not gently. Not rhythmically.

He drives into me like he's trying to bury every piece of himself inside my body—like he can't get deep enough. Like he needs to fuck the shame out of himself and the love into me.

I take it all.

I cry and shake and plead for more.

And the more I beg, the harder he fucks me.

This isn't about pain. This isn't about control.

This is about being seen.

And being wanted anyway. I give him everything in the hopes of getting all of him back.

WHAT THE FUCK DID I DO? —CONNOR

She's sobbing beneath me.

And it only makes me harder.

Every thrust drives her forward, pushes a fresh moan from her throat. Her fists are clenched in the couch cushion, her back arched, her ass red with the force of my hands, my hips.

And I don't stop.

I can't.

She asked for this. She begged for this.

And I'm giving her everything.

"Good girl," I growl, voice shredded with strain. "Look at you—so fucking perfect like this. Taking me so deep."

She chokes on a sob, and the sound does something to me.

Something unholy.

Because this is what I've fought against. What I've locked down and buried and kept behind careful walls for years.

Not the sex.

The need.

The craving to own. To claim. To possess every inch of the woman who's seen through me since day one and still asked for more.

And she's still asking.

Her voice breaks. "Please, don't stop. Need you. All of you, Connor, please—"

I lose it.

My hips snap forward and I bury myself to the hilt, grinding into her ass until my vision whites out. My hands grip her so tight I know I'll leave bruises.

And when I come, it's with a roar.

Raw. Violent. Endless.

I pump every last drop into her.

I'm panting. Sweat-drenched. Still hard inside her as her body shudders around me, broken and beautiful and so fucking mine I can't breathe.

Then I see her.

Tears streaking her face. Her lips parted. Her whole body trembling.

I pull out slowly, and cum spills down her thighs.

There are bite marks on her shoulders that will last for days. Fingerprints on her hips. There's blood on one knee somehow, and her spine has a sheen of sweat from where I held her down.

And suddenly I can't move.

I can't fucking breathe.

What did I do?

What if I hurt her?

Jesus. This was too much.

Emery shifts on the couch, turns her head and her eyes find mine. She should be looking at me in horror. She's not.

I step back and she frowns, her mouth forming words I can't hear.

Trip over something I can't even see.

Fumble with my belt, still open.

"Connor, wait..." Her hand reaches for me.

I can't stay here.

If I do, I'll break.

So I run.

Out the door, down the hall. I don't bother with the elevator. I pound up the stairs.

And I don't look back.

I don't remember unlocking my door.

All I remember is the sound of her crying—not from fear, not from pain, but from being taken. Owned. Broken open.

And the way it made me come so hard I saw stars.

I strip as I move through my condo—shoes off, shirt over my head, belt already undone, pants halfway down by the time I reach the bathroom. My reflection stops me cold.

I look wrecked.

Sweat-soaked. Jaw clenched. Lips swollen from biting them. My cock's still half-hard.

I turn on the shower. Step in. Let the water scald me. It doesn't help.

Because all I can see is her—bent over the couch, legs spread, shaking with need and crying my name. Asking me to take her. Begging me not to stop.

I gave her what she asked for.

And still—I feel like I've done something unforgivable.

Because I didn't ask. Not really. I didn't check in. I didn't stop.

I fucked her. Brutal. Deep. Marking her in places no one will ever see.

And she came apart for me.

But what if she was just caught in the storm? What if, in the clarity of morning, she realizes what that was? What I am?

I brace my hands against the tile and rest my forehead there. The water runs down my back like punishment.

I wanted to show her everything.

I wanted to let her in.

Instead, I lost control.

Not just of my body—but of us.

And that scares the hell out of me.

Because when you let someone that close, they can see everything.

Even the parts you never meant to share.

Even the past you thought you'd buried.

Even the man who danced for money and survived on hunger. And the name I swore I'd never hear again. The one that paid my tuition via G-strings and oil, and bought my first suit. The one that made me feel wanted, and used, in equal measure. The man who built his life on illusion because the truth was too ugly to name.

More than that, she saw the want I keep caged. The darkness I've worked so hard to bury. She saw the raw, unfiltered need to control and dominate.

She saw that man tonight.

And she didn't run.

But I did.

And now?

Now I don't know how to go back without falling apart.

I want to go back.

To tell her she wasn't wrong to trust me.

That I felt it too—whatever this thing is between us.

But I'm still naked in the ruins of who I used to be.

And I don't know if I deserve to be seen again.

FRIDAY, APRIL 17

I DON'T KNOW HOW TO MISS YOU—EMERY

I wake up on the couch.

Alone.

There's a blanket draped over me. My body aches in every place he touched—every place he claimed. My hips are bruised. My shoulder stings. My throat is raw from begging, from sobbing, from feeling so much it scraped me open

And I loved every minute of it, until he left.

I stretch, wincing at the tenderness between my legs, the deeper ache from where he took me apart. There's lotion smudged on the back of the couch. The faint scent of almond and sweat still clings to the air. And him.

But he's gone.

I knew the second his breath hitched, the moment he pulled out and went still. When he looked down and saw what he'd done, what I asked for, and the horror bled across his face like he couldn't recognize himself. Or worse, that he recognized something that he didn't want to.

He left before I could tell him I was okay. Before I could whisper thank you. Before I could say please stay.

I sit up slowly. There's no shame or panic. Just ache and clarity.

I know what that was. Know what it meant.

That wasn't violence. It wasn't madness. It was truth, stripped bare. That was him, finally letting go.

And me, feeling free in surrender. Not the curated version of me, not the polished expert. Me. Raw. Wanting. Willing to take the darkest part of him and still stay soft.

Because I love him.

I'm not sure when it happened. But it's there now, carved into my bones.

He's scared. Still hiding behind shame. Still terrified he'll hurt me worse if he stays.

But I'm not broken. I'm ready. So I sit for a while. Let the ache settle. Let the memory bloom and sting all at once. Let myself feel the absence.

Not as punishment. But as proof. A breath. A memory of his hands.

And then I rise. He's not the only one who has shame about the past, and I'm done letting mine define me.

IT'S A CONTRACT—CONNOR

I don't remember falling asleep.

I must've passed out sometime after the sun came up—shirtless, still half-dressed, face-down on the couch like the wreck I am.

My spine aches. My hips feel bruised. There's a dull throb in my thighs, my forearms, my jaw. A leftover burn from the way I moved. The way I held her. The way I lost control.

I didn't eat and I slept for shit.

Every time I closed my eyes, I saw her. Bent over the couch. Shaking. Sobbing. Telling me not to stop.

And me? I didn't even ask. I took. Fucked. Marked her.

Then I ran.

I scrub my hand over my face and breathe through the shame, but it doesn't help. I can still feel her under me. Can still hear the sounds she made—sounds that should reassure me. Sounds that should prove she wanted it.

All I hear is that voice in my head.

You pushed too hard.

You left her sobbing.

You fucking ran.

I've been here before. Not in her condo. Not with her. But in this spiral.

Sophomore year, when Liv told me I scared her. When she called me dangerous. Violent. Then backed away from my need like it was a weapon. She told her friends I was controlling. She didn't go so far as to say abusive, but the implication was there.

Other women said the same in softer terms. "Too much." "Too intense." "You want too much power in bed, and I can't give it to you."

And I believed them. Because maybe they were right.

Maybe I've always had too much of my father in me.

I know I didn't hurt Emery. I know she asked for it. Begged for it. Guided me through it without fear. But the moment it ended, I saw her crying—and I saw every fucking ghost I've tried to bury rise up behind her eyes.

I should have stayed. I should have held her. She may have consented, but there was nothing responsible about how I acted.

I ran. Because I'm a fucking coward.

I pinch the bridge of my nose, force a breath, and do the only thing I still know how to do when I'm bleeding out.

I power up my monitors. The comms queue loads automatically—a shared watchlist and flag system I set up with my analyst. Eyes on all my clients, plus any relevant people. Social media feeds, email flags, search engine feeds. It's all there. It's muscle memory at this point, morning triage. Most of it's routine.

Except today, there's a new flag on Emery's page.

One of the canaries sang. My chest tightens. I click. The message is clean. Quiet. Sent late last night.

The recipient: Bronson Drake. The sender: Erin. The intern. No, assistant in training.

I sit back and scrub a hand over my face. This isn't going to go over well. Emery didn't want to suspect anyone on her team. She was convinced the former Honey Pot employee, Joe Macon, must have gone out for a smoke or something. But the more I dug into him, the more it became clear—he wasn't a creep, really. He was just awkward and geeky, and likely very stoned. And the sleeping at the shop? He was waiting around to escort his girlfriend home, so she didn't have to ride the metro alone late at night.

Erin, on the other hand... I click the flag.

The body of the message includes one of the exact messages we circulated for this purpose. Almost verbatim. This isn't a misunderstanding or accidental overlap. There's no coincidence here.

She copied one of our false internal comms and sent it directly to the man who's been circling Emery since he jumped into the social media frenzy over the New York scandal.

And now I have proof. Well, some proof.

The analyst's note is brief: Confirmed match on Canary Phrase #5. Message timestamp attached.

I stare at the screen.

I always knew someone was leaking and suspected Erin, but I didn't press. I let Emery's judgment stand.

The former employee might have made sense for the event at the sex shop, but not for anything else. Erin had access and knowledge.

I should have pushed on that one. If I hadn't been so wrapped up in Emery, I would have. Not like me to let my libido do my thinking, but Emery is so much more than lust. Or was. Fuck.

I hover over the forward button, then click. Attach the file. Type a single line:

Erin is in contact with Drake. See attached.

I send it to Dee.

And I sit there.

Still shirtless. Still aching. Still reeling over what my lack of trust and fucking shame cost me.

But this part of the job?

I can still do this.

Even if I've already lost the thing that mattered most.

I TRUSTED YOU—EMERY

I barely have time to settle into the rhythm of the morning when Dee sits back in his chair, muttering "holy shit" under his breath. Alex looks up, their expression grim.

"You need to see this." Dee turns the wall monitor on, and an email flashes up.

It's a short note from Connor. No greeting.

Erin is in contact with Drake. See attached.

A stone sinks into the pit of my stomach as Dee clicks on the attachment showing an email sent from Erin to Bronson Drake.

"I don't know how Connor got this. That's not Erin's work email, but if she accessed that account on her tablet? Maybe." Dee sounds impressed. Most of that is way beyond my tech understanding, but the contents of the email aren't.

"Huh. Good to know we're going into the dungeon furniture business." It's good to see Alex's humor is still intact.

"There were two fake emails. The other claimed we're starting a service designing sex rooms." They were my ideas after I learned about the canary Connor had set. I suggested something easier. Something that felt natural and didn't sound like it was super private.

Alex cursed under their breath. "I knew I didn't trust her. I knew."

I take a long breath and let the news settle. The sting will pass in time, for now, I use it to keep me focused.

Connor had found the breach.

And he'd sent it to Dee.

I'm not sure what that means for us personally, but at least he hasn't abandoned me professionally. He's still helping protect what we've built here.

It shouldn't matter so much. But it does. I stand and pace the room while I talk.

"Start the revocation process. I want every credential stripped by the end of the hour. Email, scheduling, cloud access, building code, everything."

"On it." Alex's standard response. One I know means not only will things get done, they'll get done right, and there will be a color-coded map and probably a spreadsheet involved.

"Dee, keep digging. If she sent this to Drake, she may have sent more. Let me know what you find."

Dee hesitated, his face a mask of worry. "Been doing that, and found it pretty fast. You might want to sit for this."

I stop and drop into a chair. If Dee is telling me to sit, it's not going to be good.

He pulls up another screen.

"The video of Connor... uh... Knox... Looks like Drake sent that one to Erin, on her work email. She deleted it, but, well, y'know." He shrugs, like being a tech genius is no big deal. "It was posted to social media on an activist account tied to a coalition."

I close my eyes and count backwards from five to keep from cussing.

"It's a mess," Dee continues. "But Erin is following the activist account and is a moderator on the coalition's Discord. There are some FaceTime records deleted from the tablet, but I can reconstruct those. She was getting sloppy."

Like I needed things to get worse.

"So she didn't just leak an internal memo. She amplified a smear campaign." Alex sits back, scowling.

"Exactly." Dee shuts off the monitor and looks to me

"When is she coming in today?"

Alex checked their watch. "Ten minutes."

"Good. As soon as she gets in, tell her I want to talk to her in the front office."

I don't wait for acknowledgments. I don't need to, not from Alex and Dee. I do need the time to compose myself so I can try to be compassionate. It's possible Erin was manipulated or lied to. I doubt it, but it's possible.

Erin comes in with a bright, unbothered smile. "You wanted to see me?"

I gesture to the couch and wait for her to sit.

"We need to talk."

Erin blinks. "Of course."

Something shifts in her posture. Anyone would be tense when their boss says 'we need to talk' but this is something different. I take a deep breath and begin.

"I know you're communicating with Bronson Drake." I lay it all out. The emails. The phrase. The video of Connor. I'm not sure what I expected from Erin, maybe I hoped she'd be contrite.

Instead, she crosses her arms and glares at me.

"You're a hypocrite."

The words hit like a slap in the face, but I say nothing. I wait. Silent and listening.

"You say you believe in radical honesty," Erin continues. "But you're hiding him. Pretending you're not entangled with someone who literally gets paid to manipulate narratives. That makes you the liar. Not me."

She's not wrong on most of those points. Even if she is lacking nuance.

"You signed an NDA and yet shared internal company information. You also posted a video you knew could hurt people."

Erin's eye roll is almost comic. Her over-eager awkwardness is gone, replaced by harsh cynicism. How did I miss that duality?

"Because people need to know. You build a brand on truth, Dr. Nicole, but then you make exceptions. What I did was restore integrity."

"Was it integrity that drove you to conceal the fact that you were in communication with Bronson Drake?"

She doesn't have an answer for that one, or at least has the sense to not offer her reasons. "What you did was reckless. You weaponized someone else's vulnerability to serve your own beliefs. That's not radical. That's arrogant."

Erin lifts her chin. "Privacy enables shame. If people were forced to live transparently, there'd be no room for lies."

"If people were forced," I reply softly, "then it wouldn't be consent. And consent is the foundation of everything I do."

I stand up and shake my head. "You're done here."

As if on cue, Alex comes in from the back and holds out an envelope. "Your termination paperwork. Your final check will be in direct deposit by Monday."

Erin doesn't argue. She smiles like she still believes she's right, like she's done nothing wrong. She snatches the envelope and walks out.

I spot Dee leaning in the doorway to the back office.

"I swear you two were listening at the door."

"Maybe." Alex doesn't even try to sound contrite. Dee manages a halfway sheepish grin.

"Fine. Let's get back to work, and we might as well start looking for a new intern."

"Mind if I take that on?" Alex settles at the worktable, their eyes tight on me. I shake my head and get a slow sigh in return. "Good. As for Erin? That was... something."

"I vote we cleanse the office." Dee pops open his laptop and grins. "Or maybe exorcise it."

A tired groan slips out of me. "Put it on the to-do list between damage control and therapy."

Alex rubs their temples. "I hate that she twisted your words. Our work."

Dee nods. "Yeah. It's one thing to disagree. It's another to turn belief into a weapon."

I look between them—my people. The ones who stayed. These two understand the difference between transparency and cruelty.

"She thinks exposure equals truth," I say quietly. "But all she did was prove the opposite."

For a beat, we're all grinning like we've survived something ugly together, and maybe we have.

Dee glances up. "You know, I could always install a 'betrayal early-warning system.' Flashing red lights, dramatic siren."

"Make it play 'You're So Vain,'" Alex says.

The laugh that escapes me feels frayed but real. Alex reaches for my hand, grounding me.

"We've rebuilt before," they say softly. "We'll do it again."

And I believe them. I have to.

SATURDAY, APRIL 18

RADICAL HONESTY—EMERY

I'm still sore.

Inside. Outside. In places no one can see and places I didn't know could hold grief like this.

I haven't heard from him aside from the message to Dee.

Not a call. Not a text. Nothing.

I don't know how to chase someone who clearly doesn't want to be caught.

So I sit at my kitchen counter in Connor's hoodie—the one I wore when I came back from his place after our basement quickie turned into an evening of being taken apart piece by piece, then put back together.

My coffee's gone cold, and I don't care. When a knock rattles my door, I leap up, hoping maybe it's him. I know it's not. It wasn't his knock. I open the door to Dee and Alex. Dee's holding up a cream and pink box I know too well and Alex has a carrier full of coffees. They come in without an invite, not like they need one.

Dee waves me to the couch and in less than a minute, I've

got a steaming cup of a brown sugar and cinnamon latte in my hands then he pops open the box from Glazehole.

Alex brings plates, a knife, and a pile of napkins, then pulls a chair closer to the coffee table. "Before you say anything, let the record show: Dee did the coffee. I'm responsible for the pastries and regret nothing."

Oh shit. Alex is notoriously adventurous and will choose things by name or looks alone. A questionable practice at a local coffee and doughnut shop that prides itself on being edgy and punny.

"Is that..." I eye a pastry dripping in crushed pretzels and drizzle.

"It's a Crumb Dumpster. Of course." For all their efficiency, Alex can be like an overgrown kid at times. "And there's a Combover."

That explains the orange-glazed one topped with a wisp of yellow cotton candy sprinkled with gold flakes. The rest of the choices are their tamer fare—though tame is relative. Then I see the half dozen donut holes glistening with hot honey.

"You got my favorite!" A savory doughnut may sound strange, but their cheesy jalapeno holes are top tier.

There is nothing healthy about this breakfast, but it's heaven and exactly what I need. We divide up the bigger pastries and make our choices. For the moment, we're just three friends enjoying a Saturday morning of great coffee and even better, if slightly over the top and more than a little irreverent, doughnuts.

I bite a Fire in the Hole and can't help but moan at the perfect sweet, savory, spicy combo. This is going to need a gym trip or two. I've been doing yoga in my condo and walking for cardio, but if I keep eating my feelings like this, I'll have to step it up and hit the building's gym.

Except then I'd have to worry about running into Connor.

I drop the half-eaten hole back to my plate and wipe my hands, suddenly not hungry.

"Do you need to talk about it?"

I smile and shake my head. Dee slides over on the couch and wraps me in a big hug. It's like being engulfed by a giant, living teddy bear who brings killer dad energy to the mix. Guaranteed showing up unannounced with coffee and doughnuts was Alex's idea. They see a need; they do something about it. That something may be practical, or it may seem frivolous, but it will always serve a purpose.

While Dee? He'll respond to the emotional side first. The things he does are little on the surface, but carry big impact.

"I don't deserve you two." My words are muffled by Dee's massive arms and he releases me with a smile.

"Sure you do." Alex picks up our plates and stands. "We work so well together because we all complement each other. It's been like that since day one. That's the magic."

They drop the plates in the sink, wash their hands and return the chair, pulling it closer until they can take my hands in theirs and hold them tight.

"That's what made you and Connor so good, too."

I didn't want to hear that. I needed to hear it. A sob hiccups through me and I bite my lip, trying to stop it before it becomes another tidal wave of tears.

No one needs to ask what happened. It comes out in pieces. Not all of it. Some of it's too personal. But the core part. Connor didn't trust me with his history. And when it blew up, he ran from it. Ran from me.

"That can't be all of it." Dee shakes his head with a frown.

"It's not, but the rest is..." How can I explain the last part without telling a story that isn't mine to tell. "He can't accept his own truth, so he didn't know how to share it with me."

It's the best I can do without saying things that wouldn't

be right coming from me. I don't worry about Alex and Dee knowing personal stuff about me. With the kind of work we do, the professional boundaries were crossed and genuine friendships formed ages ago.

We finish cleaning up and Alex checks in that I'll be okay. I send them off with the promise to text if I need anything. Their visit didn't fix what was broken, but it did help me pick up the shattered pieces.

It's up to me to put them back together, and that starts with being true to myself. I shower, put on clothes, something soft and comfortable, I even do my hair and a little makeup. Then sit at my laptop and let my brain process everything.

I'm angry at Erin. Naming the emotion feels good. I trusted her. Mentored her. Made excuses for her rough edges and encouraged her to find her voice. Her ideologies are misguided and harmful, but I understand where they come from, and they're not the reason for my anger.

That comes from hurt. Erin made a series of posts minutes after walking out of the office, making it clear her entire reason for coming to work for me was access to people who are living a lie. She used me to further her agenda. Her beliefs don't give her the right to overrule the choices others make for themselves. That's what I'm angry about. My agency was taken from me, and that spilled over onto others.

Connor's agency was taken from him. I may disagree with his decision to hide his past, especially from me, but revealing it should have been his choice. No one else's.

There is no anger toward Connor. Only hurt. I'm hopeful we can overcome that hurt, because Alex was right. Connor and I complement each other in so many ways. If we can't get past this, the hurt will heal. In time.

Time to practice what I preach. Honesty and transparency. Trust. I open my email and start typing.

I tell Connor everything. No spin. No softening. I send him the files Dee saved. Tell him the whole story with Erin. I even thank him for giving us the key that unlocked the whole thing.

The hard part comes when I admit that not only did I not know, but that I should have. He was right. I was naive. I trusted too blindly. I could have, should have, dug deeper and looked harder. Maybe it wouldn't have made a difference, but I'll never know. I saw a young woman who reminded me too much of myself at that age.

I tell him I'm sorry. For not fighting harder when I should have. For believing in someone else's potential more than I believed in his warning. And I tell him I would like to rebuild, if and when he's ready.

Then I hit send.

Taking accountability for my actions doesn't absolve Connor from his. But I can only control my own choices, and this is me choosing better.

The next step is harder. Channeling raw pain and fury into something that works. I settle my fingers on the keys and type.

This one is going to ruffle some feathers, and I'd like to start by saying, I don't have the answers. I have some strong beliefs and a lot of questions. What I hope to do is spark conversation about betrayal, boundaries, and what it really means to live with integrity.

Maybe that's the real start of this post: this is a nuanced conversation and there are no easy answers. Are you ready? Let's dive in.

When betrayal hits close to home, it can trigger a lot of soul searching. What did I do wrong? It can also trigger shame. Why didn't I see it coming? That's where I'm coming from today. Reeling from some hurts and the hard choices they forced me to make.

There is a culture of betrayal that hides behind the language of integrity. People who claim the moral high ground and label it 'honesty' when what they mean is 'exposure.'

Real integrity doesn't demand that someone bare themselves to be believed. It doesn't twist vulnerability into proof. Honesty has to be chosen or it's just another form of control.

Outing someone for their sexuality, gender, career, or anything like that is not transparency.

You can't call it truth if it's been forced, coerced, or weaponized.

I believe in honesty. I've built my life and my work around it. I also respect discretion. I have to believe that consent includes the right to share our truths on our own terms.

Most of us have things in our past we're not proud of. Some are more comfortable being open. Others are not, and that's okay.

I can hear it now, 'but Emery, what about...' This isn't about silencing victims, or sweeping criminal acts under the rug. This is about a culture that delights in exposing people's personal secrets, not to protect others, but to punish, or control. Or perhaps worse, for profit.

Yes, it's nuanced. If someone preaches fidelity while having an affair, or shouts anti-LGBTQ+ rhetoric while secretly using Grindr, there's room to talk about hypocrisy.

But, what of the schoolteacher who worked as a stripper in college? Or the owner of the small-town bakery who's secretly a little, or a lot, kinky?

Do they deserve the same treatment? Does the answer change if they're a public figure? Should it?

I've seen firsthand how damaging that exposure can be. How quickly someone's past can be turned into ammunition. I will live my life honestly, but I will not allow anyone to define what that looks like for me, or for anyone else.

Let's talk. Share your thoughts, but let's keep it kind.

I sit back and reread. This works. It feels right. I don't bother going into the office, or setting up lights, or anything fancy. I arrange myself next to the window, set my phone on a stand, hit the record button, and nail it in one take.

Maybe not as polished as I'd like, and a little shaky in a few spots, with an occasional 'um' or too loud of a breath, but I'm going old school. Back to my early days of uploading posts on the fly.

It takes a minute to get the video uploaded everywhere. I stop and make fresh coffee, feeling like I got something good done today. Even if it was mostly for myself.

The comments are rolling in by the time my coffee brews. Some supportive. Some vicious. No surprise.

I don't expect Connor to comment, or even reach out, but I hope he sees it. If he's still got me on his desk of doom scrolling, he will.

He made me feel seen in so many ways, but missed the most important part. This isn't just what I do. It's who I am. And I'm done hiding.

SUNDAY, APRIL 19

WHAT SILENCE SAYS—CONNOR

The kitchen is a mess.

Maybe not to most people, but to me. Dirty dishes in the sink. A full trash can. Empty whiskey bottle tipped on its side.

In the bedroom, the bed is unmade and the hamper overflows onto the floor. I strip off my gym gear and add it to the pile. The gym is the only time I've left the condo since Friday. I stopped running and get my cardio by taking the stairs. All to avoid running into Emery in the elevator.

Silly, probably, since we lived in the same building for a while and never knew.

My water bottle's empty and I pad to the kitchen to refill, not realizing until I'm standing in front of the open fridge that I'm still naked.

The silence presses in. I stare into the fridge. Close it. Forget what I was doing.

I'm unraveling. Clean and quiet, maybe, all very professional on the surface.

I haven't opened the email she sent. I saw the subject line —Thank you, and full disclosure—and left it unread. There's a video, too. I know it went live. Haven't watched that either.

I tell myself it's self-preservation. The truth is, I'm fucking terrified.

I should get dressed. I should shower.

When the knock comes, I've got sweatpants in one hand and a towel in the other. I throw on the sweats. The knock comes again and I pull the door open without checking the peephole.

Dee.

"I let myself up. Building security knows me."

Not much I can say to that. I step aside.

He walks in, takes one look around, and exhales like the place smells of grief.

"You gonna pretend you're fine?"

I don't answer. Move to the kitchen, open the freezer, and pull out two glasses and a bottle.

Dee puts a hand on the bottle before I pour.

"You haven't talked to her." For a big guy who looks like he belongs working as a bouncer at a biker bar, he can sound remarkably gentle.

"She needs space."

His eyebrows go up. "She needed truth. You gave her spin."

I set the bottle down harder than I mean to.

"It was the right call." I tell myself that every moment of every day.

"Bullshit."

Yeah, fine for Dee to say. I'm willing to bet Emery didn't tell him everything. If she had, this would be a very different conversation.

"It was unsustainable."

"Try again." Still with that patient voice.

"I needed to protect her."

He leans forward. Quiet. Precise.

"You didn't protect her, man. You ran. You left her thinking she offered her whole self to a man who only wanted the parts he could hold without breaking."

He doesn't have to raise his voice, or sound angry. The words do all the work, landing like fists in my stomach. I blink, but don't look away.

"You think I don't know what that costs her? You think I don't know what it meant for her to give me that kind of trust?" I knew. I know. And it guts me.

"Then why didn't you give her yours?"

I close my eyes.

"You don't get it."

"Then help me."

A beat. Two. He's serious. Shit.

"She knew everything," I say. "She saw it. The parts I keep locked down. The shit I won't name. And she still..."

I don't finish.

Dee doesn't push.

I turn away. Grip the edge of the counter like it might hold me upright.

"I've never had that. Not once."

Not without strings or judgment. Not without someone expecting me to live their vision of me. Or be less intense. Less dangerous. Less me.

"She let me be the man I've always been afraid of. And I left her alone in the dark after."

Dee is silent for a long time.

"She didn't need perfect." His voice is so soft I have to listen hard. "She needed truth, and you never trusted she could handle yours."

He scrubs a hand over his jaw. "You want to know why I trust her? Why I'd walk through fire for her?"

He waits for me to look up.

"It's not just the work. Or what she survived. It's because she shows up. Even when she's scared. Even when it costs her."

He leans against the counter, mouth tilting into something between a smile and a wince.

"You think I went to that queer leadership thing because they needed a tech guy? I was somewhere between hiding and discovery, man. Freshly divorced. Still lying to myself. Emery didn't call me out—she called me in. Helped me face all the shit I'd buried so deep I didn't even know who I was anymore."

He lets that sit for a beat, then adds quietly, "Alex, too. Back at the firm, Alex was barely hanging on. The partners were chewing them up for being too visible, too loud about who they are. Emery saw it. Pulled them onto her team before they got pushed out completely. Gave them work that actually meant something. When the scandal hit, HR told Alex to cut ties for their own good."

Dee's voice roughens. "They packed up their desk and walked out instead. Texted me, said, 'I'm in. How about you?' I didn't have to ask what they meant. I was in then and I'm in now."

He shakes his head, smiling like it still stuns him. "That's who she is. She makes people brave enough to bet on themselves. That's why we work with her."

He looks at me again, steady.

"That kind of person? You don't run from that. You show the fuck up."

I exhale, and it feels like surrender, but in a good way.

"Yeah," I murmur. "I think I get it. No. I know I do."

Dee reaches across the counter, pushes the empty glass toward me.

"Save the drink for after you figure your shit out. I'll pour us both one then."

I almost smile. And once the door closes behind him, I clean my damn kitchen. Because something's wrecked, and I can't fix it. Not yet. But I can start regaining control.

FRIDAY, APRIL 24

NO MORE EXCUSES—CONNOR

The week since Dee's visit had been a blur of damage control and hollow silence. A new client request sits open on my monitor. Snippets jump out at me and my brain goes into autopilot. Leak control. Bury the story. Narrative redirection. The same shit I've done thousands of times. The kind of thing I can do in my sleep.

Instead of hitting the 'schedule consult' button, I pause and re-read, this time with Emery's voice in my head.

Not from anything she said to me in person, but from the video she posted six days ago and I didn't have the balls to view until Dee left and I cleaned my condo, showered, and put on clean clothes.

She took my breath away. I watched the woman I thought I broke stand up and tell the truth. Not for clicks or clout or revenge. But for people like me, who don't know how to stop hiding.

I read her email right after and it gutted me all over again.

I haven't replied to her. Haven't earned the right. But I

read the email. Every word. No spin. No softening. She laid it all out—what Erin did, how she found out, what it cost her. She gave me the truth, then gave me the space to decide what to do with it.

I tried to pretend they weren't meant for me. Even the email. Like if I didn't feel them, they couldn't break me. But the next day, I read the email again. Then watched the video. I've watched it every day since.

Her voice won't leave me. It's in my bones now. In the rhythm of my steps. In the places shame used to live.

Transparency isn't a weapon. It's a choice.

I built my life on the opposite belief. On the idea that secrecy is safety. That privacy is protection. That exposure is the enemy.

But what if it's not?

What if telling the truth isn't the threat, but the way forward?

I close my eyes and press the heels of my hands against them until I see stars. There's a knot in my chest that hasn't eased since the night I walked away. Since I left her sobbing and swallowed the sick certainty that maybe I really was too much. Too intense. Too dangerous to love.

But she didn't say that. Someone else did, and I've been repeating it ever since. Living with their version of me. Accepting it as my own.

Now, I stare at the new client request and I can't bring myself to get back on that wheel. I don't want to. The thought lands solid, and right behind it comes another. I want to start over.

I flag the request for later follow up, close the window and open a blank document. The cursor blinks like a challenge.

REBRAND CONCEPT: RIVES STRATEGIES — NOTES

•Integrity as leverage.

•Transparency as protection.

•Recovery through truth.

•Apology. Accountability. Amends.

It's messy and raw and the opposite of everything I usually write. It's also risky. Some clients won't want it.

But I do.

Because I've spent years mastering the art of silence and Emery broke it in two sentences. Without shaming me or outing me. No twisting the knife. She told the truth and held the door open.

I don't know if she'll ever let me close again or if she'll forgive the silence. The running. The fear. But I can become a man who's worthy of being heard. I hit save and for the first time since I ran from her condo in a daze of arousal, fear, and shame, I exhale without breaking.

I don't know if I'll get her back. I don't know if I deserve to.

But I know it's time to stop running and hiding. Maybe I can't undo the silence. But I can end it.

SUNDAY, MAY 3

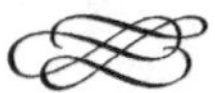

CAME ANYWAY—EMERY

I've stopped expecting Connor will show up and I've buried the hope under work—under panel prep and policy revisions and the slow, stubborn rebuilding of what my team and I have built. In regaining the trust of my clients and the partners I've worked with, and who didn't abandon me in the fallout. I've kept myself focused on what matters, on what's next. On forward.

When the knock comes, soft and unmistakable, something shifts.

I already know it's him.

I open the door and there he is. Connor Rives. In jeans and a gray t-shirt. No pressed suit. No guarded stance. Just tired eyes, a folder in one hand, and something open in his chest that wasn't there before.

He doesn't say anything at first.

Neither do I.

Finally, he swallows. "I don't deserve your time. Or your forgiveness. But I'm here."

A beat.

"I saw what you did. With Erin. With the press. With your people. You didn't just hold the line, Emery. You redrew the damn map."

I don't breathe.

He continues, voice rough. "And it made me rethink everything. How I work. How I lead. Who I am when no one's looking."

Then he takes a breath and hands me the slim black folder.

"I put together a draft. Full strategy doc. Clean-up comms. Stakeholder messaging. Press guidance, no spin. No burying. Just truth built on what you've already got going."

He holds it out to me.

"No strings. You don't owe me anything. I want to help."

I take the folder but keep my eyes on him.

He shifts like he's preparing for a blow.

I lift an eyebrow. "Just help, huh?"

A ghost of a smile. "Unless you're hiring."

I hum. "Not sure you're qualified. We specialize in radical honesty. No hiding. No secrets."

He nods, solemn. "I know. I've been practicing."

I flip open the folder and skim the first page. It's good. Too good to be free.

"So you came back because you want to work for me?"

"No." His voice is steady now. Clear. "I came back because I want to build something with you."

I close the folder. "Business?"

His gaze drops to my mouth. Then lifts. "That's up to you."

Silence pulses between us. There's work to be done and conversations to be had, but we'll get there.

I step forward and lay my hand on his chest, resting over his heart.

"Let's start here," I whisper.

His hand covers mine.

"Yeah," he breathes. "Let's."

I rise on my toes and kiss him, slow, sure, deep.

No desperation. No fear.

Just heat.

And a beginning.

The kiss slows.

But the tension doesn't.

Connor's lips linger near mine, his breath uneven. He's trying to hold back. Still afraid, maybe, of what happens when he gives in.

I don't want him to hold back.

Not from me. Not anymore.

My fingers drift to the end of his belt. I undo it with slow, sure movements. He watches me, throat working, chest rising too fast.

"I want you," I whisper.

His jaw tightens. "Emery..."

"I'm not afraid," I say. "Not of you. Not of this."

He stills.

So I press closer. My voice drops, low and even.

"It always felt good, Connor. Even then. But this time..." I slide my hands under his shirt, over his bare skin. "This time I want you to feel it too."

He exhales like I've cracked something in him.

I rise on my toes, kiss the side of his throat.

"I want you to take all of me. I know I'm safe with you."

He lets out a low groan, then backs me into the couch, hands never rough, but firm. Controlled. Focused.

He kisses me again, deep and slow, until I'm panting. Then guides me down, lays me gently across the cushions, the heat of his body pressing me into the world we're remaking—one careful breath at a time.

My dress is hiked to my waist before I realize it.

His voice is gravel.

"On your stomach."

I roll without hesitation, hips lifted slightly, knees parting. Offering everything.

He kisses my spine, one vertebra at a time. His hands trail down—soothing, grounding, worshipful.

"This okay?" he murmurs, fingers skimming over my hips.

"Yes."

His hands tighten. "Say it again."

"Yes, Connor. I want this."

I feel the shift.

The man who once held back because he was afraid to hurt me is gone.

This man?

He's still afraid.

But he trusts me now too.

His lips brush my shoulder. My spine. The nape of my neck.

I melt under him, breath catching as his hands push my dress further up. His palm smooths over the curve of my ass.

"You still want all of me, baby?" His voice is lower now. Thick with need.

"Yes." I arch slightly, aching. "I want your hands. Your mouth. Your dick. I want everything."

He hums behind me; a sound of approval and ownership rolled into one. I feel the shift—his knees spreading behind me, his chest over my back, his mouth hot and open against my skin.

One hand stays on my hip. The other?

It slides between my thighs.

He cups me through soaked lace and groans, like feeling how ready I am wrecks him.

"These panties," he says against my neck, "are in the fucking way."

Then they're gone—tugged down, discarded. His fingers find me bare.

"Fuck," he breathes. "You're soaked."

Two fingers stroke through my folds, slow and teasing. He doesn't rush—he savors. Circles my clit, then dips lower, spreading my slick, then back up again.

Every time he brushes that swollen, aching spot, my hips twitch.

He kisses my neck again. "Don't move. I want you still."

I whimper.

He hums again, then sinks a finger inside me.

God.

My thighs shake. He strokes slowly, then adds another.

And still, he talks.

"You let me in so easy," he murmurs. "Your body knows me. Missed me."

I moan, helpless under him.

"You going to come on my fingers like a good girl?" he asks, voice soft but commanding.

"Yes—please—"

He starts to fuck me with them in earnest. Slow, deep strokes while his thumb circles my clit. His mouth never leaves my neck. His body keeps mine pinned.

And I break.

I come with a cry that's almost a sob, shuddering around his hand, pulse after pulse wracking through me.

He holds me through all of it.

Kisses the back of my shoulder. Presses his palm flat to my lower back.

Only when I stop shaking does he slide his fingers free.

He doesn't ask.

He doesn't have to.

I lift my hips higher.

"I want more," I whisper. "Please."

His breath stutters against me.

I reach back and find his thigh. Grip it. Anchor myself.

"Connor," I beg, raw and open, "please... I want you to fuck my ass."

SAY IT AGAIN—CONNOR

'Please... I want you to fuck my ass.'

The words nearly knock the air from my lungs.

I freeze, still bent over her, her skin flushed and trembling beneath me. Her pussy's still clenching from the orgasm I gave her. My fingers are soaked.

But she's looking back at me now. Hair wild. Eyes glassy. Mouth parted like she's caught between praying and pleading.

Goddamn.

"Say it again," I rasp.

"I want you to fuck my ass."

Her voice is wrecked. Honest. Glorious.

"Lemme get..."

"No." She nods to the side table. "Use that. I don't want you to go anywhere."

I reach for the bottle of lotion, coat my fingers and slide them between her cheeks, already slick from how wet she is.

She moans when I tease the rim, then press in gently with one finger.

"That's it," I murmur, more to myself than to her. "Such a good girl."

She pushes back against my hand.

"You're not rushing this," I say. "You're going to beg me for every inch."

She whimpers.

I add more lotion. Ease in a second finger. She relaxes around me like she was made for this. Like her body remembers and welcomes me home.

And fuck, I missed this.

Not just the act—the control. The intimacy of it. The way she opens for me with complete trust. No fear. No tension. Just need.

When I pull my fingers out, she whines. I smile.

I shift behind her, undo my pants, and slide them just low enough. She hears the sound. Her breath catches.

Then I'm there.

Thick. Heavy. Poised at her back entrance.

"Ready?" I ask, even though I already know the answer.

"Yes," she breathes. "Please."

I push in—slowly. Just the tip.

She gasps.

Her hips arch.

I hold her down with one hand. "Stay still. Let me in."

She nods frantically. "Please, Connor..."

Another inch.

Then another.

I take my time. She earns every inch with whispered pleas and moans that damn near ruin me. Her body grips me like velvet and heat and home.

By the time I'm buried to the hilt, we're both shaking.

"Oh my God," she moans. "You feel amazing."

I lean over her back, mouth at her ear.

"You're taking me so fucking well, baby."

She shudders.

"I missed this," I whisper. "I missed you."

She cries out, her body pulsing around me.

I still. Let her ride it. Let her own it. And when the tremors fade, she lifts her hips higher, turns her head enough for me to see her eyes.

"Harder," she says. "Please, Connor. Fuck me harder."

My restraint shatters. One hand tangles in her hair. The other finds her clit, slick and throbbing.

And I move. Not slow. Not cautious.

I take. Skin slaps against skin.

Her cries get louder. Filthier. Her muscles clench around me with every thrust.

"You're mine," I growl. "My good girl. My dirty girl. You take my cock like you were made for it."

"More," she sobs. "Please—Connor—don't stop—"

I won't.

Not until I've given her everything and taken every part of her she's willing to give.

Her body trembles beneath me. Her ass clenched tight around my cock, her breath coming in sobbing gasps, her hands scrabbling for purchase on the cushion beneath her.

"Connor—"

I don't stop.

I can't stop.

My hips drive into her again and again, harder now, every slap of skin echoing off the walls. My hand stays on her pussy, stroking, tapping the rhythm her body already knows.

Her inner thighs are soaked. Her scent's all over me. I love the feel of me inside her, stretching her, filling her.

"Fuck, baby, look at you," I groan. "You're taking my cock in your ass and still begging for more."

"More—please—I need it—I need—"

I yank her upright by her hair, enough to pull her back into my chest. My hand finds her throat. My mouth is at her ear.

"You need to come for me again."

She nods frantically, eyes wild, body gone pliant.

"Do it," I growl. "Show me what it means to be mine."

One more stroke.

Two.

And she breaks.

Her scream is choked off by her own sob of pleasure. Her whole body seizes around me, pulsing so hard I nearly follow her over the edge.

But I wait.

I hold her through it, her body shaking in my arms, my name on her lips like a prayer and a promise.

Only when she slumps forward do I let go.

I ease out of her carefully. Gently. My hands shaking now.

And the second I'm free, I drop to my knees behind her.

I press my mouth to her spine. Her hips. Her thighs.

Then I roll her over, spread her legs and taste her.

Long, slow licks that make her moan again. My fingers glide through her soaked folds. Two. Then three. Then four.

She doesn't flinch. Doesn't fear. She opens.

And I lap her up like she's holy.

She cries out again, and I don't stop until she's soaked my face and gone limp in my arms.

When it's over, I don't speak.

I lift her gently, cradling her against me, and carry her to the bathroom.

I clean her like she's something sacred. Soft cloth. Warm water. Kisses to every fingerprint and bite mark.

She lets me. No words. Just the slow rebuild of something we almost lost.

When I finally pull her into bed, she buries her face in my chest and exhales like she can finally breathe again.

And me?

I don't know if this is love, but it's the closest I've ever been.

And I'm not running from it anymore.

WEDNESDAY, JUNE 3

THIS LIFE WORKS—CONNOR

The office is organized chaos, and the wild thing is, my name is on half the materials in the room now. Dee's pacing with a floor plan in one hand and a highlighter in the other, rattling off a list of renovation needs like he's drafting a battle strategy. Alex is muttering about building codes and scheduling overlaps, simultaneously texting two contractors. The new assistant is quietly conquering the digital backend with the calm precision of a Navy SEAL. Or a high school librarian. Not sure which is more intimidating.

And Emery—she's the fucking sun at the center of it all.

She's perched in a chair at the end of the table, red pen in hand, glasses low on her nose. Hair up. Mouth moving a mile a minute as she balances podcast themes and consulting packages, shooting off questions and ideas that spark like wildfire.

I watch her take a sip of her coffee, toss a smile over her shoulder at me, and suddenly it's hard to focus on anything but the curve of her spine and the memory of her screaming my name last night.

This life? It works.

I used to thrive in silence. In solo power. In being the one in the room who saw what others missed, who controlled the flow of information and kept my name off the record.

This is noisy. Messy. Personal. And I like it more than I ever thought possible.

Alex tosses a tablet on the table and groans. "Can we all agree that if y'all launch an intimacy space consulting division, I get final approval on aesthetics? Because if I see another red or black leather chaise, I'm walking."

Emery snorts. "It's about safety and mood. We're not running a dungeon warehouse."

I lift a brow. "Yet."

That gets a laugh from Dee, who mutters something about the first line should involve lockable storage that doesn't scream 'adult toy box.'

"I am never hearing the end of this, am I?" The ribbing doesn't bug me. Hell, it's deserved.

"Lots of people combine a playroom and a home office. How about close the damn closet doors if you're gonna ask someone to stop by and pick up a file you forgot? I don't need an eyeful of your toy collection. I've already seen hers." Dee waves a hand at Emery.

She doesn't blush, just lifts her shoulders and shakes her head with an apologetic grin. She meets my eyes and smirks. "Can I write off sex toys as a business expense?"

The reactions from Dee and Alex tell me this isn't the first time that's come up. Emery leans in and nudges me with her elbow.

"I mean, at this point, we're both going to need better home office set ups," Emery continues.

She laughs, but it's not a joke. I swallow hard and debate how much to say right now, in front of her staff. Our crew. I decide to hedge.

"There's that unit upstairs. Top floor. Two offices. Two bedrooms. Two and a half bathrooms. Lots of storage. Great windows. Rooftop access."

We've talked about that unit. She's been grumbling about needing more space. And how frustrating it is to cart things between our places. Hell, she's practically moved into my condo as is and only uses her place as a home office and storage.

"Speaking of expansion," Dee says, tossing a folder onto the table, "will you two please finalize the plan for combining these two office spaces? It's kind of hard to talk to contractors when things are still in flux.'

Emery gives me a nod and I open the folder Dee slides over, then tap the third plan on the list. "This one. A large, shared workspace, two private consulting rooms, expanding the kitchen, and a recording space. With soundproofing."

Emery tilts her head. "Soundproofing, huh?"

I smirk. "It's a recording studio. That's the norm."

She glances at me. Just a flick of her eyes.

But it lands like a brand.

Because last night? I had her on her knees in the shower, mouth slick and greedy around my cock, nails digging into my thighs like she never wanted to let go.

And this morning? She's radiant and ruthless and absolutely in her element.

My good girl.

My partner.

Fuck.

I take a sip of coffee and watch as she tucks a curl behind her ear. She looks at me, tips her head and stills.

"Think we could swing it?"

It takes a beat for me to realize she's not talking about the office.

"It's not about swinging it. It's an investment." I'm hoping to buy some time, but Emery's got that demanding look on her face and I'm not sure I want to have this discussion around the whole team.

"Do you trust me?" I know the answer, but it's still a dangerous question.

She arches an eyebrow and gives me the soft smile that says she's all in. That look kills any lingering doubts and seals the deal. I've found something precious and I am never walking away from it.

"You know I do."

"Good. Then wrap this up and let's get out of here. I want to show you something."

She switches gears in an instant, and we're on the way to our building within ten minutes. I've never been so nervous in my life.

LIKE IT'S ALWAYS BEEN THERE—EMERY

Connor doesn't say much on the ride home, and he pauses in the elevator, finger hovering over the buttons.

"Your place." I step closer and lean in to kiss him. He punches the button then wraps his arms around me and I drown in his kisses. When the doors open, he doesn't move to get out. Instead, he braces his foot in the door and looks at me, eyes dark and expression unreadable.

"Emery, I love you."

Hearing those words in his deep, gravel-and-smoke voice takes my breath away. I blink and try to pull in air. I don't know how in the hell I got so lucky.

He shows me every day that he loves me. In how he backs Dee in meetings. In how he listens to Alex and lets them run the numbers their way. In how he never once condescends to our new assistant, just thanks her by name and tells her she's killing it.

He showed me when he said he wanted to be part of something. When he stayed even after the fallout. When he let me see every crack he thought made him unlovable.

Hearing the words is different.

"I love you, too." It comes easily. Like it's always been there. Like it belongs to us, and only us.

Connor's smile goes a mile wide, then he bites his lip and for a moment looks like a kid who's about to tell some delicious secret.

"About that unit upstairs. What do you think?"

Something in his face tells me there's a lot more to this than him asking my opinion. "If we can swing it, I'm in."

I didn't think his grin could get any wider but it does. He pulls his foot away from the elevator door and pushes the button for the top floor. Then he says nothing. Just stands there with that goofy grin lighting up his ridiculously handsome face and staring at me like he thinks I hung the moon.

The doors open, he takes my hand, turns to the right and stops in front of a door. He fishes in his pocket and comes out with a key, then hands it to me.

"Like I said, it's an investment. In us." He tips his head toward the door.

"You... how..." I take a slow breath, trying to calm my breathing before I try again. "You bought the place? How?"

Connor points at the doorknob and raises his eyebrows like he's waiting for me to do something. I slip the key in the lock and turn, then step into a broad, and empty, living room.

The door closes behind me and Connor leans back against it, arms crossed. Those damn forearms. Distracting.

"Call it presumptuous, but I figured it was a safe gamble." He cups my hands in his and smiles. "So, what do you think? Still all in?"

"You still haven't told me how." I know he's successful, but being able to drop a down payment without blinking is a surprise.

"I've got good equity in my place, already have a buyer lined up, and I have good savings. Can we swing it? I already have. I'd rather not have to keep swinging it alone, and I can still back out. Closing hasn't happened. I only have keys because the seller is a former client."

He's thought of everything. Which shouldn't surprise me. I throw my arms around his neck and kiss him, hard.

"You're infuriating sometimes. Yes, I'm all in." I kiss him again, then pull back and look around at the bare floors. "So, are we going to christen the kitchen counter? I'm not too keen on the idea of the floor."

Connor's smile transforms to a look I know oh so well. Dark and dangerous. And hot as hell.

"Do you really think I'd leave that to chance?" He takes a step back, then points to the hall. "Second door on the right."

Of course he prepared. This is Connor. I find the door and open it, then gasp. Soft light fills the space from the big window, but it's the bed in the middle of the room that holds my attention. Or more precisely, the familiar sight of Connor's toy bag sitting on the bed.

"Strip." His voice sounds behind me, sending shivers down my spine and heat between my legs.

"Yes, Connor." I kick off my shoes.

THE LEASH DROPS—CONNOR

She's out of her clothes in less than a minute. No questions. No fear. Just trust in me. That alone nearly undoes me. She stands in front of me, naked and open, and it takes everything in me to maintain control. I need to check in. Need to be sure.

"I want to reclaim something tonight." The words come out ragged, but Emery's eyes never leave mine. "I didn't trust you with all me. Not with my past. Not with my desires. And because of that, I hurt you. I hurt us."

"Connor..."

I hold my hand up to stop her. I know she'll tell me it's okay. We've had the talks, rebuilt the trust. But not all the way.

"I love how we are. You are enough, always. No matter what. You told me you wanted to see all of me, then you saw what I was like when I let go of control."

I take a slow breath before I continue. "Whatever you say, I will live by. You are everything to me, and I will never do anything to jeopardize that. Do you want that? All of me. No holding back. No leash. You're the only brakes."

"Show me." Emery locks her gaze on mine and sinks to her knees in front of me. Her head tips back and her lips part. "I want all of you. I'm yours."

Her words hit low in my gut and pull a growl from my throat. For the first time in my fucking life, I don't hold the leash. I drop it.

"Sit on the edge of the bed."

She obeys without question and I pull out cuffs and straps. I cuff her hands together and place a cuff on each ankle, but leave her sitting where she is. I hold up a blindfold and a gag. We've used soft cloth gags before, but this one is molded silicone and will fill her mouth.

Emery nods and bends her head down. The blindfold goes

on, then the gag, and I check in. Curl her hand in mine and squeeze three times. Her fingers tap back. Two firm taps. Then I tuck a red silk handkerchief into one wrist cuff.

"Show me."

Emery tugs the silk out and waves it.

"Good fucking girl. You're perfect like this. Not because you're powerless. Because you trust me with your power." I tuck the silk handkerchief back in place. "Nod if you're ready."

She gives a single sharp nod. I don't ease in. I devour. I push her down and start with my mouth. Her thighs. Her breasts. Her hips. I suck until I feel the skin swell, bruise. I bite, hard. Mark her in places only I'll see. I want my name written on her in fingerprints and teeth.

She moans behind the gag, writhing, hips tilting in the direction of my mouth, my hands. I tease her nipples. Fingertips then tongue, then a pinch, and a suck. The sounds she makes around the gag have me raging hard.

Her pussy is dripping, begging, clenching on air.

"You were made for this," I growl. "Made for me."

I slide a hand down her belly, spread her pussy wide and spit. No warning. Just raw want. Push two fingers into her with no warmup then lean down to whisper every filthy thing I plan to do.

"I'm going to ruin you tonight, baby. That means fucking every hole you've got. I'll use mouth, my cock, my hands, whatever it takes. You're going to be wrecked and still begging for more."

She moans around the gag and I add another finger, fucking her hard with my hand until she's shaking and her moans are coming in short, high-pitch bursts. Another finger, all four in, to the knuckle and Emery starts shaking.

I pull my hand out and she makes a sound of pure frustration. I reach up and yank the gag free.

"Words," I growl. "If you want more, you beg with words."

"Please," she gasps. "Use me."

Oh fuck. I was expecting her to ask to come. Instead, she offered me everything I ever wanted. I pull her off the bed and get her on her knees, with her cuffed hands looped behind her head.

"Open!" My cock slides between her lips, stretching her mouth and I force myself to go slow and let her get used to me. Once she's taking most of my cock, I hold her head still and fuck her throat, going deeper on each thrust until tears are leaking out from under the blindfold and spit is dripping from her chin. Emery gags and chokes, but keeps going.

I tell her she's beautiful. I tell her she's mine. She moans and rocks her hips at each bit of praise.

When I pull out, she fucking thanks me for using her mouth. I call her my whore. My good girl. My hole. And she shudders like I've blessed her.

I lift her back to the bed, anchor her hands to the bedframe, spread her legs wide and clip those cuffs in place. Emery begs for my cock and I slam into her soaked pussy and fuck her with the kind of rhythm that leaves bruises on the inside.

"I love you," I pant. "So much it fucking ruins me."

Emery lets out a low wail as she comes hard, then writhes like she's trying to get away, but the cuffs hold her in place. She hasn't tapped out, hasn't waved a flag or used a safe word, so I keep going.

"Oh no, baby. You don't run from this. You take it."

Two more deep, hard strokes and she's shaking. Telling me not to stop. Begging for harder.

That's when I stop and Emery wails in protest. I cover her mouth with my hand and lean close.

"I want your ass."

I feel her low moan against my hand. "Not gently. Not slow. I mean disrespectfully hard and deep. Like it's the only hole that's ever mattered, and I own it."

I take my hand away from her mouth, kiss her lightly, then sit back "Do you want that?"

"Yes," she gasps. "Take it. Take all of me. I'm yours."

"Lift your head." She obeys and I peel the blindfold off. Emery blinks in the soft light. Her mascara is smeared under her eyes and her hair is a mess. And she is gorgeous. I unclip the ankle cuffs and flip her. There are reasons I cuffed her hands together and attached them to a single point.

Then I push her legs apart and cuff them back in place. Anal with legs wide open is harder than with the legs together, but I have every confidence Emery can take it.

I lube her roughly—three fingers, fast. She gasps and pushes back, moaning words of encouragement. When I can work four fingers in I pull out and thrust my cock into her ass with one hard stroke.

She lets out a sob and arches back, giving me everything.

"Look at you," I growl. "So full. So good. So fucking mine."

"Yes, Connor! Harder please!"

Her voice is wrecked, cracking and breathy, but sure.

"If you insist." I pound into her. The time I lost control with her was nothing compared to this. It's deep. Unforgiving. Brutal. The difference is this time, I'm in complete control and I trust myself, and Emery.

I wrap an arm around her and roll her clit between my fingers.

"Oh that's so good. More please. More."

She tips her hips and I slide four fingers into her pussy, resting my thumb on her clit.

"God, you're stuffed full and your cunt is dripping. You love this."

She's beyond words, breaking beneath me. Screaming. Coming again.

And I don't stop.

I ride her through it, through tears and bliss and incoherence, whispering filth and praise and love like they're the same language. And with us, they are.

Because this? This is who I am. All of me. Given to her freely. And she takes it like the fucking queen she is.

When I finally break, it's with her name on my lips and my heart in her hands.

And I don't run.

I undo the cuffs and hold her, then kiss every bruise I gave her.

She doesn't ask if I'm okay. She cradles my face in her hands and kisses me slow and tender.

HE SEES ALL OF ME—EMERY

My body is shaking, skin stinging with love-shaped bruises, muscles spent and boneless as I'm curled against his chest.

And I've never felt safer.

He holds me like I'm fragile. Like I'm breakable. But he knows I'm not.

Connor rises and disappears into what I imagine is a bathroom. That's confirmed when he comes back with a warm washcloth and cleans me carefully, softly, whispering praise into my skin. His hands linger on every mark, every bite, as if kissing them would make them permanent.

"I didn't scare you?" His voice is low and raw, but I don't hear doubt. Just him checking in.

I shake my head. "You showed me what it means to love without limits."

He exhales like I've given him oxygen. "Do you want some ice in a washcloth or anything?"

His fingers skim between my legs again, brushing over tender skin and I suck in a sharp breath. This kind of sex would leave me sore even with an average man. With Connor? The deep ache is no surprise.

"Maybe?" I'm sure it would be nice, but I'm not ready for him to get up and move again. Not even for a minute. "Is there even ice here?"

His eyebrow quirks up. "Have you known me to leave things to chance?"

He has a point. I lay my head on his chest and trace my fingers along the line of fine hair that goes down his stomach.

"You're everything I was afraid to want," I whisper. "And everything I'll never let go of."

He pulls a blanket over us. Wraps himself around me.

I fall asleep in his arms, completely his—and completely myself.

EPILOGUE—APRIL 16
THE FOLLOWING YEAR

MAKE IT A MEMORY—CONNOR

The ocean's a mirror tonight.

Moonlight spills across the waves. Steel drums thrum against the bass. Someone down the beach is moaning too loud to be subtle, and someone else is cheering them on.

It's that kind of resort. Clothing optional. Judgment not allowed. Pleasure the purpose.

And tonight, I'm about to take off my clothes in front of a few hundred people.

Not for the first time.

When I did it before, it was survival. Hustle. A performance I hid behind because the rest of me didn't feel good enough to show.

This?

This is for Emery.

For us.

To lay bare every inch of who I am and say, without flinching, I love you. All of me. Even this part. A year of rebuilding, of rebranding, of learning to work together, live together, love together. There's only one thing missing, and that's what tonight's about.

"You ready?" She's already barefoot in the sand, her crimson halter dress hugging curves I plan to bite later.

Her eyes sparkle. Her hair's wild from the salt air. She looks like something ancient and sacred. Like a goddess walking into battle.

I take her hand. "Depends. Are you planning to behave?"

She smirks. "Not remotely."

Her podcast's been climbing charts. Her practice, our business, is thriving. She promised this trip was vacation, but she's already mentioned a future episode about adult resorts and ethical exhibitionism.

"One live show," I murmur. "That's it. Then I'm confiscating your mic and tying you to the bed."

"Promises, promises," she says, and bites my shoulder.

The beach party pulses with light and music. The DJ's halfway through a dirty remix. Bodies writhe in the sand. Emery and I dance.

She's not trying to tease me, but every sway of her hips, every hitch of breath when I whisper in her ear, makes me want to fuck her in front of everyone here.

When the DJ gives the cue, I lean in close.

"I've got a surprise. Come with me."

She raises an eyebrow. "What did you do?"

"Trust me."

I lead her to the riser stage lit by tiki torches and help her up onto it—front and center, a lone chair in the middle of the platform. No arms. Low slung. Sturdy. Perfect for what's coming.

The DJ takes her hand and guides her to the chair. Nods to me.

I change in a makeshift area behind the DJ booth. The suit

is matte black with pinstripes that shimmer with glitter. Tailored to precision with tearaway seams. It's the same style I used to perform in.

But this time, it's not armor. This time, it's a different kind of seduction.

I used to hate this part of me. Resent it. Hide it. It nearly cost me everything. Now I wear it like a crown, because the woman out there loved me through my worst. Tonight, I show her what it means to be fully seen.

THIS IS OURS—EMERY

The music shifts to something low and sultry, heavy on the bass.

And then he walks out. Connor, looking like temptation come to life in a full black suit that flashes and shines in the flickering light. Hair tousled. Brow furrowed in focus.

He moves with that quiet intensity that always undoes me. And right now, every eye on the beach is locked on him, but he's only looking at me.

He circles my chair, then stops in front of me, leans in, and murmurs against my ear:

"Rule number one. No touching."

Goosebumps rise across my skin.

The beat drops and Connor begins to move. This isn't just dancing. This is Connor commanding attention and reveling in it. He peels off the jacket slow, letting it slide down his arms, revealing the crisp lines of his shirt. His hips pulse once to the beat. The man is walking sin.

Then the tie. He drapes that around my neck, using it to pull me close for a slow grind inches from my lips before he stops and moves on to the shirt buttons.

Each undone with maddening care. He keeps his eyes on

mine as he exposes his chest and abs. The shirt hits the stage. His last few weeks of extra gym time make a lot more sense.

The crowd whistles and cheers. I can't breathe.

He steps between my knees, palms braced on the seat beside my thighs, and grinds.

It's precision-controlled, filthy perfection. His dick's in the perfect position to make me forget we're not alone. He dips low. Lifts his hips. Strokes up the seam of my pussy through my dress with nothing but the roll of his body.

And then he smirks. Sexy as fuck, and he knows it.

He backs off, circles again, then rips off the pants with a single snap of his wrists.

Fuck.

The G-string is minimal and looks like it's in danger of losing the battle to contain a dick I know oh so well. The crowd loses it.

I don't care about anything, or anyone else. As far as I'm concerned, we're the only two people in the entire world. The rest is background noise as Connor focuses on me with the intensity of a big cat stalking its prey.

He's back between my legs in seconds, dancing filthier, closer. His face hovers over my chest. Then he buries it in my neck. I can feel his breath. Smell his cologne. His hands slide up my thighs, parting them wider, exposing me to the open air.

He lifts me enough to sit on his lap as he straddles the chair backwards before settling me over his hips. Then he grinds.

His dick drags against my ass. My dress hikes up. His hands press my hips down. He's fucking me with clothes on and I've never been so turned on in my life.

Then, like it's nothing, he scoops me up and lays me on the stage.

Crowd roaring.

Face up, hair fanned across the boards.

In some lightning-fast move that steals my breath, Connor slides between my legs, lifts my knees, and uses his body to flip me.

I'm face down. Ass up. Gasping. And he's straddle my hips, grinding and pulsing to the beat.

He leans over. Bites my shoulder.

Then flips me back and drags me into the chair like I weigh nothing.

Kneels between my legs.

Sweating. Breathing fast and hard. Glowing.

And pulls a velvet bag from behind the chair.

The crowd quiets.

Connor's eyes are soft as he holds my gaze.

"One year ago, I let shame keep me from telling you the truth. I let fear convince me I didn't deserve love. But you—" his voice breaks, then comes back stronger "—you showed me what it means to be whole."

He opens the bag. The ring glints in the torchlight.

"Emery. I love you beyond words. Marry me?"

I'm crying.

Laughing.

Nodding so hard my hair sticks to my cheeks.

"Yes. Yes, fuck, yes!"

He lifts me into his arms. Carries me off the stage, G-string and all.

The crowd's still cheering.

But all I can see is him.

COMING NEXT: FIRE & HONEY

CHAPTER 1

WEDNESDAY, JUNE 30—RAINE

The zipper stuck halfway across the suitcase. Of course it did. Because the universe had a sense of humor, and she was the punch line.

Raine yanked it free and the sound ripped through the furnished apartment like a reprimand. She stood there, sweating in the still air, surrounded by furniture that wasn't hers. Rental art prints of fog-soft bridges, a couch that smelled faintly of someone else's perfume, a stack of neutral throw pillows that were anything but comfortable.

Two months of a short-term rental and applying for jobs but hearing nothing back. She'd gone to work every day, smiling as if she wasn't one step from panic and wishing humiliation came with an expiration date.

Spoiler: it didn't. All because she stupidly not just dated, but moved in with her school administrator.

"So this is my mid-thirties." Thirty-five tomorrow and her celebration consisted of packing her life into the back of her Prius before heading home.

No. Not home. It's the farm and it's temporary.

She did a final sweep and dropped her keys on the counter. The clink a final punctuation on this chapter.

Outside, the evening breeze sent a chill through her as she wrestled her things into her hatchback and stared at the sole evidence of her existence: three boxes, two suitcases, and a bag of toiletries. The sum total of years of her life.

The GPS offered two routes north. She didn't need directions; it was the same road she'd taken seventeen years ago on her way to college. Still, she let the calm voice guide her, something steady when everything else inside her felt broken.

The freeway unspooled beneath her headlights. Miles of concrete, the hum of tires, the drone of some random music she cued up, desperate for any sounds to drown out her thoughts. The lights of San Francisco thinned into darkness and pines replaced billboards as she climbed into the foothills above Santa Rosa. A faint tang of smoke from some distant fire threaded through the open window, sharp and familiar. The smell of summer campfires and festivals. Memories of her youth.

By the time she passed the Petrified Forest, her throat ached from holding herself together. She slowed as she rounded the last bend, then pulled into the gravel turnout, headlights bouncing off the wooden sign hanging over the farmstand.

Hearth & Haven Farm

Fresh Eggs • Goat Cheese • Community Events.

Someone had twined fairy lights around the sign.

Mom, of course.

The air filled with the sound of crickets and the rustle of the wind shifting through the live oaks and pine. Every bit of it bittersweet, even after so long away.

She shifted into drive and crept down the road. The simple A-frame farmhouse stood out against a scatter of stars. A single light glowed golden on the porch, and for one ridiculous moment Raine considered backing up and pretending she'd taken a wrong turn.

Instead, she parked in front of the house and sat until her pulse slowed enough to fake composure.

The door creaked open before she'd popped the rear hatch to pull out her suitcase. Faye Matheson stood framed in the light, her once-blonde hair streaked with gray, wearing a flowy skirt with a paint-streaked t-shirt. Behind her stood Laurel, Raine's second mom.

"Hey, sweetheart." Her mother's tone was cautious, the way you spoke to a stray animal that might bolt. "Long drive?"

Raine forced a shrug as she hauled her suitcase up the steps. "Long enough to rethink all my life choices twice."

"Sounds like you need wine." Her mother took Raine's hand and pulled her toward the kitchen.

"God, yes." Raine allowed herself to be led, then sat at the old wooden table, cradling a glass of mead. She should have known when her mother said wine, she meant the honey wine they made here at the farm.

They didn't ask questions. Her mother wrapped her arms around her daughter with quiet, devastating love. As if a simple embrace could dissolve every wall Raine had spent years fortifying.

Her throat closed. She let herself lean in for a heartbeat,

then pulled back before she could break. "Okay, Mom. Enough. You'll make me sentimental."

"Can't have that." Mom hoisted herself onto the kitchen counter, her feet swaying.

The kitchen looked smaller than Raine remembered, or maybe she was bigger now. She was older for sure, and disappointment weighed heavy. Copper pots hung from the same hooks, herbs drying near the window. The table bore a few fresh nicks and at least one new stain, proof of a life that kept happening without her.

Laurel got more glasses and poured mead for the two of them. She settled into her usual seat at the end of the table, spine straight, eyes soft but sharp. Raine clutched her glass, wishing this were all a dream.

"You look tired."

"Thanks. I was going for post-apocalyptic chic."

Her mother snorted. "You nailed it. All you're missing is a flamethrower."

"Don't tempt me." Raine took a swallow of mead that burned pleasantly down her throat.

For a while, the only sounds were the tick of the old clock and the soft rustle of night through the open window. The air smelled of summer soil, the lavender around the porch, and the always present faint sweetness of peaches and goats' milk soap.

Her mother eyed her slowly, then shook her head as if she could see right through the brave front Raine had put up. "Eat anything today?"

Raine shook her head. "Didn't seem worth dirtying a dish."

That earned her a maternal eyebrow from Laurel. Raine sighed and added, "I'll scavenge tomorrow. Promise."

Laurel nodded, satisfied enough. Faye swung her legs idly. "You planning to stay a while?"

"Only until I get my feet back under me," Raine said quickly. "School starts up late August or early September, so, as soon as I find a new job..."

"Okay."

"I mean it."

Mom lifted her hands. "People always find their footing in a month or two. Especially after..."

Raine arched a brow. It wasn't like her mother to leave something hanging. "My grand tour of bad decisions?"

Mom gave her a look equal parts sympathy and mischief. "I was going to say a rough patch."

"Same difference."

The words tasted brittle. She tipped the glass again, watching the wine circle the bowl. "I need to regroup, that's all. Then apply for a job that doesn't involve a prep-school old-boys' networks."

"You don't have to explain." Laurel's voice was soft with understanding.

"I know." Raine smiled, quick and hollow. "But if I don't, it feels like I ran home because I couldn't hack it."

"You came home," Laurel said simply. Always the practical one. "That's all."

Raine swallowed hard. The easy answer shouldn't hurt so much. Changing the subject seemed like a good idea and her darting eyes landed on the hand-painted sign over the pantry door—Hearth & Haven.

"We used to joke that it sounded like a retirement community."

"It does." Mom's voice filled with her usual mix of pride and odd humor. "But it's the family business and the tourists love it. Just like they love the lights on the sign out front."

"Your mother still thinks they should spell something. Preferably something risqué." Laurel nudged Faye's foot.

"And you still hate it when I climb anything taller than a stepladder." Mom retorted, nudging back.

Raine managed a laugh. "Good to see some things never change."

Her chest tightened again. Love was never in short supply here. It was the rest of it she couldn't handle. The reminders of what, or more precisely who, was missing. She rubbed at the ache just below her collarbone, a restless gesture she couldn't stop.

Laurel watched her, eyes narrowed. "You want to tell us what happened?"

"It's boring." Raine softened the sharp words with a half-smile. "Girl meets boy, girl trusts boy, boy turns out to be an absolute dumpster fire. Academic edition."

Mom winced. "Ouch."

"Yeah. Pretty much that."

They let the silence stretch until it stopped feeling like an interrogation. The crickets continued outside, a steady, high hum that filled the cracks between words.

Raine stared at her reflection in the window. A woman who looked too old for mistakes and too young to feel this hollow.

"I thought I had it all figured out. The plan, the person, the future. Turns out, I was wrong."

Laurel rose and crossed to her, placing a hand on her shoulder, squeezed once. "You're good at surviving. The rest can wait."

Raine closed her eyes, just for a moment. The touch nearly undid her.

Mom slid off the counter and began fussing with the tea towels, folding, then re-folding them in a different way. "You'll stay in your old room. Bed's made. The goats will start yelling around six, so sleep fast."

Raine laughed softly. "Just like old times."

"Except this time you can swear all you want. We're over that phase."

"Finally, some perks."

Her mother hugged her again, then released her. "We're glad you're here, Raine."

She nodded, throat too tight for words.

When they left her alone, she lingered at the table, tracing the grain of the wood beneath her fingertips. Outside, the porch light hummed, moths tapping against the glass. Through the open window drifted the low chorus of night creatures and the faint jingle of wind chimes.

She stared into the dark until her eyes blurred.

Temporary. Just until I can stand again.

But the house smelled like safety, and the sound of the fields reached for something deep in her chest. When she rose, she washed her glass, dried it, and put it back in the cupboard, because it was something she could control.

Then she turned out the light and let the dark hold her, the faint taste of mead on her tongue and the word temporary echoing in her head like a prayer she didn't believe as she climbed the stairs.

Chapter 2

Thursday, July 1—Zephyr

Morning came like it always did in Haven's Corner, a thin, quiet breath before the world remembered how to move. The Wilde Nest yawned awake with him in the pre-dawn hour. Zephyr Wilde flicked on the lights, casting a soft glow over the long wooden counter. The scent of citrus cleaner still hung in the air under the sharp, deeper, darker promise of coffee.

He moved through the opening ritual on muscle memory. Towel over one shoulder. Grinders loaded, ovens clicking and ticking as they heated. Out the front windows, the world was still soft with morning mist shadowing the trees.

The Wilde Nest sat on a sharp rise, perched halfway between Santa Rosa and Calistoga. The first, or last, building in Haven's Corner, depending on which direction you were coming from.

He cued a playlist. Something funky this morning, heavy bass and bright horns. He liked being the first one up to meet the sun. Each day a fresh start, no matter what yesterday had brought. Marla and the rest of the crew came in through the back and set to work with bright good mornings. She grabbed the chalkboard, checked Zeph's scribbled notes, and bent to scrawl the specials.

"You sure you wanna put a peach emoji on the menu?" He tamped espresso for her usual start of shift flat white.

Marla rolled her eyes then returned to her work. "I'm not drawing anything fancy. Cal's guaranteed to smudge the thing somehow."

"Cal could smudge air if you gave him half a chance."

She huffed a laugh and added a little heart next to the peach. He pretended to be annoyed, knowing it was what she expected.

The front door opened at six like clockwork. Doris Nguyen from the post office down in the valley shuffled in, bun already crooked. "Morning, Zeph. Half-sweet almond oat milk latte?"

"Sure you don't wanna mix it up today?" The steam wand was already submerged in the oat milk he'd poured the second her silhouette hit the glass. Doris liked to pretend she wasn't predictable; he liked to pretend he didn't keep track of everyone's preferred coffee order and emotional state.

Next came Cal, boots worn, grin wide, Wilde Nest ball cap pulled low. "Smells like heaven in here. You hiding those scones, or can regular folk get one?"

"Two for locals." Zeph nodded toward the pastry case Marla had just filled.

"Guess I'm double-fisting breakfast." Cal slapped a tip in the jar without looking, like he always did.

Behind Cal, Ivy and Lena slipped into their usual corner booth, fingers laced, hair still damp from morning showers. They owned a tiny vineyard clinging to the hillside above the valley and they argued about barrel materials the way other couples argued about thermostat settings. Zeph set their French press on the counter before Marla took two steps in their direction.

Half the area ran on routine and caffeine, and he was the one who kept at least one of those running smooth.

Conversation rose and fell, familiar as an old song. Heat wave coming. Grapes maturing fast on the valley floor. Kids from the summer camps causing trouble, tourists arriving for the wineries and Old Faithful. Somebody grumbled about a yoga retreat blocking the only decent parking near the trailhead. Someone else insisted the new bakery in Santa Rosa was poaching customers.

Zeph let it all wash over him as he tamped grounds and pulled shots. He didn't have to say much; people talked more honestly when he listened and slid the right drink in front of them at the right time.

Cal leaned in and cupped his hand near his mouth like he was whispering a secret. "The Mathesons had a visitor last night. Drove in late. Quiet car. One of them electric things."

There was nothing quiet about his words. As expected,

half the café perked up and tuned in. Cal was usually the best source of juicy gossip.

Doris chimed in first. “Late? Laurel and Faye are such morning people.”

“It was after ten.” Cal confirmed in a delighted tone. “Couldn’t tell if it was a man or a woman. Just saw the headlights turn up the lane.”

Ivy peered over her mug. “Maybe a new farmhand?”

Lena smirked. “At that hour? Maybe a lover. Though it’d have to be someone remarkable. Ash was a hell of a man. Loved both of them like it was his purpose in life. Not many people could live up to that.”

A soft chorus of sighs followed at the mention of the late Ash Greenway. He’d died two years before Zeph moved to town, but twenty-five years later, the town still talked about him like he might walk in and order a coffee.

Gossip dissolved into talk about the upcoming Faerie Festival. Two months away and the buzz of excitement was already in the air. Zeph jotted a note on the pad by the register to bake muffins for the first volunteer meeting.

He liked the Mathesons. Faye with her hurricane-of-joy planning style that was heavy on creative and light on planning; Laurel steady as granite behind her. Their honey and peaches sweetened half his summer menu. If a mystery visitor meant more business, more energy, he was all for it.

Still, he caught himself glancing out the window, toward the road that wound through the trees and led to the farm a mile east. Just shadows and sunlight on asphalt. Nothing unusual.

He shook it off, smiling to himself. Haven’s Corner could spin a pair of headlights into a full-blown legend before breakfast.

Cal wiped crumbs from his beard. “Faye’s gonna need half

the county to pull that festival off this year. Heard she's adding another stage."

"She is," Doris said. "One for the dance troupes, one for musicians. My niece is trying to get a slot. She's been practicing on our porch for weeks. Neighbors are divided."

Zeph refilled Marla's coffee carafe, the dark stream steady and sure. "More music means more caffeine. Can't complain about what's good for business."

He said it lightly, but his brain was already slotting pieces into place. Extra beans, more ice, compostable cups, backup filters, staff schedules during the festival. The Wilde Nest ran on instinct and spreadsheets, a combination most people didn't expect from someone who wore friendship bracelets, painted his nails when the mood struck, and laughed easily.

A cluster of field hands came through the door, dust on their cuffs, shoulders loose from the cool morning air. They settled along the counter, greeting him by name. Zeph switched to Spanish without thinking, trading jokes and weather updates as he passed out brimming mugs of coffee and offered up the pan dulce Marla had discovered her neighbor baked.

Chairs scraped, spoons clinked, napkins crinkled, and a baby giggled while an exhausted dad mainlined espresso. Someone waved a thank-you across the room; someone else mouthed later about the school fundraiser donation jar he'd left by the register.

It was chaos, but it was his chaos.

He caught Ivy's head turn toward the counter, a sure sign she wanted more coffee. Marla was busy taking orders, so Zeph grabbed the pot and slid in beside Ivy at their booth. "Top-off?"

Lena winked, pushing her cup closer. "You're a mind reader."

"Café owner and barista," he said with a grin. "Comes with a minor in emotional triage."

Ivy tilted her head, eyes sly. "I bet. Speaking of emotions, any new crushes, Zeph?"

He laughed, shaking his head as he poured. "We doing this again?"

"It's been months since you were dating anyone," Lena said. "You're too pretty to spend nights alone counting beans."

"Don't insult the beans. They're excellent company."

More laughter. He didn't mind being the target; their nosiness was its own kind of affection. He'd long ago accepted his role as the town's sunshine boy. Everyone's second-favorite flirt, after their partners of course. Single as ever, but safe. Always.

"Dating app tried to match me with a real estate agent from Santa Rosa. Her hobbies were listed as 'networking and smoothies.' I closed the app and made banana bread instead."

"That's why you're still single," Ivy said, mock-serious. "You can't eat banana bread forever."

"I don't know," he said. "Good banana bread's a hell of a perk."

The door chime jingled again and Zeph excused himself, drifting back behind the counter in three easy steps. Two travelers stepped in, weighted with backpacks and yoga mats, that bleary early retreat look stamped on their faces. They ordered matcha lattes, leaned into each other, and let their eyes wander over the local art on the walls—photographs of vineyards at sunset, paintings of sunflowers, a charcoal sketch of goats mid-leap that one of the Faerie Festival volunteers had done last year.

He loved watching new people fall a little in love with Haven's Corner before they even realized it was happening.

By the time the morning rush thinned, sunlight had carved bright stripes across the tabletops. Zeph wiped the counter in slow, practiced strokes, the rhythm almost meditative. He paused at the windows where the honey jars sat lined on a shelf. The light caught them just right, turning them into tiny amber and gold suns.

A smile tugged at him. He shopped small and local as much as possible. Hearth & Haven supplied honey and spiced peach preserves that tourists bought by the jar to take back to San Francisco and LA like a piece of the valley they could keep. The café and the farm fed each other in ways that weren't just about ingredients.

He straightened one honey jar, letting the between-rush quiet settle around him. Mornings like this made him ache for someone to share them with. Someone who understood the small holiness of flipping on the lights, hearing the grinder roar to life, then watching the first car pull into the lot while the fog still clung to the trees.

It wasn't desperation. Not even loneliness. More like an empty space in his life, waiting for the right piece. And if there was one thing he'd learned, trying to wedge in the wrong piece just because he didn't like the gap never worked.

The bell over the door jingled again. Cal, back sooner than expected, the delivery truck keys hooked on his finger. Doris trailed behind him, clearly having decided one latte wasn't enough to face a stack of small-town mail.

"Told you," Cal crowed. "Whole town's buzzing. Someone saw a suitcase on the Matheson porch this morning."

Zeph shook his head, chuckling. "Considering the house is a good ways off the road, that 'someone' would be you, driving all the way up the lane when you picked up the produce. Pretty sure gossip's the only reason you took the delivery job."

Cal had the grace to shrug, not quite ashamed. At forty, he was too young to retire but a back injury meant he couldn't handle the fields anymore. The delivery route let him be everywhere without being in charge of anything. Perfect for a man whose hobbies included information sharing.

"Admit it," Doris said, accepting the to-go cup Zeph slid her way. "You're curious, too."

"Curious, sure. But visitors happen."

Cal chuckled and tipped his cup in salute. "This feels different. I'll drop the boxes out back."

They left in a scatter of bell chimes and morning sun, and the café settled into its mid-morning rhythm—clean surfaces, low music, Zeph humming under his breath as he moved.

Whoever the late-night visitor was, he'd meet them soon enough. Haven's Corner wasn't big; strangers didn't stay strangers for long.

By lunch, the customers shifted from the hard-working local crowd to lingerers and tourists. From the kitchen drifted the smell of roasted nuts, peaches, and sugar caramelizing in yeasted sweet rolls.

On cooler days, Zeph kept the windows open to let the breeze sweep through, welcoming the scent of pine and dust and faint whiffs of vineyards and farms. Today was already shaping up too hot so the AC hummed, fighting the rising temperature.

He hauled in the produce crates Cal had left by the back door, restocked the pastry case with the last of the scones, and lined up a new tray of muffins. Outside, the tourist crowd thickened. A group of hikers in neon gear took selfies under the Wilde Nest sign. Two dads negotiated a peace treaty between twin toddlers over a cinnamon roll the size of a plate. A woman in a floppy hat asked if the peaches were organic, and Zeph answered with easy patience, explaining how Hearth

& Haven rotated their fields, tended their orchard, how half the valley had hives from Faye and Laurel.

It wasn't a sales pitch. It was a small hymn of loyalty.

The gossip still circled his thoughts. Whoever had arrived at the farm had stirred up the town overnight. He let his eyes close for a second and pictured it: the porch light glowing in the darkness, a quiet car pulling in, gravel crunching underfoot as someone stepped out and breathed in that first lungful of Haven's Corner air. A visitor who felt like change.

The idea sat strangely sweet in his chest, like the first sip of hot coffee after a long night.

"Zeph, you daydreamin' again?"

Marla leaned on the counter next to him, one hip cocked, order pad in hand.

"Strategic planning," he said. "I multitask beautifully."

She snorted and handed him a dollar bill folded into a tiny paper crane before tucking a fresh towel into her apron. "Looks like Doris left you another bird."

He added it to the growing flock perched along the front window ledge—tiny wings casting crooked shadows on the sill, a whole migration of gratitude. Then he leaned back against the counter and let his gaze travel out the wide front windows and the clear, blue sky above the trees.

All around was the non-stop hustle of wineries and the tourism machine that fed the surrounding communities, but here, everything felt calmer. Like the town existed on its own little perch between soil and sky.

The talk about the farm's late-night visitor had him looking at his world with new eyes. The café, the farm, the little town in the hills—they were his anchors. His chosen gravity. He didn't want out.

But under the calm, under the easy rhythm and practiced charm, there was a readiness. An anticipation and sense that something was about to shift, not bigger, not elsewhere. Just the next piece of this good life sliding into place.

The thought made him grin, slow and certain.

"Bring it on," he murmured, and turned back to the counter as the bell over the door chimed again.

Fire & Honey
coming summer 2026

ALSO BY ROXANNE BLACKHALL

Charm City Connections

Book 1 ~ Complementary Colors

Book 2 ~ Intersecting Paths

Book 3 ~ Brewed Awakening

Logan County Love Series

Book 1 ~ Rekindled

Book 2 ~ Scorched

Book 3 ~ Arrested

Bristol Park Series

Book 1 ~ Abbeydon Attraction

Book 2 ~ Abbeydon Academy

Book 3 ~ Abbeydon Abandon

ABOUT THE AUTHOR

Roxanne Blackhall writes contemporary romance with heat, heart, and emotional grit. Her stories center sharp, self-possessed women and the men who meet them as equals—sometimes guarded, sometimes bold, always all in. She writes open-door romance that's as explicit as it is emotionally layered, where intimacy has weight and pleasure is never the whole story, it's the doorway.

Expect filthy banter, hard-earned vulnerability, and intimate scenes built on enthusiasm, agency, and connection. Some of her characters lean a little adventurous, but the happily ever after is always guaranteed.

A former magazine editor from San Diego, Roxanne now lives in Baltimore, where she traded AP Style for character arcs and spends her days crafting complicated love stories with endings that feel earned. When she's not writing, she's cooking something indulgent for friends, glass of wine (or cup of coffee) nearby, forever believing in grand gestures and good food.

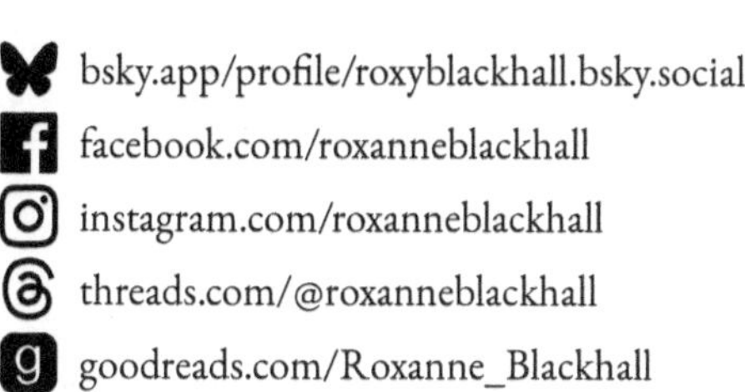

www.ingramcontent.com/pod-product-compliance
Lightning Source LLC
LaVergne TN
LVHW091022080826
845145LV00002B/325